Dreams

OF HOME

Linda McGinnis

Copyright © 2013 Linda McGinnis

All rights reserved.

ISBN: 0989227405
ISBN-13: 9780989227407

For my father, Dale, World War II Veteran,
member of the Greatest Generation,
and forever my hero.

ACKNOWLEDGMENTS

I am grateful to many friends,
for their support and encouragement as I travelled
on this journey into the past:
to Vera Barlow, who helped with research;
to Carol Callaway, who painstakingly edited my words;
to Katherine and Richard Yoshimura,
and Mildred Hironaka,
who welcomed me into their home and their hearts;
and to Grace Stephens,
my inspiration, my mentor, and my dear friend.

.

CHAPTER 1

Crying was out of the question. No matter how miserable she might be, a respectful Japanese girl did not cry in public. And the dock at Honolulu harbor in June of 1941 was very public. Of course, she wasn't entirely Japanese, only half. And half white. They even had a name for it in Hawaii: *hapa haole*. The other half was never mentioned.

Sixteen-year-old Grace Kawakami and her family were seeing her cousins off on the ocean liner, SS *Lurline*. Grace's uncle had accepted a position at a Los Angeles law firm, and was moving his family to California.

"There they are!" Grace cried, pointing up to a boat deck far above the pier.

"Where?" Grace's brother, Richie, bent slightly to follow the arc of her arm.

"I see them," said her brother, Tom.

Her two older brothers flanked Grace like armed guards. She could see that her cousin, Naomi, was yelling something at them from high above. But the music of the Royal Hawaiian Band playing on the pier behind them, made it impossible to hear anything from the ship.

To make matters worse, a squadron of Navy planes soared overhead, practicing maneuvers, as part of Hawaii's war preparedness drills.

Richie looked up, squinting into the bright sunlight. "Warhawks," he said to Tom, identifying the aircraft.

"I wish they'd do their maneuvers somewhere else," Grace's mother said.

"That wouldn't make much sense," Tom said. "If we're attacked..."

Their father's reproachful look ended his sentence.

Last minute arrivals hurried toward the gangplank, bumping into each other with packages and suitcases. On the ship, passengers draped with colorful, fragrant, flower leis crowded at the ship's railings, waving to friends and family on the dock. Rainbows of bright streamers showered down from the ship, covering the well-wishers with crisscrossed chains of confetti that seemed to anchor the ship to the pier. Every time a ship arrived or left the Honolulu harbor, the "Boat Day" celebration brought out the Royal Hawaiian Band, a myriad of flower vendors, and dozens of spectators.

Naomi's sister, Chiyo, threw a string of yellow confetti from far above. Grace reached out and caught the other end of the lifeline that her cousin held at the railing. The two girls, more like sisters than cousins, smiled at each other, their eyes promising to remain close despite the distance that would soon separate them.

Grace thought she felt the pier move and then realized it was actually the ship beginning its inevitable push toward the open ocean. As the ship slipped out of its berth, the streamer she was holding broke, and Grace felt a piece of her heart tearing away.

"Bye," she cried, waving at her cousins. She clamped down on the tears that threatened behind her dark eyes.

Flower vendors, who only minutes before were busy selling leis to departing passengers, headed to the adjacent pier where they would soon meet the next arriving vessel.

"Come on," Tom said. He and Richie walked to the end of the pier, winding between the mobs of people, waving and calling farewells to the girls. But Grace's feet felt nailed to the ground, and she stood mutely with her parents.

Lilly put her arm around her daughter's slight shoulders. "They'll write," she said, "and they can come and spend the summers here," she added brightly.

However, Grace knew that passage was not cheap; she doubted that she would see her cousins any time soon.

"They'll be back," Ken said quietly. "My sister is going to hate Los Angeles."

Grace's aunt might indeed hate L.A. However, Grace knew that her uncle and Naomi would love it there. It seemed unlikely that the Fujitas would be moving back to Hawaii.

"Are we going to the store, Dad?" Richie asked when he and Tom rejoined them.

"Yes. After we drop off your mother and Grace."

Tomoaki, known to all as Tom, was nineteen and had just finished his freshman year at the University of Hawaii. Richie had graduated from U.H. with a degree in management and was now employed full time in the family business. Both young men had grown up working at the store, aptly named Kawakami's. Ken had been grooming them from an early age to take over, just as Grace's grandfather had trained him.

"We need to look in on your parents before you go to the store," Lilly said to her husband as they walked out to the parking lot. "Grandfather isn't recovering as well as I'd expected."

Lilly was a nurse and worked at Queen's Hospital where she had taken her training. She was an unusual woman in 1941 Hawaii, having both an advanced college degree and a foreign born husband. Her parents had been killed in an automobile accident when she was twenty. Her father was a minister, and Lilly had been reared in a strict, religious home. Their deaths had shaken her faith so badly that she had turned her back on the church. Lilly thought that if there was a God, he would have known that she needed her parents more than He did.

She finished her nursing course, met Ken on a tour at the Bishop Museum, and began dating him shortly thereafter. They shared a love of language, history, reading, and movies, and they soon found each other's company both comfortable and comforting. After many months of seeing each other, friendship grew into love. Theirs was not an easy relationship, even in Hawaii. Many of their friends doubted the wisdom of their decision to marry. Ken's mother was opposed to the union and had never reconciled herself to the idea of a Caucasian daughter-in-law. However, time had proven them a good match and despite their cultural differences, the marriage prospered.

"I'm sure Dad will be fine," Ken reassured his wife.

Ken's father had recently had a stroke. Although it had been mild, he was still weak and lacked any appetite. Grace's grandfather had brought his family to Hawaii in 1910 when his two children were teenagers. The import business he had started long ago was now doing very well and had become a family concern. Ken, as well as Grace's brothers, all worked there. Grandfather's failing health was another reason that her aunt was unhappy about leaving the islands.

"I'm concerned about him, Ken," Lilly insisted.

"Try not to be. I'm sure he'll rally."

Grace's father always looked on the bright side: her cousins would come back; her grandfather would be fine; the sun would shine tomorrow. She loved his optimism, although at times, it frustrated her. Sometimes it seemed like he didn't take things seriously.

By the end of the week, it was clear that Grandfather was not going to be fine. He had continued to weaken, and late on the Saturday after her cousins left, he lay like a paper doll under a thin blanket in the hospital bed. Grace's grandmother sat in a chair next to the bed, her back rigid. Grace's father stood on the other side, his hand resting gently on his arm.

Grandfather's eyelids fluttered suddenly, and he forced them open. He looked directly at his wife. "Take my ashes home." Grace saw the muscles in his neck contract with the effort it took to speak. "Promise me."

Her grandmother's whispered response was impossible to hear, but her grandfather melted back into the pillow, and before long, his spirit was carried into the next world.

"That's the way he would have wanted it," Ken comforted his daughter later.

The family was sitting at the table in her grandmother's kitchen, discussing what needed to be done during the critical upcoming three days. Grandmother and Grandfather lived next door where, until the week before, her cousins had also lived. Her grandparents were Buddhist, and though they followed the rites of their religion only casually, death was a serious matter. Grandmother, whose family was *samurai*, had been stoic and quiet all day. The *samurai* were the military aristocracy, whose behavior was carefully prescribed, for women as well as for men. Worthy *samurai* were loyal, honor bound, courageous, proud of family, and *never* showed fear or emotion.

"Actually," Richie said, "I think he would have liked to live to a hundred."

"*Shikata ga nai*," their grandmother said. Grace had heard the familiar phrase her entire life. It meant "there's nothing I can do about it," or "some things cannot be helped," or, in extreme situations, "there is no hope." Grace was never exactly sure which of the translations was accurate.

"I'm taking his ashes back to Japan," Grandmother said without preamble.

"He never said anything to me about that before today," Ken said, looking from his mother to his wife. "Did he ever mention it to you?" he asked Lilly.

Grandmother grunted. "Why would he tell *her*?"

"I just meant he'd never talked about it," Ken said in deference.

"Well, he talked to me about it," Grandmother argued. "And that's what I'm going to do."

"You can't go to Japan alone," Ken said, in a tone somewhere between respectful and rebellious.

"Why not?" the woman asked, her voice raising just enough to let him know she was displeased.

"Mother, please be reasonable," he said carefully.

"I can go with her," Richie offered.

Lilly glanced at him with dismay, but she said nothing.

"It's late," Ken said, standing. "We can talk about it tomorrow."

Lilly and the children stood, taking his lead.

"Do you need anything else, Mother?" Ken asked.

She shook her head.

"Goodnight, then," he said, and patted her tenderly.

Grace followed the others out the backdoor, across the short walkway, and into their own house, where they'd lived since before Grace was born. Their entire neighborhood was occupied primarily by Japanese families.

"It was kind of you to offer," Lilly said to Richie once they were in the house, "but you've never been to Japan. You have no idea what it's like there."

"I can speak Japanese, Mother. I'm sure I can manage."

"Let's give it a night," Ken said to them. "We'll talk more about it in the morning."

Grace said goodnight and went into her room. She did not want to get into the middle of an argument. She brushed her long, dark hair, pulled on her pajamas and slipped under a sheet. She could hear the rest of the family as they prepared for bed and, eventually, went into their rooms. Before long, the house fell silent.

Grace woke to the sound of loud voices, something that rarely happened in her family. Although she heard her parents arguing, she couldn't hear what it was about. They were in the kitchen, which was right next to her room. It was the middle of the night, and she was alarmed. Something was wrong.

She got up quietly and snuck into the hallway where she stood, unnoticed, and listened to them argue.

"She can't go alone, Lilly," her father said.

"You go with her!" Her mother's words were short and sharp and shrill.

"I can't leave the store." Her father's voice, though loud, sounded flat and emotionless, as if he had said the same thing a dozen times. "Richie will be fine. He speaks Japanese fluently. He can do some business for me while he's there."

"It's not a good time for them to go. Things with Japan are too unsettled. They're already at war with China."

"You worry too much, Lilly. Everything will be fine. They'll be back by the end of the summer."

"Why can't they come back right away?"

"They have to be there to commemorate the forty-ninth day."

Grace knew that in the Buddhist tradition, the all-important forty-ninth day after a death represented the period of time it took for a soul to pass from earth to heaven.

Lilly didn't respond, and Grace could imagine the look of resignation on her mother's face. When she heard a chair move, Grace quickly ducked back into her room. The argument had ended. Richie would go with Grandmother to take Grandfather's ashes back to Japan.

"Great!" Richie was saying when Grace went into the kitchen the next morning. "If we go through Tokyo, I can visit those two porcelain manufacturers and find out why our shipments are always short."

"You won't have a lot of time. I'll need you at the store before Tom goes back to school in the fall."

Grace poured herself a cup of tea and sat down next to her mother. Lilly looked tired and defeated; she said nothing. Grace could see the concern on her face, and knew that Richie did, too.

"Don't be upset, Mom," Richie said. "We'll be back before you know it. I'll even bring you a nice souvenir," he added, with a grin that looked exactly like their father's.

Lilly smiled wanly at her eldest child. In her eyes, a mixture of pride and fear fought for supremacy. "I know you'll be careful, but I can't help being concerned. Relations with Japan are so strained right now. I just wish..." her voice trailed off.

"I'll check on tickets today," Ken said. "We'll need passports for both of you. Mother's must have expired years ago."

"We'll have to get expedited service," Richie said.

Ken turned to his younger son, who had been listening quietly to the conversation. "I'll need you full time at the store for the summer."

"Whatever you want, Pop."

Grace saw both her parents cringe at the colloquialism, although neither said a word about it. Tom was the only one of the three Kawakami children to use slang. Both Ken and Lilly tried to dissuade him, but the casual words kept popping up in his speech. The Kawakami children had been drilled in both English and Japanese; their parents had insisted they learn to speak each language properly.

"Classes start the second week of September. I'm all yours until then."

Ken gave his son a sharp look.

"And after that, too, if you need me," Tom added quickly.

"Thank you."

"I can help, too, Father," Grace said.

"I'll be counting on both of you."

Grace's father booked Richie and her grandmother on the ship Kamakura Maru, which was returning to Japan from San Francisco by way of Hawaii. They'd be leaving on July 7th and arriving in Yokohama on the 18th. They had return passage on the Asama Maru on August 30th. Grace thought it sounded like a great adventure despite her mother's fears.

"It won't be difficult to take a train from Yokohama to Osaka," Ken assured his wife. "At that point, the family will be there to take care of things."

Grandfather had three brothers who lived in a small town not far from Osaka, where they had all grown up. Ken sent a telegram informing them of Grandfather's death and telling them to expect Richie and Grandmother.

So, the family stood on the pier at Honolulu Harbor for the second time in less than a month, saying goodbye.

"Send us a cable as soon as you arrive," Lilly said to Richie as Grace draped an orchid *lei* around his neck.

"I will, Mom. Please, don't worry. We'll be fine."

Grace's grandmother, dressed in a dark *kimono,* stood rigid and silent at Richie's side. She was a tiny woman, with wispy gray hair pulled back at the nape of her neck. She rarely smiled, and since Grace's grandfather had died, she seemed to have no expression at all.

"I'll miss you, Grandmother," Grace told her. "I wish you didn't have to go."

The old woman nodded and patted Grace's arm.

"It must be done, Grace. *Shikata ga nai,*" her father said.

When the final boarding call came over the loudspeaker, Richie bowed gracefully to his parents and put his arm gently around his grandmother. "We'll see you soon," he called over his shoulder.

Again, they stood and watched a huge ship pull their family apart at the pier. Grace saw tears play at the corners of Lilly's eyes. She wiped them quickly away and waved to Richie, who stood tall and handsome at the ship's railing.

"Be safe," Lilly called, her voice choking.

"Bring me something Japanese," Grace cried, trying to make her mother laugh.

Grace ran the length of the pier with Tom, a tiny, two-person escort seeing the lumbering ship out of the harbor.

"Will they really be okay?" Grace asked her brother.

"Sure," he said.

The hesitation in his voice made her uneasy.

She thought about it for a few days, but then forgot about it. Like her father, she preferred to think about the positive aspects of the trip; like a child, she wondered what treasure Richie might bring her.

Grace and Tom worked at the store for the next week; Grace in the office, and Tom waiting on customers and stocking shelves. Kawakami's was popular with the Japanese as well as with the Chinese, the Koreans, and the Hawaiians. Ken's studied mix of textiles, porcelain, clothing, and ethnic foods appealed to a broad spectrum of the multi-cultural population. He was also a shrewd businessman and knew that keeping open accounts for people who had fallen on hard times, made for loyal customers in better times.

"Thank you, Mrs. Nagoya," Tom said as he handed a woman a large bag. "I hope to see you again soon."

The lady bowed just slightly. "You will," she assured him.

"Do you mind if I go to lunch?" Grace asked her brother as the door closed behind the woman.

Tom looked surprised. "You're going out?" They usually ate lunch together in the office.

"I want to get a couple of things at the drug store. I won't be long."

"Go ahead. Just don't get lost," he teased.

Grace walked down the street, happy to be outside in the middle of the day. She looked in the windows of the stores on the block, one of which featured the very latest fashions. *Naomi would love this*, she thought, noticing a chic dress in one of the displays. She hadn't heard anything from her cousins since they'd left for L.A., and had to keep reminding herself that they were busy registering for school and moving into the house her uncle had rented.

"Gracie!" she heard from behind, and she turned.

"Vivie!" she cried. Her best friend, Vivian Ozawa, caught up with her. "You did it," she said, touching the soft curls that framed her friend's face. "Is it really a perm?"

"Yes. What do you think?"

"I like it."

"Thanks."

While they were the same height, Vivian was heavier than Grace; more muscular and athletic. Grace thought the new hairstyle softened her appearance.

"Where have you been?" Vivian asked.

"My dad needed me to help out at the store since Richie went with my grandma. I told you that."

"I didn't think you meant every day, all day."

"I know. We've been busy. For some reason, people are buying a lot more than usual. Everybody seems nervous." Grace looked around as she spoke, not entirely sure why she was uneasy about their conversation.

"My mom is doing the same thing," Vivian said quietly. "What do you think is going to happen?"

"I don't know. I'm almost afraid to think about it."

"Where are you going?" Vivian asked.

"To the drug store. Come with me."

"Okay."

Like Kawakami's, the drug store seemed busier than usual. Grace selected a bottle of pale pink fingernail polish, a hairbrush, and a pad of stationery.

"Is that it?" the cashier asked her.

"Yes."

After paying, they walked back toward Kawakami's. "Let's go to the movies on Saturday," Vivian said.

"I don't know if I can. I'll ask Dad."

"We don't have to go in the afternoon. We could go at night."

"My parents still don't like me to be out alone at night," Grace said.

"Ask Tom if he'll go with us. They wouldn't mind that, would they?"

"No. I think that would be okay. I'll talk to you later and let you know."

Grace knew something was wrong the minute she walked back into the store. Tom and her father were talking quietly in the stock room; there were no customers in sight.

"What's happened?" she asked.

Her father held a cable in his hand. He read the message to her. "Grandmother had heart attack this morning. Resting comfortably in ship hospital. More when we arrive Yokohama."

"But…" Grace stammered.

"She'll be fine. She's strong, and Richie will take care of her."

Grace looked at Tom, who nodded in agreement with their father.

"Let's get back to work," Ken said, and turned to go back to his office.

However, things were feeling less and less fine to Grace.

A week later, Richie sent another cable. Grandmother was recovering, but still needed to be hospitalized. They were in Yokohama. Although Grandfather's brothers had come to the city to help out, there was little anyone could do except wait. She was getting excellent care and seemed to be in good spirits. She merely wanted to get out and go to the family home with Grandfather's ashes.

They'd just finished eating dinner when the cable arrived. Grace stopped clearing the table when Tom said, "If you want to go over, Grace and I can run the store."

Lilly looked alarmed.

"I can't do anything more than Richie can," Ken said. "But thank you for the offer, son."

Grace plunged her hands into the hot, soapy water and began scrubbing the plates. She could just imagine her tiny grandmother, lying in a hospital bed surrounded by nurses and doctors, and poor Richie, trying to keep her from jumping up to take Grandpa's ashes home. If her grandmother was determined to do something, nothing could stand in her way.

"Couldn't one of Grandpa's brothers take the ashes back?" Grace asked.

Ken laughed. "They could if my mother would let them. She promised she'd do it and that's the way it will be."

Lilly was silent as she began drying the dishes. A knock at the door startled her, as though her mother was waiting for the next blow.

"That's probably Hiro," Tom said. "He wanted to go play ball at the park."

Tom had met Hironori Sato his first week at the university, when they'd both joined the Reserve Officers Training Corps. Recently, all entering male freshmen were required to join ROTC and participate in it for at least two years. It was another part of Hawaii's preparedness efforts, given the uncertainty of the world situation.

"Hey," Hiro said when Tom opened the door.

Grace glanced quickly at him, appreciating, as she always did, how handsome he was.

"I'll be home later," Tom said, slipping on his flip flops as he left.

As in all Japanese households, the Kawakamis took their shoes off at the door, one of the many traditions of an Asian home. It was such a habit that Grace often found herself barefooted in her Caucasian friend's houses, as well.

"Can I go over to Vivian's?" Grace asked when she finished the dishes. "She wants me to go to a movie with her."

"Of course," her mother said. "Just don't be out too late."

The evening was warm, and the trade winds were picking up as Grace walked down the street to Vivian's house. They'd known each other since the first grade and had been close friends for many years. Vivian was an only child. Since her parents were considerably older, they seemed to worry excessively about her. She had fewer freedoms than Grace, and in many ways, was far more traditional.

"Hello, Grace," Vivian's mother greeted her. "Please come in."

Grace made a slight bow to the woman and slipped off her flip flops. "Hello, Mrs. Ozawa."

"I'm in my room," Vivian called out.

Grace went into her friend's room and found her sitting on her bed, looking at a movie magazine.

"Isn't Clark Gable dreamy?" Vivian asked.

"I guess so. He seems so old," Grace said, picking up another of the magazines strewn on her friend's bed.

"Well, who do you like?"

"Tyrone Power."

"You're right. He's good looking, but I've been in love with Clark Gable ever since I saw *Gone with the Wind*. Speaking of movies, I thought we were going to go tonight."

"We are. It isn't too late, is it?"

"Not if my parents come with us. Would you mind?"

"Of course not."

"*The Philadelphia Story* is playing downtown. I know my mom would like to see it."

Both of Vivian's parents wanted to see the movie, so the four of them went together. On the way home Vivian said, "I think maybe Cary Grant is more handsome than Clark Gable." She looked at Grace. "Well?"

"What?"

"What do you think?"

"I still like Tyrone Power," Grace said.

Vivian's mother laughed. "I agree," she said.

When Grace got home that night, her parents were already in bed. Tom was in the living room listening to the radio.

"Did you and Hiro have fun?" she asked him.

"Yes. Listen, Grace, I know Dad keeps saying that things are going to be fine." He paused and then said, "I think he's saying that for Mom's benefit."

Grace frowned at her brother. "Are you talking about Grandmother?"

"I'm talking about everything. Hiro knows some of the older guys in ROTC, and they say that things are heating up."

"What do you mean?"

"I mean…" he hesitated, "I mean with Japan. The military is gearing up, and some of the guys are convinced that we're on our way into this war."

"With Japan?" Grace asked, her voice shrill.

"Hush! Not so loud. Yes, with Japan. If we do, things are going to change fast."

"How?"

"First of all, the authorities will close the store."

"What? Why?"

"Because we do business with Japanese companies, and we won't be allowed to do that. Besides, we wouldn't be able to get stock replaced anyway."

"Did you say something to Dad?"

"We talked about it tonight. He actually admitted he's been expecting it. He didn't seem surprised. The thing is, we need to make provisions for ourselves, since we'll lose the income from the store."

"How do we do that?" Grace asked, panic bubbling up in her chest like soapsuds.

"We'll be bringing some things home and stashing them here and next door. We'll want extra supplies for ourselves as well as things to barter. We can't be obvious about it, and we can't talk about it with anyone else. I wanted you to know so you understand." He looked at her closely. "This has to be kept in the family."

"What about Richie and Grandma?"

Tom looked grim. "I have no idea. I wish they'd never left."

Grace lay in bed that night wrapped in worry. Her whole world had turned upside down in less than a month. Her grandfather, gone; her cousins, gone; her brother and grandmother, gone. What, or *who*, was next?

CHAPTER 2

"Take the bag in the house, Grace. Don't look around. Don't be nervous. Just go into the house." Tom spoke calmly, but there was an urgency in his voice.

Grace opened the car door, fighting the impulse to look to see who might be watching. She and Tom and their father had just come home from the store, where they'd packed seven bags with essentials to have on hand in case supplies on the island became scarce.

Once inside, they put all the bags on the kitchen table.

"I'll take most of it next door tonight," Tom said.

"Be sure to open everything so they don't look brand new, son. We don't want it to look like we're hoarding."

"It feels like we're being so paranoid," Grace said.

"Cautious," her father amended.

Two weeks had passed since they'd heard about Grandma's heart attack. They'd been busy with customers making large purchases at the store. At the same time, Ken had made a list of necessities they were now bringing home to have in reserve.

"We're lucky that Grandma lives next door," Grace said, as she and Tom carried the bags to the other house that night after dark.

When they entered through the back door, Tom sniffed loudly. "It smells like an old lady's house in here."

"It's because it's been closed up so long. I'll open the windows, and we can let it air out."

She began opening the windows as Tom stocked the food in the cupboards, put the fabric in their grandmother's linen closet, and stashed the rest of the goods on shelves in the tiny garage behind the house.

"Grandma is going to wonder what in the world happened when she gets home," Grace observed as they walked back quietly through the back yard.

"She'll understand. The uncles are probably doing exactly the same thing in Japan."

"Has Hiro heard anything more?" Grace whispered. "About war, I mean?" War had been on her mind for days. It consumed her thoughts and invaded her dreams. But she was afraid to mention it; afraid that saying the word out loud, might somehow make it happen.

"*He* hasn't said anything, but I've heard customers talking in the store. People are nervous. It's strange, though. They never talk about it in English."

All three Kawakami children spoke fluent Japanese. A vital part of their upbringing included Japanese school, every Saturday, from the time they were very young. There, they had learned not only the language, but the traditions and mores of their father's culture, as well. Chiyo, Naomi, and Vivian had also attended. In fact, most of their friends' parents had insisted on this traditional education. Japanese language schools were prevalent throughout the islands, and many children attended at least through the eighth grade.

"What will happen to Richie and Grandma if war starts while they're in Japan?"

Tom looked away.

"What!"

"I suppose it depends on Grandma. If she's still sick, Richie won't leave her." After a pause he added, "In which case, they'll be stuck in Yokohama. If she can travel, they'll go to the mountains. Richie would be safer there, I think."

"Do *you* think we'll go to war?"

The frown on Tom's face said it all. "I don't see how we can avoid it."

Since 1938, the hostilities in Europe had been in the news nearly every day. Over the past three years, Adolf Hitler had ordered German troops to invade Poland, Finland, Denmark, Norway, France, Belgium, and Holland. Although the United States had proclaimed neutrality, there was growing pressure worldwide for America to join Great Britain in the fight against Germany.

During that same period, Japan had invaded China and Manchuria and continued to attack islands in the Pacific. Grace couldn't understand any of it. Why couldn't countries be content with what they had? Why did they always seem to want more? Was it power? Land? What?

She lay awake that night, fighting off thoughts of disaster. The idea of war was bad enough; imagining her brother and grandmother in foreign territory, thousands of miles away, was unbearable. And not only foreign territory, *enemy* territory. Her grandmother was *samurai*. Still, how could she not be afraid?

At breakfast the next morning, Grace ventured a question. "Will we celebrate *Obon* this year?" One of the most important holidays of the Buddhist calendar, during *Obon*, families honored the spirits of those who had died. The date of the festival, a five-hundred-year-old tradition, was based on the lunar pattern and took place in July or August.

"Yes, of course," her father said. During the holiday, families visited the cemetery to clean and maintain their ancestors' graves and to say prayers for the deceased. Grace especially loved the *bon-odori*, a joyful event where everyone in the community celebrated by dancing together around a high wooden scaffold. For this special occasion, women wore *yukata*, the colorful, lightweight summer *kimono*.

Grandma had always taken charge of the plans for *Obon*. Grace realized that her mother would not know all the intricacies of the day, and Aunt Makiko wasn't there to take over. She felt a sudden sadness; more than half her family was gone, and every day things seemed to be getting worse.

When Grace, Tom, and their father arrived home that evening, Lilly was cooking dinner. "Grace, there's a letter on the table for you from Chiyo."

She glanced at her mother. "Do you need me to help with dinner?"

"No. Go ahead and read your letter."

She tore open the envelope, and began reading out loud.

"Dear Grace,

You can't imagine how big and busy Los Angeles is. We have a small house in an area called "Little Tokyo" that's close to my new school. Many Japanese families live in this area, which you might gather from the name. Naomi will take the bus to UCLA, which is only a few miles away. We both registered last week and will start classes on September 2nd, I'll be taking English, History, Math, Science and PE. I looked in their school yearbook and found some clubs that sounded interesting. I'm going to join the Camera Club.

Naomi loves it here already. She says it's more interesting than Hawaii, because there are so many more things to do here. She met a girl named Allison when she went to register, and is already friends with her. So far everyone is very nice, although I haven't made any friends yet. I miss you. Please write soon.

Chiyo"

"Chiyo is so shy," Lilly said. "I'm afraid that it will be harder for her to make friends than it will be for Naomi."

"She'll meet people at Japanese school," Ken said.

Grace made a face. She'd been overjoyed when her parents had allowed her to quit Japanese school the year before. Chiyo, on the other hand, had continued, and insisted that she liked the classes.

Ken noticed her grimace. "I know you never liked it. Chiyo always did, and that will help her now. Tradition and culture give you a way of belonging in the world...a way of being that..." He stopped, seeing his wife's cautionary look. "Anyway, it will help Chiyo."

Grace was glad to have avoided his lecture.

"I wonder what they'll do for *Obon*," Tom said.

"There's a temple near them. I'm sure Makiko has already made several connections, and if I know her, some elaborate plans," his father replied.

After dinner, they sat together in the living room, listening to the news on the radio.

"Tensions continue to increase between the United States and Japan," the announcer said. "On the local front, the Mayor of Honolulu has appointed a committee to do an analysis of ways to meet the food needs of Honolulu in the event of possible shipping interruptions."

Ken glanced at his wife. "You bought more rice, right?"

"Yes. I went across town last weekend. I thought it was a good idea to go somewhere they didn't recognize me."

Tom chuckled. "And someone from across town no doubt came here to our market."

Grace disliked these discussions, which seemed to be happening more and more frequently. They were talking like war was on the horizon—both for them here in Hawaii, and also for Richie in Japan. Why couldn't the stupid governments work out their differences like civilized people?

Ken was quiet for a bit, and then he said, "Lilly, I want you to open a bank account in your maiden name."

"What?" his wife said, startled.

"There's no telling what will happen if war starts, but I'm pretty sure there will be problems for the Japanese here, if it does. We'll have some protection if you have money of your own available."

"But why my maiden name?"

"Because it isn't Japanese."

She frowned at him. "Have you heard something you're not telling us?"

"No. I've heard fear talking. But I think the smart thing for us to do is to prepare while we can. It's like having insurance. It's a precaution."

Her father's words were prophetic; on July twenty-sixth, the United States froze all Japanese assets, and Japan retaliated by freezing US funds in Japan.

Once again, the family sat in the living room talking about the latest turn of events.

"Thank heaven I have a job," Lilly said.

"We're U.S. citizens," Tom complained. "How the heck can they do this to us? We have a business to run!"

Ken shook his head. "I'm not a citizen. They're not doing it to you...they're doing it to *me*." He looked at his wife. "You opened the account I asked you to, right?"

Lilly shook her head. "I meant to," she began.

"You *didn't*?" Ken asked, his voice strained and sharp.

"I'll do it tomorrow. I'll have to take time off work. It isn't all that easy."

"Lilly, you need to understand how important this is!"

"I'll do it."

"How will we run the store, Pop?" Tom asked.

"We'll make do with what we have in stock for as long as we can. *Shikata ga nai*," he said with a shrug.

"I'm glad Richie and Grandma's tickets are already paid for," Lilly said. "Richie won't have any access to funds in Japan either."

"The uncles will make sure they have anything they need," Ken assured her.

Grace pushed down the panic she felt more and more often when she thought about her brother. They hadn't heard anything more from him since the cable telling them Grandma was in the hospital. She tried to imagine what he was doing every day to keep busy. How could he keep busy and stay out of sight? He must know that the authorities would notice him if war broke out.

"What about Yoshi and Makiko?" Lilly asked.

"We have to hope that the firm will pay him in cash. Unfortunately, they won't have free access to *their* bank accounts now, either."

"How does the government expect us to live?" Grace asked, her voice shrill.

"They aren't thinking about us. It's a political move, meant to hurt the government. Sadly, it's the people who are hurt most in decisions like these."

"Well, they'll have to make some exceptions, or the entire Japanese population of Hawaii will be on the streets," Tom said.

"Let's concentrate on us," Ken told him. "Your mother will get a new account, and then we'll be able to access money more easily. We'll keep the store open as long as we're able, help our customers, and prepare ourselves the best we can."

"Will we go to war, Daddy?" Grace asked, not only sounding like a child, but feeling like one as well.

"Only if the United States has no other option."

The next week, a letter from Naomi detailed the difficulties the Fujita family was facing in Los Angeles. Lilly read it aloud at the dinner table.

"Thank goodness we already paid my fees for the year, or I wouldn't be able to attend UCLA this year. Father says his job is secure, and the firm is taking care of ensuring his salary, but things have changed here. People on the street and the bus look at me differently these days. One good thing: a neighbor asked me to babysit for her, so now I have a little pocket money. I'm saving it for the fall in case I need any extras at school.

I miss every one of you. I'm sorry about Grandfather. It's hard to imagine that I'll never see him again. I'm sure that Grandma will recover quickly. She's *samurai*, after all. Let us know what you hear from Richie. Write soon. Naomi."

"Wow!" Tom said. "Naomi is working. Times *are* tough."

"It won't hurt her a bit," Ken said. He'd always felt his oldest niece was a little spoiled. "Hardship builds character."

"I bet Grandma would agree with that," Grace said.

The following Saturday, Richie sent another cable saying that Grandma was still in the hospital, and that the doctors thought she might be there another week. He closed with, "All is well. Uncles taking care of everything. Will write soon."

"I don't like it," Lilly said, pacing between the dining room and the living room. "She should be well enough to travel by now. It's been two weeks. There's something the doctors aren't telling them."

"She's old. She's just lost her husband, and she's had a heart attack. Her system is in shock. She'll be fine, Lilly. Try not to worry. She'll be fine."

"You keep saying that, but it doesn't seem right to me."

Ken started to respond, and then Grace noticed he stopped himself. She was glad. She didn't think she could stand hearing "She'll be fine," one more time.

The day before *Obon* began, Grace met Vivian for a soda at Benson Smith's, the drug store fountain where locals often gathered.

Vivian took a long sip of her Coke. "Are you ready for the festival?"

"Pretty much. It feels so weird without my grandparents. Last year Grandma said she'd buy me a new *yukata* when I turned sixteen. Since she's not here..." Her voice trailed off. *Yukata* were worn in summer when the heavier, silk robes called *kimono*, were too warm. Although *yukata* were much less expensive than *kimono*, Grace didn't want to ask her parents for a new one. Money was now a huge concern.

"When will she and Richie come home?"

"They have passage on August 30th. That is, if Grandma can travel."

"Is she still in the hospital?"

"As far as we know." Grace paused a moment, and then said, "I didn't realize I'd miss Richie so much. The house feels weird without him there, sort of off balance."

Vivian nodded, and yet Grace knew she couldn't understand. Richie was the favorite child, as first-born sons often were. He had a loving, generous nature, and was constantly looking out for his younger brother and sister. He'd always been the center of the family. Now they were trying to make a wheel work with no hub.

When they had finished their sodas, they walked home together.

"I'll see you in the morning," Vivian said.

"Come over as soon as you're ready, okay?"

"I will."

When Grace woke the next morning, she was every bit as excited about *Obon* as always. She dressed carefully, and then did her best to tie the *obi* sash around her middle. Lilly helped as much as she could, but her hands did not know the intricate movements so familiar to Grace's grandmother. An *obi* could be as long as twelve feet, and was nearly impossible for one person to tie.

"You look beautiful," Ken told her. "Your grandparents would be proud."

"*Arigato*," Grace said. She felt the mystical tug of her ancestry as she and Vivian left for the celebration.

As usual, the three day festival sped by, and the final night was coming to an end. The crowd of dancers crushed in around Grace and Vivian, who had drawn as close as possible to the *yagara,* the high, wooden scaffold at the center of the festival grounds. Only the dance leaders moved in front of them, demonstrating the steps and actions to the surrounding throng.

Vivian started laughing at Grace. "You're doing it backwards!"

"I am not," Grace insisted, although she realized then that she was.

Vivian moved easily in her bright green and white *yukata,* which was printed with purple and yellow hash marks. Her equally bright orange *obi* was carefully tied and matched the *geta*, or thonged, wooden sandals she wore. Grace wore a crimson colored *yukata* with a black and gold *obi,* and black *geta.* They smiled as they danced, copying the familiar movements and gestures they'd seen all their lives.

Tom squeezed in beside them. "Where have you two been? I've looked for you everywhere."

"We were with Mom and Dad until about half an hour ago," Grace said.

"Dance, Tom," Vivian urged.

"Are you kidding? I can't dance. Let's go have some stir fry noodles."

The girls shook their heads.

"We just started dancing," Grace said.

"Dance with us for a while first, and then we'll go with you to eat," Vivian told him.

"Oh, all right," he said, waving toward Hiro, who stood at the edge of the crowd.

The vibrant colors of the *yukata* moved around Grace like a giant kaleidoscope. The steady beat of the drums echoed in her chest, and found its way to her feet. Joy spread from her heart to her lips. She saw Hiro dancing at the side, safe from the eyes of their friends. Grace knew how easily he was embarrassed whenever he attracted attention. He was handsome, but so shy that she could almost feel his discomfort.

When the music stopped, they joined Hiro.

"Aren't you hungry?" Hiro asked the girls, who both nodded.

"I want stir fry," Tom said.

"You can have that any time," Hiro said. "I want *andagi.*"

"Yum," Grace said, imagining the taste of the sweet fried dough made especially for *Obon.*

They walked to the food booths, where they stood in line to buy plates of the much loved treats.

The culmination of the festival was Grace's favorite part: the *Toro Nagashi,* or floating lanterns. Family members set illuminated paper lanterns out to float down the river, symbolizing the spirits of their ancestors returning to the world of the dead. Grace stood with the others, watching as dozens of lanterns rocked gently on the water, and thinking of her grandfather and the mystical journey he had begun.

"Do you think that Grandpa knows we're here?" she whispered to Tom.

The light of the lanterns reflected in his dark eyes. "Absolutely."

A light breeze caressed them as they walked home, watching fireworks light up the sky.

"It's not the same without Grandma and Grandpa," Tom said.

"And Richie," Grace added.

"Richie and Grandma will be home in two weeks," Lilly said. "Then things will be better."

When Grace got up the next morning, the look on her parents' faces told her that things were *not* better. Her mother and father sat at the kitchen table; between them lay the morning paper. Bold headlines read: "Shipping Suspended between the United States and Japan."

"Does that mean passenger ships, too?" Grace asked, struggling to keep her voice under control.

Her father nodded. Her mother simply stared.

"What will happen to Grandma and Richie?" She sounded like someone had a hand around her throat.

"We don't know yet," Ken said.

"We do know," her mother said harshly. "They're stuck. They're stuck in a country that's at war with half the world!"

Grace sat down heavily. "What are we going to do?"

"There's nothing we can do," her mother said.

Tom came into the kitchen. "What's wrong?"

Ken handed Tom the newspaper.

"Not good," he said, scanning the headlines.

"Not good?" Lilly repeated. "*Not good?*"

"It isn't his fault, Lilly. Don't take it out on him."

Grace looked from one to the other. "Why is it so bad? Richie hasn't done anything wrong. He and Grandma can stay with the uncles until...until..." She stopped, not sure until when.

"It's more complicated than that," Lilly said. She looked at her husband with despair.

"The thing is," Ken began, "Richie is a Japanese citizen. He'll be treated just like any other citizen."

"How can he be a Japanese citizen? He was born in Hawaii. He's a US citizen!" Grace insisted. She looked at her brother for reassurance.

"Actually," Tom said, "we're both."

Grace looked at him, surprise registering on her face. "We?"

Tom looked at his father, who shook his head.

"Since I'm a Japanese citizen," Ken began, "Japan considers any child of mine a Japanese citizen. It doesn't matter where you were born. At the same time, since your mother is an American citizen, and you were all born in American territory, the United States considers you a U.S.

citizen. Unless you denounce one or the other, you have dual citizenship."

"Hiro is in the same situation," Tom said. "Lots of the guys in ROTC are. Their parents are Japanese, but they were born here. So, they're both."

Lilly looked miserable. "I wanted your father to file the papers to renounce your Japanese citizenship. Grandma and Grandpa didn't want us to cut those ties, so we decided to wait until they were gone."

Grace thought for a bit. "Well, if he's a Japanese citizen then he should be okay. Right? I mean, they wouldn't arrest him or anything like that."

"No," her father said. "They wouldn't arrest him. That would almost be better."

"They would draft him," Tom said.

"Draft him?" Grace said, confused. She looked at her father who seemed to shrink into himself.

"Japan is at war," Tom said. "If the Japanese military wants you, they take you, no questions asked. They don't care about his U.S. citizenship. To Japan, he's just another young man the right age for the army."

"So," Lilly said, "since he can't come home, his best chance would be to try to hide out with the uncles."

Grace thought of her brother, sitting in a chair in the hospital next to his grandmother's bed. "He won't leave Grandma, will he?" she whispered.

No one answered her, but the reality hung clearly in the air.

Richie was *samurai*.

He would never leave Grandma to save himself.

.

CHAPTER 3

During the next several days, Grace watched the tension increase between her mother and father. If he asked a question, she answered with only one or two words. Her mother rarely spoke at all. Tom tried to keep a conversation going during meals, but with little success. By Friday evening, Grace wanted nothing more than to get away from them.

"I'm going to Vivian's," she said to no one in particular. She slipped on her sandals at the front door.

After a silence of several seconds, her father said, "Please don't be out late." Grace wondered if he even knew what time it was. "Okay."

She and Vivian decided to walk to the park.

"Maybe some of the guys are playing ball," Vivian said.

Since Vivian played both softball and tennis, she was more interested in sports than Grace. Grace would have been happy to watch pigs roll in mud, if it got her out of her house that evening.

They heard cheering as they approached the ball field.

"Hey, Marjorie!" Vivian called, waving to a girl who sat with a group in the stands.

"Hi, Vivian. Come sit with us," her friend yelled.

The two girls climbed up the bleachers and sat down by Margie and two other girls.

"You know Grace, don't you?" Vivian asked.

"Of course. We both had Mr. Freeland for Algebra last year," Margie said. "Naturally, Grace got an A."

Grace smiled self-consciously.

Just then, one of the players hit a homerun. Half the crowd jumped to their feet, cheering.

"I bet you can't wait for school to start, eh Vivian?" Margie said.

"I guess."

"You brainy kids would always rather be in school," Margie insisted.

"She likes vacation as much as we do," Grace said. "Just because she gets straight A's, doesn't mean she doesn't need a break."

"Uh," Vivian said, "I'm right here." She looked at Margie. "I love vacation. Especially because I have time to read books I like."

"I'll bet you're reading some highbrow thing like the Greek tragedies," Margie said.

"Hardly. I'm reading *The Grapes of Wrath*."

"You're reading it in Latin, right?" Margie said.

Grace laughed. She knew Margie was an excellent student except in math, a subject she detested.

"If you weren't in the Honor Society, I'd take this more seriously," Vivian told Margie.

"There's a big difference between *doing* the work and *liking* the work," Margie said. "You actually like it."

"You're right about that," Vivian admitted.

A high fly ball to center field got the crowd to their feet. Half of them cheered when the player there missed it.

"Say, Grace," Margie said quietly, "I heard that Richie is in Japan."

"Yes."

"What's going to happen to him?"

"We have no idea. It doesn't look like he'll be able to leave. My mother is so upset, she can barely talk about him."

Margie lowered her voice. "It's getting scary. The newspapers keep saying we're going to war. My dad doesn't believe it, but there sure are a lot of people who disagree with him."

Grace thought about what Tom and Hiro had said, but decided not to mention it. No point making things worse.

After the game, Grace and Vivian walked home.

"Let's go to the movies tomorrow," Vivian said. "*My Favorite Wife* is playing, and you know how much I like Cary Grant."

"Okay. I should be able to get away for the matinee."

"I'll meet you at noon. We'll have lunch before we go."

Grace walked down the block to her own house, now dark and quiet even though it was only nine o'clock. She guessed that Tom was out, and her parents had gone to bed. She wasn't tired, and was glad that she had a good book to distract her. She changed, got into bed and opened her copy of *Goodbye Mr. Chips*.

However, it wasn't long before her mind had drifted to Richie and her grandmother. She wished she could talk to them. Japan might as well be the moon, it was so far away. What would happen if they went to war? What if Richie got drafted? Maybe he could find some American soldiers and surrender to them. But what if they didn't understand? What if they shot him?

She slept fitfully, the specter of the unknown lurking in the shadows of her dreams.

A cable arrived the next evening. Ken opened it quickly and read aloud, "Grandmother slightly improved. Doctor encouraged. Travel possibly week after next."

They had barely finished dinner, and Grace was starting to wash the dishes.

"He's smart," Tom said. "He doesn't mention where they'll go."

"I'm surprised he was able to send it," Ken said. "They told me at the telegraph office that nothing could go through."

"Maybe it's easier from there," Tom said.

"Maybe the shipping embargo is different there, too," Grace said brightly.

"It's not," Lilly told her. "I spoke to Betty Wong at the travel agency. Nobody can leave there for any U.S. territory. She did say that they'd be arranging for people to travel back to their homes, if they were stranded somewhere."

"Then Richie *could* come back!" Grace said.

"Gracie," Tom said, "he's a Japanese citizen. They aren't going to let him leave."

She felt like he'd thrown a bucket of cold water in her face.

They were all quiet for a while. Ken shifted in his chair. "Has Hiro heard any more scuttlebutt?"

Tom shook his head. "The ROTC seniors have been pretty tight-lipped lately. He's not sure what that means."

"Everybody's nervous," Ken said. "I see it at the store every day. People don't talk as much, or as loudly as they used to. And they talk more in Japanese and less in English. A lot of time, I see them look around before they say something."

"The same thing is happening at the hospital," Lilly said. "Everybody is on edge. They get angry easily. Nobody has any patience. One of the doctors bit my head off the other day, simply because I asked him about an order on a chart."

"All we can do is try our best to understand," Ken said, and Grace braced herself for the 'things will be fine' speech. To her surprise he said, "I'm afraid it's going to get worse before it gets better."

During the last week of summer vacation, Grace realized she'd barely thought about school starting up again. At the end of the spring term, she'd been looking forward to her junior year of high school. Now that Richie was stranded and Chiyo was miserable, school didn't seem nearly as important to her.

"Wouldn't you like to get some new clothes for school?" her mother asked her at breakfast on Wednesday. "What about Saturday? Vivian could go with us if you'd like."

"Sure," Grace said without much eagerness.

"While you're at it, get her a new pair of shoes," Ken said. "Sturdy shoes."

"Sturdy shoes?" Grace asked. "Why, for heaven's sake?"

"I want you to be prepared."

"Prepared for what?"

"For whatever comes. I'm not sure what, but all the information that the military is putting out lately says to have sturdy shoes. Sandals don't give you any support or protection."

Grace couldn't imagine what her feet might need protection from, but the tone of her father's voice kept her from asking any more questions. He had changed in the weeks since Richie and Grandma had left; her questions seemed to annoy him these days.

On the way downtown that weekend, she asked her mother, "Is Daddy mad at me? He seems so grumpy when I talk to him."

"No sweetheart," her mother said gently. "He's just worried. He doesn't like to admit it. It's his nature to believe that things will be fine, and they aren't fine right now."

"You mean he's worried about Richie?"

"He's worried about all of us. And the store. Things are so uncertain right now, and there is more and more animosity toward the Japanese." She paused and then said, "He thinks we'll be at war by the end of the year."

"Do you?"

"I don't know. I certainly hope not. The situation with Japan isn't improving though, and Europe is a mess. Hitler has to be stopped somehow. I'm not sure France and England can do that on their own."

Grace couldn't think of what to say. The world around them was falling apart.

Her mother looked at her. "Try not to worry, Grace. There's nothing that we can do about any of it. Our only job is to be ready to face whatever might come. Your father wants to make sure we have all the supplies on the Preparedness List that the Major Disaster Council put out. Aside from that, we need to try to think positively."

Even looking for new clothes didn't make Grace feel better. They returned home with two new dresses, a skirt and blouse, and new shoes and socks. Grace put them all away with little interest.

"I'm going down to Vivian's" she told her mother. "She asked me to stay for dinner if that's okay."

"Of course. Have fun," she added brightly.

Vivian was reading, but when Grace came in, she put the book aside and asked, "Did you get anything at the store?"

"I bought a couple of dresses, and a skirt and blouse. Oh, and a pair of saddle shoes."

"My mom said she thought I had plenty of clothes."

"She's right. You have more clothes than anyone I know."

"One of the advantages of being an only child."

Grace curled up in the chair next to Vivian's bed. "Do your parents ever talk about war?"

"Probably. But never in front of me."

"My dad thinks we'll be in it before the end of the year."

"Really?"

"Yes. Tom hears things from the ROTC guys, too."

"Like what?"

"Like it's only a matter of time."

Vivian glanced away, and then turned back to Grace. "What about Richie?"

"Tom says they won't let him leave because he's a Japanese citizen. We're dual citizens. Have you ever heard of that?"

"Yes. I'm both, too. My parents wanted me to keep my dual citizenship. They want me to have the same tie to Japan that they have."

"Do they want to go back? Move back, I mean?"

"No. It's more about the tradition, I think. Or, better put, the culture. They'd never go back. Life was difficult for them there. But the United States won't allow them to become citizens, so if they renounce their Japanese citizenship, what *are* they? They would literally be without a country."

The two sat in silence.

"This is a lousy way to spend our last weekend of vacation," Vivian said. "Let's go get a root beer float."

"You're right." Grace said. "Enough of this morbid talk. Let's go have some fun."

On Monday, Grace and Tom attended Honolulu's Labor Day Parade with their parents.

"Listen to this," Ken said that night when he was reading the evening paper. "There were more than seven thousand Unionists who marched in the parade today."

Grace laughed. "I thought it would never end."

"They're organized to protect all of our rights, Grace," Tom said.

She said nothing. She'd had enough of politics.

The next morning, Grace was ready for school early. Her mother had offered to drop Vivian and her off on her way to the hospital. Grace ate a bowl of cereal with a banana, and then brushed her teeth and her hair. She let it hang down straight, even though she knew it would be warm and muggy by ten o'clock. The first few weeks of school were always a challenge because of the humidity. She looked forward to November, when the days were milder.

"Ready?" her mother asked.

"Ready."

She and Vivian went to the Back to School assembly together, and then met with other friends outside the auditorium. McKinley was a large school with more than three thousand students. Every nationality on the island was represented, including Hawaiian, Caucasian, Japanese, Chinese, Filipino, Korean, and mixes of them all. Each fall, clubs and organizations offered students the opportunity to pursue their talents and interests outside the classroom. Following the assembly, the groups set up tables with flyers detailing their activities. Club members gave interested students information sheets along with registration forms.

"Are you on yearbook staff this year, Grace?" Ruth Hanoi asked her.

"I am. So you'd better be careful what you do, because I'll be hanging around taking pictures of people all semester."

"It can't possibly be as bad as Chiyo was last year. She and that camera were everywhere. I bet she slept with it," Vivian said.

"I bet you're right," came a voice from behind Grace.

She turned. "Beatrice! I thought you were moving to the big island."

"I was. Then, my aunt and uncle said I could stay with them so I could finish my senior year here. I couldn't refuse."

"That's so good of them," Grace told her. "I'd hate to miss graduating with my class."

Beatrice and Grace were both in Junior Red Cross. Their mothers had met in nursing school, and had worked together at Queen's Hospital until Beatrice's father was transferred to Hilo the past spring. The family moved to the big island in June.

"Are you joining another club, Grace?" Beatrice asked.

"No. But I need to know about everything that's going on around campus, so that we include it all in the yearbook."

The girls walked along the line of tables and displays, greeting friends and picking up flyers from the various groups.

"You should join choir," Grace said to Beatrice. "It's so much fun."

"If I could carry a tune, I would. Unfortunately, my voice sounds like Olive Oyl."

Vivian laughed. "Mine, too. On the other hand, with so many kids in the group, maybe they wouldn't notice our voices. There must be more than two hundred singers."

"About two hundred and fifty," Grace corrected.

"And everybody reads music?" Beatrice asked.

"Just about," Grace said.

The morning bell rang, signaling that classes would start in ten minutes.

"See you at lunch," Grace told Vivian, and she turned to head for her first period course.

Grace set the table that evening while Lilly prepared dinner. Tom and her father came through the door just as the clock struck six.

"Why so late?" Lilly asked.

"My fault," Tom said. "I had to stop and buy some supplies for school. They're less expensive in town than they are on campus."

"How are your classes?" Grace asked, as they sat down at the table.

"Fine. Big. Lower division classes are always crowded, especially at first. After a few days, people figure out their schedules and drop out of their double-booked courses. What about you?"

"So far, so good. I have Mrs. Wallace for Core Studies."

"Lucky you. Everybody says she's the best. I got stuck with Miss Johnson. What a crone."

"Tom," Lilly said, "I don't like to hear that kind of talk about a teacher."

"Sorry. Anyway, you'll like Wallace," he told Grace with a sly wink.

She did her homework after dinner and then took a shower. When she came out of the bathroom, she heard a familiar sound coming from Tom's room. She peeked in the door. Tom was working at his short wave radio.

"Wow! I haven't seen you use that thing since you were in Radio Club at McKinley."

"It dawned on me that I might be able use this to get in touch with Richie."

"Do the uncles have a radio?"

"I doubt it. But radio operator hams know other hams, and I might be able to make a connection somehow."

"That's a great idea." Tom was the problem solver in the family. Grace loved that about him. "Thanks, Tom."

He smiled at her.

"See you in the morning."

"'Night," he said, returning to the radio.

Tom continued his attempts all week, with no success.

On Saturday, a cable arrived from Richie that said, "Grandma improving; not yet able to travel."

"I wish he'd tell us how *he's* doing," Lilly said that evening at dinner.

"He's fine, Mom," Tom reassured her. He glanced at Grace. "I've got an idea. Let's play Monopoly tonight."

Grace started to say no thanks, when the look on her brother's face made her change her mind. "That sounds like fun. Don't you think so, Mom?"

Lilly looked from one child to the other and grinned. "I'm game. What about you, dear?" she asked Ken.

"You're serious? We haven't played Monopoly for years. What's up?"

"We don't have to if you don't want to," Tom said. "I just thought it would be something different."

Ken stood up from the table. "I agree." He patted Tom on the shoulder. "If I remember correctly, I used to be the big winner whenever we played."

"That was during the dark ages."

"I'll be the banker," Grace said as she and her mother cleared the table.

"Later, we'll listen to *The Shadow*," Tom said, turning on the radio. "Where's the game, Mom?"

"I have no idea. I'm not sure we even have it any more."

"It's in my room," Grace said. "I'll get it."

The evening sped by, and Grace was soon yawning. "I'm beat. I'm ready for bed. Besides, Daddy has all the property anyway."

"I'm with you," Lilly said. "Next time, *I'll* be the banker."

On Monday, Grace found letters from both Naomi and Makiko in the mailbox.

"Do you want to hear this?" Grace asked as she opened Naomi's.

"Of course," her mother said.

"Fire away," Tom told her.

"Classes have started at UCLA, and so far, I like all my professors. Allison and I are in the same English and Psychology sections. Books are expensive and heavy! The student body is very active - there are so many clubs and organizations, I don't know where to start. The first football game will be on September 20th, just like UH. Maybe we'll meet in the playoffs. Ha! Dad is very busy at work. Mom is hoping to be called in to substitute teach. Chiyo is writing, so I'll leave it to her to tell you her news. Tell my friends hello. Naomi."

"What about Chiyo's letter?" Ken asked.

"There wasn't one from her. Maybe we'll get it tomorrow."

"I'll read Makiko's," Lilly said, opening the second letter.

"Dear Family,

Life in L.A. is busy. People are always doing something. Nobody seems to relax; I get tired just watching my neighbors. I was hired as a substitute in our local school district, although I haven't been called in yet. This week I visited the La Brea Tar

Pits and saw some of the bones recently excavated. Yoshi and I went to the Grauman's Chinese Theater, which is built like a giant, red pagoda, and looks completely out of place here. My favorite spot so far is the Farmers' Market, where I can find all the foods we like. I hope everyone is well. Write when you can. I miss you all. Makiko."

Lilly chuckled. "She doesn't sound as unhappy as I'd expected. Maybe L.A. it isn't so bad after all."

"So long as Yoshi and Naomi like it, it won't matter what Makiko thinks," Ken said. "There are two squeaky wheels in that family, and it sounds like they're both well-greased."

Grace read Chiyo's letter when it arrived the next day.

"School has started, of course. I don't like it at all. People aren't very friendly to me. I joined the Camera Club, and that is the only thing that's any fun. I wish I could quit school, and just take pictures all day. It's hot here. There's too much pavement. I miss you so much. Please write and tell me everything you are doing.

Chiyo."

"Well, *she* certainly doesn't sound happy," Grace said. "I feel bad I haven't written more. I need to do better."

As soon as she'd finished her homework that night, she wrote a long letter to Chiyo. She told her about her classes, taking pictures for yearbook, the music they were singing in choir, and what she and Vivian had been doing.

She ended with, "I'll try to write more often. Please forgive me. I miss you, too. Grace."

Before long, the weeks were measured by exams, and the upcoming football games. The university team, The Rainbows, was having its best season in years. It wasn't until the final game that they suffered a loss.

"It looks like we'll make it to the Shrine Bowl," Tom announced to everyone on Thanksgiving. "I think we'll be playing Willamette on December 6th."

"Oh, I want to go," Grace said.

"Sure. We should all go," he said.

"Not me," Lilly said.

"I think that your mom and I will go to the movies that night," Ken said. "I don't want to fight the crowd."

The night of the big game, Grace realized how right her father had been. The event was sold out: more than 24,000 spectators filled the arena. Since the stadium was only a few blocks from their house, Tom and Grace, and Hiro and Vivian, walked there together.

"Do you think we have a chance of winning?" Grace asked Tom on the way.

"I heard the guys are pretty wound up. And, they have had a great season. I think the odds are actually pretty good."

They found their seats, and settled in for the game.

Willamette put up a good fight, but the players were no match for the Rainbows. The University of Hawaii won, 20-6.

The four friends walked home, ecstatic over the victory.

"I'll never forget tonight," Grace said, turning around and walking backwards to face the others.

"Me either," Vivian agreed.

"It was the most exciting game I've ever seen," Tom said. "No kidding, it was the best."

"You don't get too many nights like this in a lifetime," Hiro said. "I doubt if any of us will forget December 6th."

CHAPTER 4

Grace loved Sunday mornings. She loved the quiet tranquility when the family relaxed and enjoyed a few hours without work or school. Her favorite days were when her father made breakfast, usually pancakes, because it was so unusual to see him in the kitchen. Sometimes she helped him, and sometimes the boys helped, but in either case, Sunday morning had become her mother's time off.

"Who wants another pancake?" her father asked, his red and white apron covered with batter.

"I do," Tom said.

"Not me," Lilly told him. "I'm stuffed."

"Me too," Grace said. "You eat, Daddy."

"Okay," he said. His voice sounded content and proud, as if he'd done a full day's work when it wasn't yet eight o'clock. He served himself and sat with them at the table.

"So, what's up today?" Ken asked, pouring syrup on his pancakes.

"I have to study," Tom said. "Finals are just around the corner."

"Me, too," Grace told him. "And then maybe see a movie with Vivian."

"I need to do laundry," Lilly said.

In the distance, Grace heard several explosions. She looked at Tom, alarmed.

"It's just Sunday morning maneuvers."

Their conversation continued. So did the explosions. Outside, children's voices turned to parents' shrill screams.

Ken went to the front door, opened it, and stepped out on the porch. A neighbor yelled at him. "Get back inside. It's an attack!"

Ken turned and looked at Tom, confused.

Tom frowned. "Impossible. It's maneuvers." He switched on the radio and tuned in KGMB just as announcer, Web Edwards, said, "This is no drill! This is the real McCoy."

"Oh, my Lord," Lilly said.

Pancakes rolled over in Grace's stomach and threatened to reappear unbidden. She grabbed her mother's arm. "What do we do?"

"We're going to be fine," Lilly said, her voice calm. But her mother's eyes searched the room, almost as if the enemy might come in through the wall.

Tom rushed to the front door.

"Don't go out!" Lilly cried.

"I'm only going to look for a second."

"Tom!" she yelled, but he was already out the door.

Moments later he was back. "My God, Pearl Harbor is black with smoke. Those planes that just flew over had the Rising Sun on them!"

Ken sat down heavily. "It can't be. What are they thinking? Japan can't win a war against the United States!"

Grace watched her father turn into a frail, old man, the apron like a shroud on his collapsed form.

"Grace," Tom said. "Get changed. Put on pants, those new shoes, and a shirt with sleeves."

She wasn't about to leave the room. She wasn't about to be out of sight of her family. What if they bombed their house? What if everybody was killed?

Lilly hustled her down the hall. "We can't stand here doing nothing." Grace was in a daze as her mother pulled out her clothes. "Come with me. We can change together."

Moments later, Grace heard Edwards say, "All Army, Navy, and Marine Corps personnel are ordered to their stations." When they returned to the living room, Ken hadn't moved. He sat hunched over the radio. "All police and firefighters are called to duty. Report immediately!"

Tom came in the back door from the garage, his arms full. "Dad, you need to get changed. At the very least, we have to be ready in case we're evacuated."

Ken looked up at his wife. "I can't believe it. I just can't *believe* it."

"Dad!" Tom said sharply.

Ken looked up at him.

"Go and get changed, Dad. People out there need help."

Ken stood as if shaken from a trance. "Yes, of course," he said, and he hurried toward the bedroom.

"Help me, Grace," Lilly said, quickly clearing the dishes from the table.

"Where's that preparedness list, Mom?" Tom asked.

"In the bottom drawer of the desk, right in the front."

Grace washed the dishes as Tom started a pile of supplies in the corner of the living room: flashlights, gloves, tarp, first aid kit, matches, and water jugs, reading each item aloud as he added it to the stack. Grace's anxiety grew as the stack grew.

Ken returned to the front room. "Thank you, son," he said, glancing at the accumulation of necessities. He turned up the radio. "I don't want to miss anything."

An explosion rocked the house. Grace screamed and dropped the glass she was washing. It shattered on the floor, sending shards of glass flying like shrapnel.

"They're bombing here!" Tom cried.

"Mom…" Grace said, terror tripping her tongue. "I'm scared!"

"We're okay, Grace," her mother soothed. "It was a mistake. There's no reason for them to bomb civilians." She shot Tom a warning glance.

Tom opened the front door cautiously and went out on the porch. "There's a fire *mauka.*" He pointed toward the mountains. "It looks like it's over on King Street."

Grace shuddered. That was only four blocks away!

"I'm going to see if I can help," Tom said, grabbing a pair of gloves.

"Tom, no," his mother said.

He looked at her. "Mom…"

"Yes…of course…you need to see if you can help." Grace heard reluctance mixed with pride in her mother's voice.

"I'll go with you," Ken said.

Tom looked at Grace, and then at his mother. "Do you want one of us to stay here with you?"

"We'll be fine," Lilly said calmly. "You be careful."

The two men went out the door, and Lilly began to clean up the broken glass.

"I'm sorry," Grace said numbly, looking at the mess.

"It's not important."

Grace began drying the dishes, moving in jerky motions, like a marionette on strings.

"I'm going to fill the bathtub with water," Lilly said. "It's one of the things they've been drumming into us at work."

"What else should we do?"

"Check that list Tom found. See what else we need."

Alone in the living room, Grace could barely keep her mind on the list. She kept checking the door, listening for any sounds outside. Would the next person through the door be a friend or an enemy?

Grace's body tensed as she read the heading on the paper: "Preparedness for Major Disaster." She glanced down the page to the section entitled "In case of evacuation," which detailed clothing and food to include in an evac kit. She found some of the foods, put them in a bag and added them to the growing mound. She shook with each explosion or sound outside. When her mother finally returned to the room, Grace's breath escaped like a popped balloon.

"Do you think we'll be evacuated?" Grace asked.

"We're not in the evacuation area. But if the fires get worse or the authorities decide it isn't safe here, we'll have to leave. Get some extra clothes into a bag. I'll do the same."

Although Grace's room was right next to her parents', she felt a hundred miles away from her mother. She packed a change of clothing in a small bag, then added a hairbrush and her book. The thought of the familiar ritual of reading before bedtime, soothed her.

Some of the things on the list seemed ridiculous. A jacket. When would you ever need a jacket in Hawaii? Unless you were up on the Pali, the high mountain. She stuffed a jacket in the bag.

One explosion after another shook Grace's world. Web Edwards repeated, "This is an attack. Stay under cover," over and over.

"I smell smoke," Grace said. She rubbed her arms, trying to keep her mind from losing contact with her body.

Lilly rushed to the window. "God help us."

"Mommy?"

"There are fires everywhere!"

"Should we leave?"

"Absolutely not! We stay here unless we're evacuated."

Lilly stepped away from the window. "Bring your bag out here with this other stuff," she said, pointing to the pile Tom had assembled.

Her father came in through the front door just as Grace dropped her bag on the floor.

"Are you okay?" he asked Lilly, briefly hugging her. The small gesture shocked Grace almost as much as the bombing: her father never showed any outward affection.

"We're fine," his wife assured him.

"It's a mess out there. An apartment on King and McCully was destroyed. There are fires all over the place, but nobody's coming to fight them. All the trucks must be at Pearl. Neighbors are dragging garden hoses around, trying to do their best."

"Where's Tom?" Lilly asked, glancing past him, and out the window.

"He'll be here in a minute. He got burned. You'll need to take a look at him."

Lilly immediately went into the pile of supplies and found the first aid kit.

"Burned?" Grace repeated.

"It's his arm. He's fine, but I think it should probably be covered."

Tom came in, breathless, filthy, and spattered with blood. When he saw the look on Lilly's face, he glanced down at himself. "It's not mine. I'm okay. It's only a little burn."

He pulled off his gloves, and offered his mother the burned arm. The wound covered nearly the full expanse and width of his forearm.

"Oh, Tom," Grace cried.

"It's okay. Mom will fix me up."

Lilly cleaned the wound carefully, applied ointment and bandaged it loosely.

Just then Web Edwards announced, "All doctors, nurses, and volunteer aides must report to work immediately."

Grace's head snapped around and her eyes fixed on her mother.

"That's me," Lilly said quietly.

"Do you have to go?" Grace asked. Her voice, small and scared, was a stranger.

"You know I do."

"I'll drive you, Mom. You shouldn't walk."

Lilly changed into her nurse's uniform and picked up the bag she had packed. "There's no telling how bad it will be, or how long I'll need to stay."

She hugged and kissed Grace, and gave her a long look. "I'll be fine, and you'll be fine." She leaned close and whispered something Grace had never heard her say before. "You're *samurai*. Remember that today."

Grace watched Tom drive her mother down the street. Although the explosions had diminished, Grace now tasted the smoke that hung heavy in the air.

"Are you going back out?" she asked her father.

He looked at her tenderly. "No. I'll wait until Tom gets back. I won't leave you alone, Grace."

It took Tom nearly an hour to drive the two miles to the hospital and back. "The streets are a disaster," he told them when he got home. "The ones that haven't been hit are jammed with traffic. Some people are acting crazy, and others are acting as if nothing is happening. I saw one guy headed toward the beach with a surfboard!"

"Tom, listen," Ken said. He pointed to the radio. "Once again, ROTC cadets: all units are called for duty. Report at once to headquarters on the University campus."

"No!" Grace said.

"Yes." He smiled at her gently. "This is what we've been training for, Gracie."

"But your arm…"

"Grace! People are dying. Nobody's worried about a little burn."

He changed quickly into his uniform.

"Stay with Dad. You'll be okay, and so will I," he told his sister.

"I have no idea when I'll be back," he said to his father as he opened the door.

"Be careful, son," his father said. And then, in a voice barely audible, he added, "I love you."

Grace looked at her father as if he, too, might disappear. "You aren't leaving now, are you?"

"Not unless we go together."

They listened to the radio and the explosions, one shock escalating into the next. Announcements calling for emergency personnel to report to work were repeated again and again.

After what seemed to Grace a long forever, the explosions stopped.

Grace sat quietly waiting, listening, wondering. After a time she said, "Should we go see if anyone needs help?"

"I think that's exactly what we should do." He picked up one pair of gloves and handed her another. "You know, it could start again. The bombing."

She looked at him. She thought of her tiny, tenacious grandmother. She thought of her mother's admonition. And she thought of how wonderful it would be to hide somewhere.

"We don't have to go. We can stay here," he said.

"We can't help anyone if we stay here."

"No, we can't."

"Then, I think we need to go," she said, putting on the gloves.

They walked north toward King Street, where smoke hung in the air like a cloud of desolation. Grace could hardly take a breath without coughing.

"Is this where you and Tom went?"

"Yes."

She didn't know what to expect, but she knew she wouldn't like it. Silently, she called on the spirits of all her grandmother's ancestors to help her.

The corner of King and McCully looked like a scene out of Dante's Inferno. Charred houses had collapsed, and flared with fire. Neighbors used garden hoses, doing their best to control the outbreaks.

A man in tattered clothes perched on a chair in the middle of the rubble, holding his head, and mumbling to himself. A girl knelt at his side trying to comfort him. Nearby, a woman sat nursing a baby, and crying. "He's still in there. He's still in there," she kept repeating.

Ken crouched down next to her. "Who?" he asked.

But she just kept repeating the same thing.

Another neighbor stooped and addressed her by name. He spoke to her in Japanese, and she finally looked up. She shook her head and said, "My husband."

Grace stumbled, and would have fallen if her father hadn't caught her by the arm. She looked down at her feet and saw that she'd tripped on a crumpled tricycle.

Across the street, Grace watched two men lift a young woman off the ground, and put her into the back seat of a car. She was covered with blood; her head lolled back, and her arms and legs hung down like a rag doll's.

Ken put his arm around Grace's shoulder, and turned her around. "Don't look."

"Is she dead?"

"I don't know. But it won't help to look."

The men got into the front seat of the car, and drove off toward the hospital.

That was when Grace noticed two other bodies, each covered with a sheet and attended by silent mourners.

"Isn't there something we can *do*?"

Ken began asking people what they needed. They helped one man look for his family, found some crackers for a hungry child, and water for three boys whose parents were fighting the fires. He and Grace did what they could, which seemed insignificant considering the catastrophe they faced.

Grace saw a young couple sitting on the side of the street. They were filthy. A makeshift bandage on the man's arm was oozing blood. She pointed them out to her father.

"Is this your house?" Ken asked, as they approached the pair.

The man nodded.

"Is there somewhere you can go?"

The hollow-eyed man shrugged. "We could go to her parents' if we could get to our car." He gestured toward the collapsed garage.

"I have a car," Ken said without hesitation. "Come with us, and we'll take you."

The two looked at each other. "Let's go with them," the man said gently. "They can take us to your parents' house."

The young woman looked at the garage, and then back at the man. She nodded silently.

Grace and her father led them slowly back to the house.

"Grace," her father said, "take..." he stopped, not knowing the young woman's name. He cocked his head with a silent question.

"Dorothy," she said.

"Take Dorothy in and help her wash up. Give her something clean to put on."

"You need to wash your face," he said gently. "Your mother will have a heart attack if she sees you like that."

Grace led Dorothy into her room. They were nearly the same size, so Grace handed her a pair of pants, a shirt, and some sandals. "These should fit you." She showed her to the bathroom, and gave her a small towel and washcloth.

"I'll wash them and bring them back," Dorothy said when she came out of the bathroom. She had changed and washed her face, and held her soiled clothes in her hand.

"It's no problem," Grace said.

Her husband had washed his face and hands in the kitchen sink. He took his wife's clothes. "This is very kind. Thank you," he said.

The streets weren't as congested as Grace expected. Dorothy's husband, Paul, directed them toward a wealthy neighborhood near Diamond Head, far from Pearl Harbor.

When Dorothy's mother saw her, she began to cry. She hugged her daughter and son-in-law, as Dorothy's father pumped Ken's hand vigorously. "Thank you," he said. "We could see the fires and we were worried sick. Our car is in the shop. I had no way to get to them."

"Please, come in," Dorothy's mother urged. "We can't begin to thank you enough for your kindness."

"I think we'd better go," Ken said. "There are bound to be others we can help."

Dorothy gave Grace a tentative hug. "Thank you so much," she said, her voice barely a whisper. "I'll never forget you helping us."

"Take care of yourselves," Ken told them.

"And you be careful!" Dorothy's father cautioned.

Ken turned on the radio in the car just as Edwards said, "All citizens are ordered off the streets. Do not use your phone; the lines are needed by emergency workers. Keep calm. Stay tuned to this station for further bulletins."

Grace and her father sat in the living room the rest of the day, listening to the bulletins on KEMB. Legionnaires were ordered to report for duty. Retired military were asked to help. Civilians were warned, again and again, to stay off the streets. During the quiet moments, the station played The Star Spangled Banner and other patriotic music.

The heavy bombing had long since ceased, although there were periodic sounds of heavy artillery fire.

"What are they shooting at?" Grace asked.

"I don't know."

"Will the Japanese come back?"

Her father's face twisted. "I hope not."

"How will Mother get home?"

"I'm sure someone will bring her."

"What about Tom?"

"I don't know, Grace."

Her father's voice sounded weary and defeated.

Grace stopped asking questions.

Late in the afternoon the radio announcer said, "Governor Poindexter has announced that the Hawaiian Islands are now under Martial Law. A curfew has been declared. *No one* is allowed on the street after six pm or before six am. Anyone ignoring curfew will be arrested immediately."

"It's after five now," Grace said with alarm. "How will Tom and Mother get home?"

"I doubt that they'll be home tonight. I'm sure they're both very busy. Try not to worry. Mom's at the hospital, and Tom's with his ROTC unit. They will both be safe."

Grace wanted to scream at him. Nobody's safe. Not them and certainly not us, she thought.

"It's been a long day. We need to fix some supper," Ken said. He went in the kitchen and began taking things from the cupboards. Grace set the table for the two of them, and watched her father do something she'd never seen before: prepare dinner. He made rice, fried Spam and sliced pineapple.

They ate in silence; the only sounds in the room were the periodic announcements on the radio. As they finished cleaning up, a brutal knocking shook the front door.

Ken got up and opened it cautiously. Two men in military uniform pushed him roughly back into the room.

"Kenji Kawakami?" one asked.

"Yes," he answered, looking bewildered.

"You need to come with us."

"Why?"

"No questions," the other said sharply.

"Daddy!" Grace cried, rushing to his side.

"My daughter is here."

"That's too bad. You're coming with us." They pushed him out the door.

"Daddy!"

Ken twisted around as best he could to see his daughter. "Go to Vivian's, Grace. You'll be safe there."

She hurried after them out to the street, trying to reach around the men to touch him.

"Did you hear me? Go to *Vivian's*," he yelled.

The two men shoved him into the back seat of the dark-colored car, and slammed the door. Neither one looked at her before getting into the front and driving off.

CHAPTER 5

Grace's heart pounded, each beat like a tiny explosion blowing up inside her. Every muscle in her body strained to run after the car, but her father's words hung in the air, and she breathed them in as painfully as she had the smoke.

The street was deserted. The house was deserted. It was almost six, almost curfew. More than anything, Grace wanted to disappear, to crawl into the shell of yesterday and never allow this day to dawn.

She took one last look down the block, and balled her hands into fists. "You are *samurai*," she said aloud.

She went into the living room, picked up the bag she'd packed earlier, and left the house. She walked down the street as fast as she could, and when she reached Vivian's house, rapped loudly on the door.

Vivian's father opened it a crack, and peered out.

"Grace?"

"May I come in?"

He pulled her inside quickly, and slammed the door.

Vivian was sitting on the couch by her mother, but jumped up the moment she saw Grace.

"What's wrong?"

Grace slumped into a chair. "Everybody's gone," she shuddered, the warrior *samurai* escaping with her words.

"What?"

"Grace," Mrs. Ozawa said, kneeling down in front of the girl. "Grace, what's happened?"

"They took my father."

"Who took your father?"

"Two men."

"What men?"

"Two men in uniforms. They came to our house and said he had to go with them."

"Where did they go?"

"I don't know."

"Where is your mother?"

"At the hospital."

"Where is Tom?"

"I don't know. He went with ROTC."

Mrs. Ozawa looked at Vivian. "Get her some tea, dear." She turned her attention back to Grace. "I'm sure that everyone will be fine. You'll stay here, of course."

"Why do you think they took my father?" She looked from Vivian's mother to her father. "He didn't do anything wrong. We were out helping people. He didn't do *anything*."

"It's probably nothing," Mr. Ozawa said. "I'm sure they just want to talk to him. He'll probably be home tomorrow."

"Talk to him about what?"

"I don't know. A lot of Japanese men were picked up today. Nobody was told why. I'm sure it's only a formality."

"Thank you," Grace mumbled when Vivian handed her the steaming cup of tea.

"Did you leave your mother a note?" Mr. Ozawa asked.

"No." She shifted in discomfort. "I should have. I didn't think…"

"She won't be home until tomorrow anyway. Curfew is in effect until then. I'll take a note down first thing in the morning," he told her.

They heard a rifle shot outside. Grace began to shake; the tea cup chattered in her hand.

"It's okay, Grace," Mrs. Ozawa said.

"I'm cold."

"I think she might be in shock," Mr. Ozawa said softly. "Vivian, go get her a sweater. Grace, try to drink your tea."

Suddenly, they heard planes fly over, followed by rapid gunfire.

"Are they back?" Grace stammered, spilling the tea.

"I don't know," Vivian's father said. "If they are, the military will take care of it. We're safe here."

Grace had seen the apartment building on King. She knew nobody was safe.

Vivian draped a heavy sweater over Grace's shoulders. "Drink your tea," she encouraged her friend.

Grace lifted the cup to her lips, the hot liquid familiar and soothing.

"Have you had dinner?" Mrs. Ozawa asked.

"Yes."

Time dragged by. The only sounds were the far-off noises from Pearl Harbor and an occasional challenge from a block warden, when someone turned on a light. They had been warned all day that blackout would be strictly enforced.

"I should have left a note," Grace said absently. "I didn't think of it. I was scared. It was already getting dark."

"It's okay," Mr. Ozawa said. "Nobody will be coming home tonight. Not with the curfew. I'll go over first thing. Besides, anyone who *knows* you would look for you here."

Silence sat in the room with them like a malignant stranger. Grace had no idea how late it was. The only connection she had to time was the ringing of the grandfather clock in the corner. She couldn't concentrate on it long enough to count the chimes.

Grace had long since finished her tea, when Mrs. Ozawa said, "I think you girls should go to bed now."

"Are *you* going to bed?" Vivian asked her.

"In a bit."

"I'll stay in the living room tonight," Mr. Ozawa said. "I don't want to miss it if anyone knocks on the door. And, we need to keep our clothes on, just in case we have to evacuate. I doubt if we will," he added hastily, "but it would be good to be ready."

"Come on, Grace," Vivian said, taking her friend's hand.

Grace let herself be led into Vivian's room. She'd spent the night there many times and was familiar with the house, even in the dark. Grace sat down on the bed where she always slept when she stayed over. "I'm not sleepy," she said.

"I'm not either."

"Are you scared?" Grace whispered.

"Yes. Are you?"

Grace nodded, then realized Vivian couldn't see. "Yes."

There was nothing else to do except lie down. Grace's mind swirled. She tried to imagine where her father was, what her brothers were doing, and when her mother would be home. She drifted alone in the darkness, hoping the rest of her family was not as desolate as she was.

After a long time, Vivian asked, "What do you suppose is happening in California? Do you think they're getting bombed, too?"

"I have no idea." Grace was struggling to understand what was happening to her family, much less to anyone else. "At least they're all together."

Minute by minute, time ticked away. Silence buzzed in Grace's ears like a persistent fly.

A sharp scratching on the window screen brought Grace bolt upright. She held her breath. Then, again, the scratching, like someone was trying to find a way in.

"What is that?" she croaked.

"It's the rose bush," Vivian said.

"Are you sure?"

"Yes. I hear it all the time. I asked my dad to trim it."

She wished she had a knife, or a baseball bat.

"This is awful," Vivian said. "The night is never going to end!"

"Can you see what time it is?"

Vivian got a flashlight from her desk, and hid under her blanket. "It's four-thirty."

"How can time pass so slowly?"

"Do you want to get up?"

"And do what?" Grace asked. "We can't see."

Silence settled back on them; sleep did not.

Gradually, the blackness turned to a reluctant gray. Grace heard sounds coming from the kitchen and then a soft knocking on the bedroom door.

"Vivian?" Mrs. Ozawa gently opened the door.

"What's wrong?" Vivian asked, alarmed.

"Nothing. I thought you'd be awake. Would you girls like some tea?"

"Yes, please," they both said.

They got up and went into the kitchen.

"Did you sleep at all?" Vivian's mother asked.

Vivian said no, and Grace shook her head.

"Do you want to write a note for your family, Grace? Vivian's father will take it over for you. He's going to go see what he can find out about your father."

"What should I say? I don't know where he is."

"Say that you're here, your father was taken for questioning by the authorities, that Tom is with ROTC, and your mother is at the hospital. That way, whoever comes home will know everything that we know."

Grace wrote the note as Mrs. Ozawa suggested.

Mr. Ozawa came into the kitchen. "I'm going to the temple, and then downtown to ask about Ken," he told his wife. "I'll leave Grace's note on the kitchen table."

"Thank you," Grace said. She was glad she'd done the dishes and the table was bare. Anyone who walked in would see the note easily.

"Be careful, dear," Mrs. Ozawa said, as she walked her husband to the door.

"Stay here. I'll be back as soon as I can."

The grandfather clock struck six as he closed the door behind him.

The radio crackled to life shortly after Vivian's father left.

"All schools in Hawaii will be closed until further notice. Citizens are expected to stay away from sensitive areas, and follow directives given by military personnel. Keep your radio on and tuned to this station. Bulletins will be updated as needed."

"No school," Vivian said. "That's so weird, so different."

"Everything is going to be different, I'm afraid," Vivian's mother said. "Our garden club has talked about this."

"What do you mean?" Vivian asked.

"Since martial law has been declared, the military will be in charge of everything. They'll tell us what we can and can't do. All the laws become military laws; if we break them, we'll be arrested and taken to a military court." She was quiet for a moment and then said, "There will be rationing. We'll have more military personnel and more war workers here before long. The housing shortage will get worse. There will be restrictions on our movements. The worst part of it is that martial law means ordinary citizens have no rights."

"Like my father," Grace said.

"Yes, I'm afraid so," Vivian's mother said. Silently, she fixed them rice and pickled vegetables, and although Grace had no appetite, she ate.

After cleaning up the kitchen Vivian said, "Let's write to Chiyo and Naomi. They'll be worried about you, and wondering what's happened here."

"I wouldn't know what to tell them."

"You can tell them what you know: the island was attacked, your father was taken for questioning, you helped a couple whose apartment was bombed, that Tom got his arm burned in the rubble, that your mom went to work at the hospital, and that you spent last night here."

Grace took the paper Vivian offered her. "Okay."

"You write Naomi, and I'll write Chiyo. They can share the letters."

They sat together at the table, each telling their own story of the attack. Writing it, putting it on the page, made it seem unreal to Grace. She remembered every moment, but it simply didn't seem possible. Grace did her best to describe the chaotic scene at the apartment, and meeting the young couple they'd helped. She told her cousins about Tom leaving, her mother leaving, and her father being taken away. She said she hoped that they were okay, and that California hadn't been bombed at the same time.

"I wonder when the mail will go out again," Grace said.

"Whenever it goes, these will be the first."

When Vivian's father returned, they gathered in the living room.

"Dozens of Japanese were taken into custody yesterday: priests, language teachers, newspaper men, business men, and many of our community leaders. No one was told why. It looks like they're being held at the Immigration Office. They aren't allowed visitors."

"What else?" Mrs. Ozawa asked.

"Hundreds of military men were killed. Pearl Harbor is a disaster. Some ships were sunk, some terribly damaged. Some are still burning." He shook his head in dismay. "Only a couple of ships escaped. The hospitals are overflowing. Schools are being used for emergency medical and evacuation centers."

Vivian and Grace stared at him.

"You need to go to the grocery store," he said to his wife, "and try to get what you can. People are already lined up outside markets. Things are going to go fast."

Grace thought about how they'd been stocking up on things for months and was proud of her father. At least they had food.

"We can go with you, Mom," Vivian offered.

"No," Mr. Ozawa said. "Grace should stay here. Just in case any of your family comes home," he said, looking at Grace.

So, she stayed at the house with Vivian's father, while Vivian and Mrs. Ozawa went to the store. The hours dragged by nearly as slowly as they had during the night. Vivian and her mother finally reappeared, carrying heavy bags.

Mrs. Ozawa collapsed into a chair. "What a mess! The line was down the block and around the corner from the market. They only let a few people in at a time, and they limited how much we could buy."

"Everyone was talking about an invasion," Vivian said. "Do *you* think that they will come back?" she asked her father.

He shook his head. "I doubt it. The time for that has passed. We're on alert now. There are ten times as many people out there with firearms, watching the beaches and mountains. I don't think so."

Grace wondered if he believed it, or was merely saying it for their benefit. A few people on the beach with guns could hardly have stopped the attack.

A sudden knock at the door startled them all.

Mr. Ozawa opened it and said, "Ah! It's so good to see you, Lilly. Come in."

"Mother!" Grace cried, jumping up. She ran to her mother and hugged her fiercely.

"You're all right!" Lilly said. She looked at Vivian's parents. "I can't thank you enough for taking her. I had no idea that Ken would be arrested. Have you heard anything about what's going on?"

Mr. Ozawa told her what he'd learned that morning. "Anyone who has gone to the Immigration building has been turned away. May I suggest that you not try? Let me go for you again tomorrow, and see what I can find out."

"Thank you, Shigeo. I would appreciate that."

"When do you have to go back to the hospital?" Vivian's mother asked.

"Tomorrow morning."

"No!" Grace cried.

"Grace can stay with us as long as need be. Day or night, she's always welcome."

"How can I ever repay you, Edith?"

"That's nonsense. You'd do the same for us. Are you hungry?"

"If you don't mind, I need to get some sleep. I was up all night. I'd like to go home and take a nap. I'll talk to you later."

"Yes, of course," Vivian's mother said. "Call me. We'll figure out the best way to make sure Grace is safe."

Grace got her bag, thanked the Ozawas, and said to Vivian, "I'll talk to you later."

Outside, Grace discovered a world dulled by a somber gray sky. Few people were on the street. The smell of smoke was thick and strong, and filled every breath. They walked quickly, neither one wanting to be out any longer than necessary.

Once home, Lilly pulled Grace over to the couch and sat down with her. "It must have been awful for you to see your father treated like a criminal."

"He told me to go to Vivian's."

"Yes. That was exactly the thing to do."

"Last night was awful. I was so scared. You were *all* gone!"

"I'm sorry, Grace. I had no idea that your father would be taken away."

"Why do you think they took him?"

"I don't know."

"Is it because Richie is in Japan?"

"Oh, I doubt that. More than likely, it's because of the store, because he does business with Japan."

"That doesn't make him a *criminal*."

"No. They might think it makes him suspect, though. They probably want to ask him some questions, and after that, they'll let him come home."

Grace hesitated and then asked, "What happened at the hospital?"

Lilly didn't answer.

"What..."

"It isn't easy to talk about. Not even to people who were there."

"Did a lot of people die?"

"Yes."

"But you tried to save them."

"Yes. But there were just so many. And the injuries were so awful..."

Grace laid her head against her mother's shoulder. "I'm sorry."

Lilly patted her.

"When do you think Tom will come home?"

"I don't know that either. We're at war now. We have to think of it as if he's in the army. It may be a while before he comes home."

Grace looked up at her mother. "Are you scared?"

"I'm not scared right now. At the hospital, we were too busy to be scared. I'm not scared about your father, because he hasn't done anything wrong. I'm not scared about Tom: he's smart and he'll be careful. Mostly, I'm scared about Richie. I'm sure he'll be drafted, and I'm afraid that...I'm not sure. I don't know anything about the Japanese military. I suppose I'm afraid of what I don't know."

They sat quietly for a while. Lilly leaned her head back and closed her eyes.

"Are you tired, Mom?"

"Exhausted."

"You should take a nap."

"I want to take a shower first."

After her mother had bathed and changed her clothes, she went in and lay down on the bed.

Grace went into the room with her. "Could I sleep with you?"

Lilly patted the bed next to her. "Of course."

"Should I lock the door?"

Lilly gave a short laugh. "The military would come right through it if they wanted to come in. So, you'd only be keeping out our friends."

Grace relaxed for the first time since the bombing. She put her head down on the pillow, and drew in the soothing scent of her mother's perfume. She let herself drift. It was okay now: her Mom was home.

CHAPTER 6

Grace woke reluctantly from a dream where she was talking to Tom. She rolled over. When she realized that her mother was not beside her, panic rose in her like high tide.

Then, she heard her brother's voice.

"Tom!" She jumped up, and ran out to the kitchen.

Tom grabbed her and hugged her fiercely.

"Where have you been?" she asked.

"We've been patrolling in the hills. They told us that paratroopers had landed. We were supposed to stop them from getting into the city." He laughed. "We didn't find a thing."

"Did Mom tell you about Daddy?"

"Yeah. Leaving you alone like that was way out of line. Going to Vivian's was the right thing to do. I'm sure Dad's fine. He hasn't done anything illegal. I heard a lot of *Issei* have been detained, mostly leaders and businessmen."

"Do you have to go back?"

"Yes. Before curfew."

Grace looked at the clock. "That's less than an hour!"

"I know. I just came to make sure you were okay."

Lilly had been busy in the kitchen as they talked, and now put a plate of sandwiches on the table. "You have to eat."

"Thanks, Mom," Tom said, picking up half a sandwich, and taking a ravenous bite.

"Sit down for heaven's sake," Grace said.

He sat and ate quickly. "Listen, we need to keep track of each other. Grace, would you make some sort of sign-in board? We should each have a card: one side 'In' and the other, 'Out'. When we leave the house, we write the date, time, where we're going, and, if possible, when we expect to be home. That way we won't wonder or worry so much about each other."

Grace looked sideways at her brother. He was always a problem solver, even under stress.

"Speaking of which, I need to go. Write me out," he said to Grace. "I'm with ROTC. Actually, we were reorganized yesterday, and now we're the Hawaii Territorial Guard." He grabbed another sandwich, wrapped it in a napkin, and stuffed it into his pack. "For later."

Lilly and Grace stood and hugged him.

He stopped at the door and pulled on his boots. Then, he picked up a rifle, which Grace had not even noticed had been leaning against the wall by the door.

"Be careful," Grace said, feeling proud, as well as protective.

"It's my new middle name."

They watched from the porch, as he jogged down the street toward his headquarters.

From inside, they heard the announcer on the radio say, "Half hour until blackout." Tom rounded the corner, and the two women went back into the house.

"We need to make curtains," Lilly said, clearing the table. "We can't sit here in the dark doing nothing all night."

Grace thought about the interminable misery of the previous night. "How long will the blackout last?"

"As long as we're at war, I suppose. We *are* at war: President Roosevelt declared it in front of Congress today."

"I know. I heard his speech on the radio at Vivian's. He called it 'a day that will live in infamy'."

"Your father kept saying it was coming. I didn't want to believe it."

The phone rang, and Lilly jumped to answer it. "Hello?"

Lilly's disappointed look told Grace that it wasn't her father.

"Yes, Edith. We're fine. Tom was just here." She paused and then said, "I'll need to leave around six am. I'll stop by with Grace on my way, if that's okay. I'm sorry it's so early. I'm afraid it takes me a while to walk to the hospital." She paused. "Thanks, no. I can walk."

"Do you have to walk?" Grace asked when Lilly hung up.

"I walk all the time. It's only two miles."

"I could take you."

"What are you afraid of, sweetheart? The block wardens are everywhere. No one is going to hurt me."

"What if the Japanese come back? Some people think there will be an invasion."

"If there's an invasion tomorrow morning, being in the car won't help much," her mother said. She put her arm around Grace. "I know it was awful for you last night when they took your father. We won't let anything like that happen again. But I *have* to work. It's the only income we have now. And I have to do my part. I need to help the best way I can."

The radio announcer started reading another bulletin. "All grocery stores will be closed for inventory tomorrow, Tuesday. Liquor sales are now banned until further notice."

"I'm glad we listened to your father when he wanted to stock up last fall. We're better off than the people who didn't think this could happen."

"It is now black out," the radio blared. "All lights are out until tomorrow."

His voice made Grace's skin crawl, like he was telling them to hide in the dark from a malevolent monster.

Grace slept in her parents' room that night. She put on pajamas, just as her mother did. However, she insisted on locking the front door. While her mother was changing, Grace hid a knife under the bed. If Tom had a rifle, she wanted *something* for protection.

Mr. Ozawa greeted them at his door the next morning. "I'll check again today and see if there's any word about Ken," he told Lilly.

Vivian's father was a public school teacher, and since the schools had been closed, would not be going to work.

"Thank you, Shigeo. I'm not sure what time I'll get off work. Yesterday, patients kept coming and coming. They were still coming when I left. A pathetic parade," she added soberly.

"Don't worry. Grace is fine here."

"I'll see you later," she said to Grace.

"Bye, Mom. Be careful."

"I will."

As soon as Vivian and her mother were up, Mr. Ozawa called a family meeting. "Just because there's no school, doesn't mean you girls shouldn't study. I want you to schedule a time to do that every day. Then, we need to figure out how you can contribute in the community. The Red Cross is asking for help," he said, looking at Grace. "They've set up canteens at the schools to feed the volunteers. Another possibility is babysitting in the neighborhood, so some of the moms could volunteer."

The two girls looked at each other.

"Okay," Vivian said tentatively. "We need some time to talk about it."

"Of course," he said.

"I'll need your help today," Vivian's mother said. "I have to get material to make curtains, so we don't have to sit in the dark all night."

"We need those, too," Grace said. "I wish I'd asked Mom for some money."

"We'll get enough material for both houses. You girls sew well enough that we'll have them done in no time."

Crowds of women choked the aisles at the department store, all wanting fabric for curtains. By the time Mrs. Ozawa was waited on, there was no black material left on the shelves. Instead, she chose a dark navy blue material, with a second piece of lighter blue for the lining. She bought twenty yards of both. The girls each carried one of the heavy packages home, while Vivian's mother carried the rest of the notions.

On the way home, they walked by several houses where residents had actually painted their windows black.

"That means they're blacked out in the daytime, too," Edith said.

"I bet someone is in trouble for thinking up *that* idea," Grace giggled, laughing for the first time in days.

"I suppose if you're working all day it doesn't much matter. But at night, since it's so warm, if you open the windows for air, you'd have to turn out the lights anyway."

While they were at the store, they heard stories of block wardens screaming at people whose curtains didn't cover their windows, and banging on the doors of others, whose curtains blew aside in the evening breezes.

Mrs. Ozawa carefully measured each opening, and designed the curtains so they would cover the windows completely. They brought Lilly's sewing machine down to Vivian's house, and the girls both sewed, as Edith designed and cut. They finished the windows in the front part of the house, and then carried supplies down to Grace's, and made curtains for the Kawakami's living room.

"We'll do the rest tomorrow," Edith told them. "I've got to get dinner started while it's still light."

That evening, when Grace and her mother walked into their house, Grace switched on the light.

"No!" Lilly cried, and then she noticed the curtains. She looked at Grace. "How did you ever...?"

"We went shopping today. Mrs. Ozawa designed and cut, and Vivian and I sewed. We had a little sweatshop going."

That night they sat in the living room, reading and talking long after blackout.

"This is so much better, Grace. Thank you, sweetheart."

"We owe Mrs. Ozawa some money."

"That's not all we owe her."

"I wish we could find out about Daddy."

"Mr. Ozawa said he'd keep inquiring. I'm sure the authorities will tell us something soon. Thank heaven we have such good friends."

A sudden banging on the door scared Grace into a panic.

Lilly stood, patted Grace's arm reassuringly, and walked to the front door. "Who is it?" she asked loudly, without opening it.

"Military Police. Open up!"

Grace rushed over to Lilly. They took her father. Did they want her mother, too?

Lilly opened the door. "Is something wrong?"

Two uniformed men pushed into the room.

"That's what we're here to find out."

One man started looking in the kitchen cabinets, while the other one went into the bedrooms.

"If you'll tell me what you're looking for, maybe I can help you."

"And maybe not," the officer in the kitchen said.

Grace held on to her mother's arm. She was not going to let them take her away without a struggle.

The other man came in from the bedrooms carrying Tom's radio. "Whose is this?" he barked.

"It belongs to my son," Lilly said calmly.

"What's his name?"

"Tom Kawakami."

"Where is he?"

"He's serving with the HTG."

"When was the last time your husband used this?"

"He's never used it. He doesn't know how."

"Why does your son need this?"

"He doesn't *need* it. He belonged to the Radio Club at McKinley. It's his hobby."

"Not any more it isn't," he said nastily, and he threw it on the floor by the door.

"Where is your husband?" the first officer asked.

"I think you might know more about that than I do," Lilly said. "He was taken away night before last. I have no idea where you took him."

"Lady," the first officer said in a threatening tone, but the other man interrupted. "Let it go, Hal."

Outside someone yelled, "Hey! Close that damn door!"

Lilly walked to the door. "Sorry," she called, closing it.

Grace stood near the wall, trembling and terrified. How could her mother be so calm?

"Do you have any firearms in the house?"

"No."

"Any explosives?"

"No."

"Ammunition?"

"No."

"Do you have any other weapons in the house?"

"No."

"When do you expect your son home?"

"I don't. He's helping with the war effort."

The man called Hal took a step toward Lilly. The other man stopped him.

"Tell your son to watch his step. And if you know what's good for you, you'll do the same."

"We're taking this," the kinder officer said, picking up the radio.

And with that, they left.

Grace shook so hard she nearly fell over. Lilly pulled her to the couch and sat down next to her. "It's okay, Grace. Everything is okay."

"They could have taken you!"

"They weren't interested in me. The one was just doing his job; the other one, Hal, was a bully. You can't back down from a bully. We've done nothing wrong."

"Daddy didn't do anything wrong, and they took him."

"They're afraid of him."

"Of Daddy?"

"Well, they're afraid of what they think he is, a Japanese sympathizer. He isn't, of course, and when they realize that, they'll let him come home."

"I hope it's soon."

But it wouldn't be.

On Saturday, all gasoline stations were closed to prepare for rationing, which was set to begin the following day. Lilly went to work each day, and Grace went to Vivian's. The girls studied, and helped two of the neighborhood moms, who worked at the Red Cross canteen.

Each day, Vivian's father went to the Immigration office to try to find out about Ken. Each day he was turned away.

And then, on the 17th, there was news.

"They've been taken to Sand Island," Shigeo told Lilly. He was referring to the small island in the Honolulu Harbor, used by the military. "They're building a camp there for the men who have been arrested. Nobody can see him, but at least now we know where he is."

"Who told you?"

"One of the men I teach with. His brother is an MP. He probably shouldn't have said anything, but he knew we've been frantic to know about Ken."

"Thank you so much," Lilly said.

As Grace and her mother sat down to dinner that night, Lilly said, "If they've put your father in a camp, he may not be coming home as soon as I'd hoped."

"You said he hasn't done anything wrong." Grace sounded to herself like a whiny child.

"He hasn't. But apparently, the authorities haven't figured that out yet."

The door rattled. "Mom, it's me."

Grace ran to let her brother in.

"You're locking it now. That's good," Tom said. He leaned his rifle against the wall and kicked off his boots.

"I'm so glad you're here," Lilly cried. "Can you stay for dinner?"

"Yep. I'm here for the night. First, I want to get out of this uniform."

When he reappeared in shorts and a tee shirt, he asked, "Where is my radio?"

"The MPs paid us a little visit," Lilly said, and she told him the story.

"I'll never see *that* radio again. It's ironic, don't you think? I'm out risking my life to protect the city, and they're in here stealing my stuff." He laughed. "It's crazy out there. Rumors are spreading like the flu. It's nuts."

"Will they come after *you*?" Grace asked.

"No. They got what they wanted."

"What have you been doing?" Lilly asked as she served him dinner.

"Guarding bridges, or water towers, or the power station. It's something different every day."

"Are you scared?" Grace asked him.

He looked at her. "Sure. Sometimes. Especially at night. Guys get trigger happy and shoot before they shout. Mostly it's okay," he said with a shrug. He took a large bite of fish. "Have you heard anything about Dad?"

Lilly told him what Vivian's father had learned that day.

"Well, that's better than shipping him stateside."

"Speaking of stateside, I finally got a letter from Chiyo today," Grace said.

"What did she have to say?" Tom asked.

"She was worried about us and hoped we were okay. She says things have really changed there. People at school don't talk to her at all. Some people even yell 'Go home, Jap' at her. They get dirty looks everywhere they go; salesmen ignore them. She hates it there. She wants to come home."

Tom shook his head, frustration oozing from his pores. "As if it was our fault; as if *we* wanted this war. Poor Chiyo. She was unhappy *before* this all started."

"Why don't they just come home?" Grace asked.

"It won't be easy now. They're bringing war workers here. The authorities aren't going to want to bring families back, especially Japanese families."

An announcement came on the radio saying that the military had ordered the evacuation of all farmers in the Pearl Harbor area.

"At least we can stay in our own house," Lilly said.

"You're right, Mom. We have to be grateful for what we *do* have," Tom said.

Tom left early the next morning. "Sign me out," he said to Grace. "You did a good job on that board."

She had forgotten to show it to him and was pleased he had noticed it anyway.

"Will you be home for Christmas?" she asked.

He thought a moment. "My gosh, that's next week. I have no idea. I'll try, Gracie."

Grace and Lilly watched him as he walked down the street, his rifle slung casually over his shoulder.

"Be careful," Lilly called after him.

As soon as he had rounded the corner, Lilly said, "We have to get going, too."

"What do you think's happened to Richie?" Grace asked as they walked to Vivian's. She thought about her oldest brother all the time, but she hadn't wanted to upset her mother by asking about him.

"Tom seems certain he would have been drafted by now. Japan is fighting in so many places. A healthy young man his age wouldn't go unnoticed. I pray that the Lord will watch over him."

Grace had rarely heard her mother speak in religious terms, and it surprised her. "That doesn't sound like you, Mom."

"I guess when times are this uncertain, you go back to your roots. It's what my mother would have said. At this point, I'll take all the help I can get."

There was a note in the mailbox when they got home that evening.

"Listen to this," Grace said.

"Dear Grace,

I've washed your clothes and would like to return them to you. I'm living with my parents now, since Paul enlisted in the navy. They would like you and your family to come for lunch on Sunday. Would that be possible? Please leave a reply for me in the box, and I'll pick it up tomorrow. Tell me if Sunday is good, and how many of you can come. We look forward to seeing you.

Dorothy Pritchard"

"That's very thoughtful," Lilly said. "Would you like to go?"

"Yes. I doubt if I could find their house, though. I don't remember much about that day."

"Write her a note, and tell her you and I can come. Then ask her to leave directions for us in the mailbox."

On Sunday, they drove to Dorothy's parents' home, using the car for the first time since the attack.

"It feels funny to be in the car," Grace said. "It's been so long."

"I'm glad your father kept the tank full," Lilly said. "Ten gallons a month, per person, isn't much of an allotment."

"We're lucky we live so close to the hospital and the school, and we're used to walking."

Dorothy met them at the door with a big smile and a hug. "I'm so glad you could come. I've been wanting to thank you properly."

Grace noticed how pretty she was. Her hair was blonde and not the gray, ash-colored mop it had been after the fire. She was petite and bouncy, quite a contrast to the dull, silent woman Grace had last seen.

She led them into the house, which was much bigger than it appeared from the outside. "My parents are out on the patio. We're all so pleased that you could come today." The living room had wall to wall windows that looked out on a lush, green valley. Dorothy escorted them through the sliding glass doors onto a lovely, covered patio.

Dorothy's parents stood and greeted Grace and Lilly. "I'm James Reback and this is my wife, Sarah. You must be Grace's mother," he said, shaking Lilly's hand.

"Lilly. Yes. Thank you for having us."

"Please," Sarah said. "We want to thank you. We owe you a great debt."

Lilly handed her a small orchid plant she had brought.

"Oh, it's lovely. Thank you."

"Where is your father?" Dorothy asked, as Grace and Lilly sat down.

"I'm afraid that he was arrested," Lilly said.

"Arrested?" Dorothy repeated. "Whatever for?"

"We're not sure. MPs came to our house the night of the attack and took him away. There was no explanation. I was at the hospital. It makes me furious that they left Grace at the house, alone."

"Good Lord!" Sarah said. "That's unconscionable."

"What did you do?" Dorothy asked Grace, her eyes full of concern.

"My best friend lives down the street. I went there."

"You must have been terrified."

Grace nodded, the memory flooding over her in a painful wave.

"I'm sorry you had to go through that," James said to Grace. "Particularly after your family had helped so many people earlier."

Dorothy nodded in agreement, her head bobbing up and down vigorously. "Paul and I weren't the only ones they helped. Lots of other people who live in our neighborhood talked about how your dad and your brother were fighting the fires and helping people escape. In fact, I heard your brother got burned. How is he?"

"He's healing nicely," Lilly said. "We saw him on Thursday."

"Where is he?"

"He's serving with the HTG."

"So," James said, "have you been able to talk to your husband?"

"No. I don't think anyone has been allowed to talk to the detainees."

"Damn military. This martial law thing is ridiculous. Premature if you ask me. Taking civilian rights away is a drastic move." He looked around and cleared this throat. "And you have no idea why he was arrested?"

"We own an import business, and he has suppliers in Japan. I imagine that's why."

"Well, he didn't strike me as a threat to our country. I'll see if I can find out what the problem is. I may not be able to do a thing, but I intend to try."

"Thank you," Lilly said, looking dubious.

Dorothy shot a conspiratorial smile at Grace. "I'm sure he'll be able to do something. Daddy is a territorial judge."

CHAPTER 7

Grace had never seen a white Christmas. In fact, she'd never seen snow. Some residents of Hawaii didn't even have heaters in their homes. She and her mother were listening to Bing Crosby's song on the radio as Lilly finished fixing their dinner. Grace imagined herself sitting by a crackling fire, in a beautiful mountain cabin, surrounded by pine trees with snow falling everywhere.

"I wish Tom could have been here," she said, as she set the table for the two of them. The windows were all open, and Grace could hear children playing outside. In spite of the shortages, people had somehow managed to find presents for their children. The little ones were happily playing in the warm afternoon, with no thoughts of the war.

Lilly put a plate down at each setting. Grace made a mournful face.

"I know. Liver isn't your favorite, but that's what the butcher gave me."

Buying meat was one of the most annoying hardships of their wartime life. Customers were given no choice at the meat department. The butcher handed the buyer a package, and that was it. The day before, Lilly was given liver.

"It's not so bad with all the onions," Grace said. She didn't hate liver, although that was the best she could say about it. "I wonder if Richie is celebrating Christmas."

Her mother shook her head silently, and Grace was sorry she'd brought it up. Tom and Richie and her father, all gone. They didn't know where any of them were.

Grace ate, and then started clearing the table.

"You sit, Mom," she said. "I'll clean up."

She was drying the dishes when they heard a car stop in front.

"Yoo-hoo," came a cheery voice. "It's us. Merry Christmas."

Lilly opened the door to find Dorothy and her parents standing on the porch, all dressed in festive clothing.

"Please, come in," Lilly said. "Can I get you something to drink?"

"Some coffee if you have any," James said.

Sarah offered Lilly a beautiful, double layer cake on a crystal platter. "We wanted to share our dessert with you."

"What a surprise," Lilly said. "Thank you. I'll get some plates."

"I have some good news," James said. "One of my colleagues, a lawyer, was allowed out on Sand Island yesterday, to write up powers of attorney. He spoke to Ken, who seems to be in good health. He would like you to send him some clean clothes."

Lilly gasped and ran to James. She grabbed his hand, and shook it heartily. "Oh, thank you, James! Thank you so much."

"This is the best Christmas present possible," Grace said.

They had cake and coffee, while James told them all he had learned about Sand Island. An inquiry commission would question each detainee, and decide their fate. Civilian and military personnel would both be on the board.

"I've already applied to be on the commission, and the chances are good I'll be accepted. It helps to have friends in the military. They like the idea of an older, shall we say, seasoned judge on the panel."

Tears slid down Lilly's face. "And you're doing all this just for us?"

"I'm doing it for Ken. He and Tom put my daughter's welfare, and the welfare of the community, before their own. Ken isn't a threat to us, he's a hero to us."

Sarah laughed. "I thought judges were supposed to be impartial, dear."

James gave his wife a sly grin. "I'm the most impartial man you'll ever meet, with the possible exception of this issue."

"When do you think the commission will meet?" Lilly asked.

"I'm not sure. Most likely, not until after the first of the year. Meanwhile, get some clothes together for Ken, and write him a letter. Don't say a thing about what I've told you. Keep it light. The censors are reading everything."

Lilly agreed to have the clothes and her letter for Ken ready the following morning.

"I'll come by and get them," Dorothy said.

"I can't thank you enough," Lilly told James as they were leaving.

James looked fondly at her. "In that case, you know exactly how I've felt."

The next day, the headlines in the newspaper were bold. "By order of the military governor, all persons in the territory will be registered and fingerprinted beginning on Saturday. Identification cards will be carried at all times."

The registration line stretched down the street, around the corner and down two more blocks. Grace and Lilly walked to the designated location with Vivian and Edith.

"I thought we'd be early," Lilly said, disheartened.

"It's the same as everything else: we wait in line for the market, the butcher, ration books, gas ration cards, and even for the movies," Grace said.

"At least we only have to do this once," Vivian said.

"It's hard to believe things have changed so much in such a short time," Lilly said.

"Is your dad at this location?" Grace asked Vivian as they moved closer to the building. Teachers had been called in to provide manpower for the registration project.

"I think so."

Edith shifted from one foot to the other. "I shouldn't have worn these shoes. I didn't think it would take this long."

"Things take twice as long these days," a woman behind them said.

"I wonder if we'll ever get back to normal," Vivian said.

"Things will *never* be the way they were before the war," her mother said. "War changes people."

"Yes," Lilly said, "and sometimes, not for the better."

"It can also bring out the kindness in people," Grace said. "Look at what the judge has done for us."

"That's true," her mother said. Then she laughed. "I must be so pessimistic because my feet hurt."

Lines were unavoidable. Some commodities, like soap, toothpaste, shampoo, and detergent, were only sold at certain times during the day. Anyone who couldn't be at the store at that time, did without. Mail was irregular; some letters arrived promptly; some took weeks. All letters were censored; unacceptable passages were blacked or cut out. Letters often arrived in shreds, or so marked up they were unreadable.

While the fear of invasion had diminished, the hardships of war had increased. In an attempt to maintain the readiness of the community, air raid sirens sounded periodically, agitating an already nervous population.

Ken's letters came regularly now. Some of the other detainees had already had their commission interview, and a few had been released. The fate of others was still a mystery.

A letter from Makiko told of the difficulties the Fujitas were having in California.

"Naomi and Chiyo have been ostracized by their classmates. Chiyo hates school. The only thing that makes her happy these days is taking pictures. Naomi is registered for spring semester, but not at all enthusiastic about her classes. Yoshi is busy at work, and doesn't realize how hard it is for the rest of us. If I had wings, I would fly home."

"We would love to see Chiyo's pictures," Lilly wrote back. "Please ask her to send us some. Ken will soon be interviewed by the commission and, we hope, will be home this month."

On January 28th, while Lilly and Grace were folding laundry, they heard a bulletin on the evening news. "Beginning Tuesday, gas masks will be distributed to Hawaiian residents. All persons will carry their mask with them at all times."

"Do you think we'll get gassed?"

"I guess the military thinks it's a possibility. We've been training at the hospital on how to clean and treat people who've been exposed. Gas was used a lot in the last war, and the effects were devastating. I think they're trying to cover all the possibilities."

On Wednesday evening, Tom was sitting in the living room when Grace and Lilly got home.

"You're here!" Grace cried.

Tom barely looked up.

"Tom? What's wrong?" Lilly asked, going to sit next to him.

"I was discharged this morning. All the Japanese guys were discharged, just like that," he said, snapping his fingers. He sounded distraught and dejected. "The country is at *war*, and they're saying they don't need us."

"Oh, Tom."

"We were good enough to send into the mountains on the 7th, when they thought paratroopers had landed. But now, all of a sudden, they don't trust us."

Lilly heaved an enormous sigh. "I'm so sorry, Tom. You've all proven your worth. This is the decision of a few, frightened men. You mustn't let it get you down. There are lots of ways to help in the war effort. You'll only have to look around."

Tom didn't reply, and Grace could see him considering his mother's words. It wasn't the first time one of the Kawakami children had faced discrimination.

Grace was delighted that Tom was home, even though she knew he was miserable. She tried to engage him in her activities. He refused. "Just leave me alone," he told her again and again. Lilly's words had not helped.

On Saturday, Grace, Tom, and their mother were eating lunch, when they heard a car pull up in front. There was a knock on the front door and Dorothy's now familiar, "Yoo-hoo."

Grace went to the door, opened it, and began screaming. "Daddy! Daddy, you're home!"

Ken and Dorothy walked into the house, just as Lilly and Tom reached the front door. Lilly hugged and kissed her husband, and Tom shook his father's hand with such force he nearly knocked him over.

Dorothy wiped tears from her eyes. "He took me home, and now I've brought him home."

"My interrogation was this morning," Ken told them, "and you'll never guess who was on my panel." He reached over and gave Dorothy an uncharacteristic hug. "This young lady's father."

"Did you recognize him?" Lilly asked.

"He looked familiar, but I couldn't have told you why. I thought maybe he had been a customer. When the questioning was over and they said I was released, I didn't know what to do. I got my bag and went outside, and Dorothy was there waiting for me."

"Daddy and I planned it," Dorothy told the others. "He was determined to get him released, and I was determined to bring him home. Obviously, Daddy couldn't have brought him, being one of the panel. He and Mother want you all to come for lunch tomorrow, so we can celebrate."

"We'd like that," Ken said. "I need to thank your father properly for all he's done."

"This time I'll bring dessert," Lilly said.

"See you then," Dorothy said, and waved goodbye.

Lilly made Ken lunch, and the four sat down at the table. Lilly sat silently, fork in hand, staring at her husband. Ken ate like a man who hadn't seen food in years, all the while keeping an eye on his wife.

"Tell us everything, Pop," Tom said.

And so he did. He told of crass guards, careless companions, and cruel jailors. He told of bad food, inadequate housing, and long, miserable nights. He told of confused, frightened men, who were ill equipped to be detained, questioned, and imprisoned without explanation.

"It sounds awful," Grace said.

"No more awful than what you went through. I felt terrible deserting you that awful night. I'm so sorry, sweetheart." He put his hand tenderly on hers, and she was sure he was about to cry. "I never would have left you alone if I'd had any choice at all."

"I went to Vivian's like you told me," she said, hoping to spare him the embarrassment of tears.

"We owe the Ozawa's a debt we may never be able to repay," Lilly said. "Shigeo went to the Immigration department every day, trying to find out what happened to you."

"And I've stayed at their house every day, while Mom's been at work."

"I don't know how we'll repay everyone, but we'll have to try." After a long silence, Ken said, "Do you know what I'd like?"

"What, dear?"

"A hot bath."

"Simple pleasures are the best," Lilly said. She stood, and went to fill the tub for her husband.

Grace saw a smile on her mother's face that she hadn't seen since the night of the College Bowl game. December 6th, back when life was normal.

A week later, the military issued its most unreasonable directive: "Bomb shelters must be constructed by residents, even if materials are not available. Citizens are advised to use substitutes and ingenuity." The same day, all Hawaiian schools were reopened.

"I'm not going back to school, Pop."

They were eating Sunday supper, and discussing the two latest changes in Hawaii.

"What do you plan to do?" Ken asked him. "The store is closed."

"Dig a bomb shelter in the back yard, for starters," Tom said. "And then, I'll see who might need help digging theirs."

"Well," Ken began, when Grace interrupted.

"I can't *wait* to go back. I've missed school."

Her father's attention was diverted, as she'd hoped.

"That doesn't surprise me," Lilly said. "But you mustn't expect it to be the same."

It wasn't.

Grace noticed it her first day back. The school newspaper later estimated that nearly a third of the senior class had not returned to finish the year.

"I wonder if they'll be sorry later, that they didn't graduate," Grace said.

"Could be," Tom said. "They probably think there are other things that are more important now."

They were sitting outside on the lawn, talking. President Roosevelt had instituted year round daylight savings time, now called War Time. Grace liked the light later in the day, and

Lilly loved coming home before it was dark. They had finished dinner, and were relaxing in the cool evening.

"We're almost finished with the Ozawa's bomb shelter," Ken said. "It's been a challenge finding wood to reinforce the walls. Thankfully, Judge Reback has a lot of connections."

"Hiro has been a big help," Tom said. "The guys in the ROTC gang are hard workers."

"They've proven that again and again," his mother agreed.

"We've been talking about forming up and offering our services to the military: an all Japanese battalion. They can use us any way they see fit. We don't care how we serve, just as long as we're allowed to serve."

"That's an admirable idea, son," Ken said.

On February 25th, the Army said yes to the proposal from Tom's group. They called themselves the Varsity Victory Volunteers, since most of them had been students at the university.

"Some of the parents aren't too happy, considering the way the military has treated us," Tom told his parents. "Some of the elders think we're stupid. But personally, I think it's the right thing to do."

The VVV was assigned to the Army Corps of Engineers, and sent to be housed at Schofield Barracks, halfway across the island near Wheeler Army Air field.

"I wish you didn't have to leave again," Grace told Tom when Hiro arrived to pick him up.

"We can't do without him," Hiro told her.

"I'll come see you soon," Tom promised her.

"Can I come, too?" Hiro asked.

Grace felt her face flame. "Sure."

Tom looked from one to the other. His lack of a comment made Grace blush even more.

A week later a desperate letter arrived from Makiko. Grace read it aloud.

"The President has signed an order saying the military can move all Japanese families away from the west coast. It doesn't seem possible, but it's true. It looks like we'll be sent to a camp somewhere inland. I want to come home. Is there anyone there you can talk to? Please, Kenji. There must be something you can do."

"You could talk to Judge Reback," Lilly said. "He knows a lot of people. Maybe there is some way he could help."

"I hate to ask him for anything else after he's done so much already."

"But Daddy, he's always saying to let him know if he can help us."

"Let me think about it," her father said.

Being back in school left Grace little spare time. When she wasn't in class or studying, she was working with the Junior Red Cross. The girls helped roll bandages, and sort and wrap care packages for the troops. Her father drove her and Vivian to school whenever he could. Carrying a three and a half pound gas mask along with their books was a real challenge.

"I'm glad your father had us study while we were off," Grace told Vivian early in April. "It really has helped, since we've been so busy this semester."

"Yeah, although it's a pain to admit he was right," Vivian laughed.

"They have to get it right once in a while. With all the decisions they make, the odds are with them," Grace said.

The girls were walking home from school, enjoying the unexpectedly cool day. The weather had been unusually warm, which made the evenings miserable. Blackout curtains didn't allow breezes in to cool off the houses, and the long nights were a trial for everyone.

"What are you doing for your birthday?" Vivian asked.

"I don't know. What I'd like most is a dinner with Richie and Tom."

"Why don't we pack a picnic, and go visit Tom and Hiro?"

"That sounds like fun. I'll write Tom and see if they can get some time off next weekend."

A letter that arrived from Chiyo later that day pushed all thoughts of her birthday from Grace's mind. She read it out loud at the table that night.

"Next week we're being sent to someplace called a relocation camp. We have no choice about it. Mother is so upset. She says it like being sent to prison. We have to sell everything. We can only take what we can fit in one suitcase! I don't know why they hate us so much. We didn't do anything. I wish we'd never come here."

"Ken," Lilly said, her voice strained, "you've *got* to call James, and see if he can help."

"I'd hoped it wouldn't come to this."

"He keeps offering, Daddy. He *wants* to help."

"I don't like to take advantage of people. But it does sound like they're being sent to prison."

"It sounds like they're sending every Japanese on the west coast to prison. What is the matter with the military? The government has gone crazy." Lilly said.

"Fear makes people do crazy things."

His wife sighed deeply.

"I'll talk to James," Ken said.

That weekend, Grace and Vivian took a picnic lunch to Schofield Barracks and picked up Hiro and Tom. Vivian's father allowed her to use the car, his present to Grace, he had said. The boys directed them to a small park near Schofield and helped carry the lunch to a spot under a huge, shady tree.

"Happy Birthday, Gracie," Tom said. "What's up at home?"

"Not much. I got a letter from Chiyo. Things are bad in California. The military is sending all the west coast Japanese to camps," she said, and then shared the details of the letter.

"And this is who we're working for," Hiro said with disgust. "What do we have to do to prove we're loyal Americans?"

"More than we've done, apparently," Tom said.

"Your Dad should call the judge. Maybe he could help."

"That's what I've been telling him," Grace said. "It's worth a try at least."

"Ask him again, Grace. The judge can do something, I'm sure."

They unpacked the lunch, spread out the food and began to eat.

"What are you two doing this summer?" Hiro asked.

"I'm looking for a job," Vivian said.

"Yeah, me too," Grace said. "The question is, where? So many places don't want to hire Japanese."

"I'm not interested in babysitting again," Vivian said.

"Me either."

"Start asking around right away," Tom told them. "Get a head start on the others. I'll try to think of places you can apply." He took a healthy bite of his sandwich. "And what about your Junior Prom?"

Grace and Vivian looked at each other and shrugged.

"We don't have anybody to go with. Plus, my folks aren't ready for me to date," Vivian said.

"We can take you," Tom offered. "Nobody should object to that." He looked at Hiro with a quick glance. "What do you think?"

"Sure," Hiro said. "We could make that sacrifice for the war effort."

Grace wondered if they had come up with the idea before the picnic. Hiro was quick to agree to it, which seemed unlike him.

A month later, the four friends were dressed in their finest clothes, dancing at the Junior Prom.

"You look really pretty," Hiro told Grace as they danced to Glenn Miller's new song, "String of Pearls."

She'd never blushed so much in her whole life as she had the past few months. "Thank you." Grace had known him for almost two years. But here, in unfamiliar surroundings, she didn't know what to say to him.

"This is a nice party," Hiro offered.

"It doesn't seem like a real prom in the middle of the day." Blackout had forced the class to plan the annual event in the afternoon, instead of the evening.

Hiro squeezed her hand. "I'll make it up to you. When the war is over, I'll take you for a real night out, at night," he added, with a grin.

She smiled at him, touched by his sweetness.

"Any luck looking for a summer job?"

"I could work in the fields, but I'd rather not do that."

"Check at the hospital and see if you could do anything there. Even if you started as a volunteer, it might develop into something that would pay."

"Good idea. I'll do that."

"Or at the Royal Hawaiian Hotel. Maybe working in the kitchen. They're so busy there, now that the Navy is using it for R&R."

The most famous Hawaiian hotel had been taken over by the Navy, to give sailors a place to enjoy a few days of rest and recreation.

"Thanks, Hiro. I appreciate the ideas."

Before long, the room was so warm that Grace felt light headed. "I need to get some air."

"Come on," Hiro said, taking her hand. They walked outside and found a bench under a shady tree.

"You sure have changed a lot since the first time I saw you," Hiro said.

"I have?"

"Absolutely." He was quiet for a minute and then said, "Do you think your parents would let you go out with me?"

"I don't know."

"Would you like to?"

"I would, yes."

"It won't be right away. I'll have to let you know when I can get time off again. Maybe we could go to a movie."

"I'd like that," she said, wondering why the strange, light headed feeling persisted.

Grace was hired to work in the kitchen at the Royal Hawaiian, and Vivian found a job at a small neighborhood drug store. They both started work the Monday after school let out. They met for a soda after their first day on the job.

"It's better than babysitting," Grace said. "However, I certainly wouldn't want to work in a kitchen the rest of my life."

"I feel the same way."

"At least you don't smell like grease," Grace said, sniffing unhappily at her clothes.

"What are you doing this weekend?" Vivian asked.

"We're going to Dorothy's for lunch on Sunday."

"Has the judge had any luck getting your cousins out of Manzanar?"

"Not yet. He tells us these things take time, but that he's working on it. He's such a nice man. We're lucky to have his help."

"I imagine he feels the same way about you."

Makiko's next letter was filled with despair. She had written from Manzanar, their new "home".

"Yoshi sits and stares into space all day. Many of the men are depressed and do nothing. Chiyo has been angry and obstinate since they took her camera away. None of us are allowed to take pictures. Naomi is trying to find a college in the Midwest that will accept her. Students can leave here if they can qualify, have admission, and can find a place to live.

The camp is windy and filthy. I can't keep our rooms clean no matter how hard I try. All four of us are living in two rooms of a barracks. The walls don't even go up to the ceiling, so there is no privacy. We eat in a dining room, two thousand at a time. We stand in line for everything: meals, toilets, showers, everything. The food is terrible. Sorry to sound so miserable, but that's how it is."

Grace was practically crying. "Why is it taking so long to get them home, Daddy?"

"James is doing everything he can, Grace. The red tape is endless. There are so many people who want to leave California. He's asked us to be patient."

"I hate this miserable war," Grace said.

Ken's face was blank, as if the effort to control his emotions had cost him everything.

"It was a mistake for them to leave. Everyone knew there would be war," Lilly said.

"A war, yes," Ken said, pain dripping from his words. "That much we knew. But who could have known that Japanese Americans would be treated like the enemy?"

CHAPTER 8

"Where is Midway?" Grace asked as she read the headlines on the newspaper her father held.

"It's northwest of here," Ken said, "about a third of the way to Japan."

"I didn't know there were any islands out there."

"It's small, but the Japanese could have used it as a springboard to the west coast. So, it's a good thing we smashed them there."

Richie could have been with them; if he was, they would have smashed *him*. She couldn't stop herself from imagining her brother as a soldier in the Japanese army.

She peeled a banana, started eating it, and then glanced at the clock. "Holy cats! I'm late." She grabbed her purse. "I'll see you tonight."

"I'm right behind you," her father said.

He had been working for a friend who owned a floral shop. Kawakami's would be closed for the duration of the war, and Ken didn't know if he would be able to open it again, even then. The florist job didn't pay much, but at least he was working. Although he didn't seem unhappy about his job,

Grace knew it frustrated him to see their store falling into disrepair. They weren't even allowed to go into it.

Each morning, Grace walked to the hotel, which was only a mile from their house. The beautiful landmark hadn't changed much, although the Navy had taken it over for the sailors for R&R. Hundreds of seamen now used the facility. For them, rest and recreation included a ten day stay, and was completely free of charge. She had been concerned that her distinct features might bring unwelcome looks or comments from the guests. Apparently, they'd become used to seeing Asians, for no one had said an unkind word.

"Hey, Gracie," the cook greeted her. "Hot date last night?" He pointed to the clock.

"No. I was reading the morning paper and lost track of time."

"You owe me one. I punched you in," he told her.

As she worked, she thought about the note she had received from Hiro, telling her how much he had enjoyed the prom, and that he looked forward to seeing her again. When she told her mother about the note, Lilly was pleased. "I like him. From what I've seen, he's a nice young man. The note was sweet. I wonder if it was his idea."

Her father was another matter. He had resisted letting her go to the prom. "You're too young to date," he had said.

Lilly told her to be patient. "After a while, your father will get used to him being around. It's ideal that he's a friend of Tom's. Your dad already knows Hiro, and he likes him."

That Saturday, Tom and Hiro showed up unexpectedly. Grace and Lilly were weeding the garden in the back yard. They rushed into the house the instant they heard Tom's voice.

"At the last minute, we got the day off," Tom said. "We thought it would be fun to surprise you." He was so pleased with himself that Grace had to laugh.

"It's a surprise, all right" she said, patting the scarf she had tied around her hair, to keep it from falling in her face. She glanced down at her grubby clothes and filthy hands.

"How did you get here?" Ken asked the two young men.

"We hitchhiked with a farmer who was coming from north shore."

"And what are you up to?"

"We thought we'd take Grace and Vivian to the movies. That is, if they're interested. What about it, Grace?" Tom asked.

"As long as it's not a war movie," she said. Hollywood was already making movies about the conflict in Europe. Every time the Japanese were mentioned, they were depicted as evil monsters.

"You call Vivian; I'll check the paper," Tom said.

Vivian agreed to join them, and the four were soon on their way downtown to see *Sleepy Time Gal*.

"I'll only agree to this if we can see an action movie next time," Hiro told Grace as they stood in the long line outside the theater. They huddled against the side of the building, trying to stay out of the sun.

"Just as long as it's not about war. I hear enough about that every day at work." She looked at him. "It must be the same for you. Aren't you tired of it?"

"Actually, we don't talk about it all that much. We talk more about what's happening here in the islands than we do about what's going on elsewhere."

"Oh, come on," Tom said. "We talk about it all the time. Every one of us would like to get into it."

Grace had heard a different story. The men who were staying at the hotel talked almost exclusively about getting *out* of it.

After the movie, they stopped for a burger. The restaurant was crowded, and it took far longer than they had expected to get served.

"It looks like we'd better eat fast," Tom said when the food finally arrived, "or we aren't going to be able to make curfew."

They bolted down their hamburgers, and then had to wait in line to pay, since all the others were trying to make curfew as well.

They ran home along the back streets, avoiding block wardens and police. They stopped at Vivian's long enough to see her inside, and then sprinted the rest of the way home. The three of them collapsed on the porch when they reached the house.

"What is it they think we're going to do after six o'clock, anyway?" Grace asked when she finally caught her breath. "I think this curfew thing is stupid."

"It's all about control," Hiro said. "The military wants the citizens to know that they're in charge."

"People can get into trouble more readily when it's dark," Tom said. "We're easier to patrol this way."

"Yes, but it's light until nine o'clock now. Why don't they change curfew time?"

"If they did that, then they'd have to change it back. Then, if people didn't want to comply, they'd say they forgot, or thought it had changed again. It's simpler to keep it the same all year long."

"Speaking of changes, did you hear they're printing new money?" Grace asked.

"No. What's that about?"

"They're going to print currency just for the islands, with the word Hawaii on both front and back. We'll have to exchange the U.S. bills we have now; Dad says the old ones will be destroyed. He says that because we're totally isolated, we're especially vulnerable. If the Japanese were to take over here, they could use our currency to manipulate the entire world market."

"So many changes," Hiro said. "I wonder if we'll ever get back to normal." He picked up his gas mask and looked at it with disdain. "We could have run faster if we didn't have to haul these things around." He looked at Grace. "Have you ever even tried yours on?"

"Only when I first got it."

"Let's see how you look in it."

"No."

"Come on, Gracie. Try it on," Tom said.

"You guys first."

Hiro and Tom put on the awkward, green, rubber masks, which covered their entire faces. Built in goggles protected their eyes, and what looked like a soup can hung down from the mouthpiece.

"Now you," Hiro said, his voice muffled inside the mask.

Grace pulled the smelly mask over her head, and adjusted it securely.

"Do you like it?"

"I don't think that's a good color for you," Tom said. "Does it come in pink?"

They were laughing at each other when Ken opened the door and looked out. "What in the world are you doing out here?"

"Trying to see if they gave us the right sizes," Tom said.

"It's after curfew. You'll have to spend the night, Hiro."

Hiro looked uneasy. "I hope that's okay…"

"As long as your folks don't mind, you're welcome to stay," Ken told him.

"Actually, they don't even know I'm in town. I didn't have time to call them before we left, and I've been busy since we got here. I'm sure they wouldn't mind, in any case."

When Grace got into bed that night, she was more contented than she had been in many months. The day with Hiro had been wonderful; the night, with him sleeping in Tom's room, made the house feel as full as it had before Richie left. Hiro had held her hand in the darkened living room after her parents went to bed. She thought he might kiss her goodnight, but he didn't.

Was he thinking about it, too?

She didn't know. But she hoped he was.

The next morning, Ken and Tom made pancakes for breakfast.

"I didn't know you were such a good cook, buddy," Hiro said to Tom. "I'll have to let the guys at the barracks know about this."

"In which case I might have to tell them that my sister says you're a great dancer."

"Don't put me in the middle of this," Grace said, although she loved being in the middle.

Hiro grinned at her. "You think I'm a good dancer?"

"I might have said that."

Grace noticed her father watching their exchange with interest. "More pancakes, anyone?" he asked.

"Not me, Daddy."

"I'll have another, if there's enough," Hiro said.

"Sure, Pop," Tom said, handing Ken his plate.

Lilly looked at him and smiled. "It's so nice to have you home."

When Tom and Hiro were ready to leave, Hiro whispered in Grace's ear, "I'll see you soon, I hope."

She smiled and said, "I hope so, too."

The VVV had a busy summer, and it was the end of August before Hiro and Tom were back again. Grace was disappointed not to hear from Hiro in all that time, but she knew he had no access to a phone, and writing might have drawn unwanted attention to himself. Her social life revolved around lunch at Dorothy's, and movies with Vivian. She and Vivian often met after work for a soda at Benson Smith's.

"I'd like to see if I can graduate in January," Grace said to Vivian, as they were drinking root beer floats one afternoon. "Then maybe I could get a real job."

"Doing what?"

"I don't know. School seems like such a waste of time now, with the rest of the world fighting a war. I think I could be doing something more useful."

"Have you talked to your folks about it?"

"Yeah. We've had a few discussions. They weren't very happy about it at first. I'll need to go to work after I graduate anyway, so it may as well be sooner than later."

"Wow." Vivian said. "I thought you wanted to go to college."

"I did. I still do. But that will have to wait. With Richie and Tom gone and the store closed, we need another income. The papers are full of job openings these days. It's just a shame I'm not a welder."

Grace made an appointment with the school advisor, and with her help, worked out a plan that would allow her to graduate mid-year.

"Of course, I won't have time for choir, or yearbook, or any other electives," she told Vivian. "I'm doubled up on English and History. I'm not too worried. What else is there for me to do besides study?"

"Oh, I don't know, go out with Hiro?"

She had only been out with him once since the day they went to the movie. She noticed that her father seemed to accept their friendship and had offered no more objections to her going out with him.

"And your father hasn't complained?"

"Not once. I'm not sure if my mom talked to him about it, or if he decided on his own. It helped that Hiro has been around for a couple of years, and that he's Tom's friend."

"I wish *I* had an older brother."

"You can share Tom."

"I don't much think of him as a brother anymore."

"Really?"

"He's been so sweet lately. And you know, he looks at me differently than he used to."

Grace hadn't noticed. When they had been together the last few times, all Grace had noticed was Hiro. "Have your parents said anything?"

Vivian shook her head. "Which is perfect. I don't have to ask about dating, or explain anything."

"This has been a year of changes," Grace said.

Sarah Reback called that night and invited the Kawakamis over for Sunday lunch.

"Do you suppose the judge has news about the Fujitas?" Lilly asked, when she hung up the phone.

"I certainly hope so."

Her cousins had been at Manzanar for nearly six months now. Grace had begun to despair of them ever coming back.

"I don't think we should get our hopes up. The military doesn't like the Japanese living here any better than they do in California," Grace said.

"We can't ever give up hope; that's what keeps us going," Ken said.

He was right back to where he was before being arrested, always the bright side.

They sat on the patio at the Reback's house that Sunday, looking out over the valley below their home, which stretched out in peaceful contrast to the turmoil of the world behind them. After everyone had been served a drink, the judge cleared his throat, as he often did before speaking.

"I know you're anxious for news about your family in California. Here's the thing...the authorities have two major concerns with them coming back: housing and jobs. If we can solve those two problems, I think we can do this."

Ken and Lilly looked at each other and smiled. "The first one is solved," Ken said. "They've always lived next door to us. My parents own the house. Well, my mother now that my father died. So, they *have* a place to live."

"That's one down," the judge said.

"And, my sister is a teacher. She should have no trouble finding work. Yoshi is a lawyer as you know, and if he can't practice, he could probably teach at the university."

"Does this mean they can come home?" Dorothy asked. Her eyes lit up as though it were her own family.

"It certainly tips the scales. I need to talk to a couple of people this week, and see what the next step is." He looked at Ken. "I'll call you about it as soon as I can."

Sarah put the casserole on the table. "I'm sorry it's so casual, but you know how it is at the meat counter."

James began serving. "Why is it that we've never met your mother if she lives next door to you?"

Grace glanced anxiously at her father. She knew he had been reluctant to tell the judge about Richie and Grandma, fearing that it would strain their relationship.

"My mother is in Japan."

"Really?"

Grace watched a struggle pass across her father's face. She waited, anxious about what he would say next.

"Yes. My father died in July of last year. He wanted to be laid to rest with his parents in Japan. She insisted on taking his ashes back."

"Ah. And, she's stuck there."

"Yes," Ken said.

"That's not the worst of it," Lilly said.

Ken's face darkened. "Our oldest son, Richie, went with her."

Realization bloomed on the judge's face. "Oh, God."

"Have you heard anything from him?" Sarah asked.

"Nothing since the attack."

Grace could have sworn that she saw the exact moment the judge understood.

"You think he's been drafted," the judge said.

"I'm sure of it," Ken said.

The judge shook his head sadly. "This must be a nightmare for you. I remember how it was for us, when Dorothy was out of touch for only a few hours."

"Yes," Lilly said.

"*Shikata ga nai*," Ken said, and then looked up in surprise at his own words. "It's an old phrase. It means 'there is nothing that can be done about it'."

"I'm so sorry," the judge said. He was quiet for a bit and then said, "When the time comes and he's able to come home, I'll be here to help."

Grace saw tears spring to her mother's eyes.

"Meanwhile, we'll keep him in our prayers," Sarah said.

After a silence, Lilly asked Dorothy, "What do you hear from Paul?"

"Not too much. He's getting leave next month. Six days of R&R. We're thinking of it as a second honeymoon."

They talked as they ate, the afternoon drifting into evening.

"We've got to go," Ken said. "We're barely going to make curfew."

"I'll call you soon," the judge told them as they walked out to the car.

"Well," Lilly said, as they drove down the street, "that went better than I'd expected."

"Yes. It's great news about California, and I'm glad we finally told them about Richie and Mother."

"When you chose someone to help after the bombing, you sure chose the right person, Daddy."

"There couldn't have been a wrong person, sweetheart. I'm not sure that I made the choice anyway."

Did he? Did anyone make their own choices? Was everything pre-ordained? The question had always puzzled her. Was it free will or karma that governed their lives?

Grace had been in school for more than a week when the judge finally contacted them. He made arrangements with Ken to come by to talk on Saturday morning. Lilly had a pot of coffee perking when he arrived.

"Wow, that smells good, Lilly," he said, as he sat at the table.

"She only makes it when you come over," Ken said.

"It's so hard to get these days," Lilly said. "I know how you love it."

"I'm honored that you share it with me," he told her.

Grace saw that the judge had brought a briefcase, which he now opened.

"I think we've just about done it," he said. "There are several forms you need to fill out. I'll file them here, and then send copies to your brother-in-law to complete on his end. After that, it's up to the authorities in California."

Ken looked at the judge with eyes full of thanks. "This is such wonderful news. Thank you, James, from the bottom of my heart. I'll complete these forms, and get them back to you tomorrow."

"Don't leave anything unanswered," James cautioned. "The military seems to like nothing better than issuing denials. So, call me if you have any questions."

"Yes. Yes, I will."

Lilly set a large cup of coffee down before the judge. "Sugar or cream?"

"I wouldn't put a thing in it to ruin the taste. Just coffee, thanks." He sat back, and drank it with obvious pleasure.

The papers were filed within the week, and two weeks after that a post card arrived from Chiyo. All it said was, "We're coming home!"

Grace's school load was challenging, and she often didn't get back from classes until late in the afternoon. When she arrived home on the first Wednesday in October, she heard voices and laughter coming from her house. She opened the front door and entered the room, which suddenly turned silent.

Then Chiyo screamed, "Grace!" and ran to hug her cousin.

"You're home!" Grace cried. "You're home."

Naomi, Makiko, and Yoshi all stood to greet her.

"Does Mom know?" Grace asked her father.

"No, I couldn't get hold of her."

"We should go pick her up when she gets off work," Grace said.

"She'd probably have a heart attack," Ken said.

Grace thought a moment. "Then let's make something really special for dinner."

"I think that's a better idea," her father told her.

"Could we go shopping?" Naomi asked. "I haven't been in a real store for months."

Grace looked at her father. "Take the car," he said, giving her the keys. "Don't forget your gas masks."

"You have yours already?" Grace asked, surprised.

"Yes. They registered us, fingerprinted us, and gave us the masks before we ever got off the ship," Makiko said. "Such organization."

Naomi looked at the ugly mask unhappily. "We're only going to the market."

"It's the law now, Naomi," Ken said gently.

"Take it," her father said, less gently.

The girls left for the market, happy to be in the car, but unhappily carrying masks.

"I hope Daddy cheers up now that we're home," Chiyo said.

"He won't be happy until he's working again," Naomi said.

"I'm sure what you went through was awful," Grace said. "It'll take a while to get used to being here again. Plus, a lot of things have changed here, too. For one thing, there's no telling what the butcher will give us," Grace said. "You take what you get these days, whether you like it or not."

"Whatever it is, it will be better than what they gave us at Manzanar. *Haoles* have no idea how to cook for Japanese," Naomi said.

Grace looked at her with amusement.

Chiyo laughed, her hand daintily covering her mouth.

"Sorry," Naomi said. "*Your* mom is different."

They stood in line at the meat counter, and Grace was shocked when the butcher handed them a rather large package.

"Thank you," Grace told him.

"You're welcome," he said, looking right past her. "Hey, Naomi. I haven't seen you around in a while."

Naomi laughed. It sounded like bells tinkling.

Grace had never heard that sound before.

"I just got back in town."

"Don't be a stranger," he told her.

"Count on it," she said.

Grace tore open the package when they got home. "It's a chicken! The biggest one I've ever seen." She looked at Naomi. "I'm never going shopping without you again!"

Lilly didn't have a heart attack when she got home, but she did have a drink to celebrate the Fujitas' return. Then, she and Makiko cooked dinner, side by side in the kitchen, exactly like they used to.

"Did you call James?" Lilly asked as she sat down at the table.

"I certainly did," Ken said. "We're going there for lunch on Sunday."

"I'm going to school with Grace tomorrow," Chiyo said.

"And I'm going up to the university to see if I can register," Naomi said. "You'll come with me, won't you Father?"

Yoshi nodded at her.

Grace thought he looked drugged. He had lost weight; he looked slack and sallow and sunken. Manzanar had turned him into an old man.

They'd all become prisoners of war.

CHAPTER 9

"Come on Vivian, go with us," Chiyo said.

"I can't. I've got way too much homework."

"The football game will be over in two hours," Chiyo argued. "And then, we'll come right back home."

"Ha! You'll go for a soda, and then you'll want to go shopping. I *have* to study."

"Next time," Grace said, pulling on Chiyo's arm.

The girls were on their way to the Saturday football game between McKinley and their rival school, Roosevelt. Grace knew that she would have to work hard, later, to finish all her assignments, but she wanted to go to this game with Chiyo.

"Have fun," Vivian called as they walked across the yard.

In the week since the Fujitas had returned, Chiyo and Naomi had registered at school, Makiko had been hired at the local elementary school, and Yoshi had made connections with colleagues, who were trying to find him work. Makiko and Lilly had made blackout curtains for the Fujitas' house, and today they were taking inventory of the goods that Ken had stockpiled the previous fall.

"You're so quiet," Grace said to Chiyo as they walked to the game.

"It's hard to believe that I'm back. It seems like we were gone for years."

"A year and four months. I kept count of every day."

"We never should have gone. It was awful there."

"Were you unhappy the whole time?"

Chiyo considered the question. "The only good thing was the Camera Club. They even had a dark room at school. At first, the kids were nice to me. After the war started, everything changed."

"How?"

"Kids called me *Jap* or *Nip*. They told me I should go home. Nobody wanted to believe that America *is* my home. They think if you're Japanese, you should live in Japan."

"The kids in the Camera Club said that?"

"Not all of them, but most of the kids at the school were nasty, or just ignored me."

"No wonder you didn't like it."

"And then, we found out we had to go to the relocation camp." She shook her head sadly. "Honestly Grace, it was exactly like going to prison, except that we hadn't done anything wrong."

"Did they come to your house?"

"No. They put big ads in the newspaper and posted flyers everywhere."

"Then what?"

"We had to sell everything. People came like scavengers. They offered us a nickel or a dime for things worth way more. We had no choice…it was sell things or throw them away. Luckily, we didn't have all that much, since we hadn't been there very long. Other families lost everything they owned. Japanese weren't allowed to possess certain things, like short wave radios, weapons, or cameras. More than anything, I wanted to keep my camera. I begged Daddy, but he said no. Losing it was like losing my only friend."

Grace knew that Chiyo's camera was nearly as important to her as her life. It was her best friend.

"They took us to the camp on busses. The windows were all covered, so we couldn't see where we were going. It took hours. It was so hot. Little kids were crying, begging for something to eat, or to go to the bathroom. People were getting sick and throwing up. It smelled so awful, *I* nearly got sick."

Grace shuddered. How could people be so cruel? Even animals were treated better. How could the government justify such inhumane treatment of innocent citizens? "I'm so sorry."

Chiyo surprised her when she said, "*Shikata ga nai.*"

They saw Beatrice and Margie sitting in the bleachers at the field, and waved to them.

"Come sit with us," Margie called.

Chiyo put her hand on Grace's arm. "I don't want to talk about this in front of them."

"Of course. I understand." She felt the same way about the night of the bombing, when her father had been taken away. Talking about it just brought it all back.

The teams were well matched, but McKinley managed an early lead and won, 21-17.

"Let's go get a soda," Margie said, and the others agreed. Benson's was crowded, and they had to wait for a table. After they finished, Margie said, "I need to get home and help my mom." Beatrice and two others invited Grace and Chiyo to go with them to the movies.

"I've got tons of homework," Grace said.

"Me too," Chiyo told them. "More than tons."

"See you Monday then," Beatrice said, and she and the others headed for the theater.

Chiyo lagged behind Grace as they walked down the street. "Smell," she said.

"What?"

"Smell. It's plumeria." She reached up to a branch of the parkway tree and pulled it down, so the fragrant flowers were directly in front of her face. She drew in a deep breath, and sighed. "It's heavenly."

"Are you turning into a botanist?"

Chiyo shook her head. "The camp stunk. Really, it stunk. Even the food. They made the most awful food. We ate in a mess hall; hundreds of us all at once. The authorities chose the cooks. Our cook was a mechanic. He served bread, potatoes, macaroni and rice all in the same meal. No vegetables. Practically no fish or meat. Sometimes, we stood in line for an hour, and then they served us *that*."

"You couldn't cook in your...your..."

"Our house? That's what we called it, even though it was only two rooms in a barracks. No. There was no kitchen. No bathroom either. We had to go to the latrine to use a toilet."

Grace watched as Chiyo seemed to step back into the camp. She waited while her cousin dredged up the sordid scene.

"The latrine was a huge room. In the middle, there were two rows of six toilets, back to back. There were no partitions, and no privacy. The toilets backed up all the time, and the floor was covered with...well, you can guess what it was covered with."

Grace felt sick to her stomach.

"It stunk. All the time. I felt bad for the older ladies; they were so embarrassed. The little kids who had to pee, would dance around in line holding themselves, and crying. And then, if you were sick..."

"I'm so sorry, Chiyo. I had no idea."

"We couldn't write about it. The censors wouldn't allow it."

Grace shook her head.

"Our house was dirty all the time. There were holes in the walls where the boards had pulled apart. The same for the floor. Everything was filthy. The wind blew almost every day, and there was sand and dirt everywhere. We couldn't keep it out of our eyes or our hair. Half the time it was in our food."

Chiyo was quiet for a while.

"You don't have to tell me about it if you don't want to."

"It's okay. I'm home now."

They walked in silence for a bit. "I saw snow," Chiyo said.

"Really?"

"Yeah. It snowed not long after we got to the camp."

"Was it pretty?" Emma envisioned her dream of a white Christmas.

"Yes. For about ten minutes. But it's cold. It stings your hands. We didn't have any clothes that were suitable for snow. So we were freezing, and the house was freezing as well. It was like a shack. The wind came right through. There was a stove in the center of one room, but it didn't help much."

Chiyo's voice faltered.

"The interior walls didn't go all the way to the ceiling, so there was no privacy in anyone's house. If someone snored, everyone in the barracks heard it. If someone was sick, their coughing kept everyone awake. And if people were arguing, the entire place knew it. The authorities weren't interested in our comfort. They didn't care, and they weren't about ready to make conditions any better. We were treated as if *we* had started the war...we were treated like the enemy."

"No wonder they didn't want you to have a camera. The government doesn't want a record of what they're doing."

"I think a lot of the kids I went to school with would say that that's what we deserved for being Japanese."

"Being Japanese. That's the crime of this century."

They had reached home. Chiyo looked at Grace with a sad smile. "It's done now. I'm home. That's all that matters."

"I'm glad you are."

"And, I've got homework. So, I'll see you later."

"Yep. Study hard."

"You too, Gracie."

When Chiyo had gone into her house, Grace turned and walked down to Vivian's. She knocked on the door, and when Mrs. Ozawa answered she said, "May I pick some plumeria from the tree out back? I want to make a *lei* for Chiyo."

"Of course, Grace. Come on in."

The ancient Hawaiian tradition of *lei* making was well known in the islands. Children learned the skill when they were young, and by the time they were teens, had made many of the flower wreaths.

"Here," Mrs. Ozawa said, handing her a large paper bag. Then, she helped Grace pick about a hundred of the pink and white flowers. Their fragrance filled the air. It was one of Grace's favorite scents; it was the aroma of Hawaii, the smell of home.

"How are the girls doing?" Mrs. Ozawa asked.

"Pretty good. They didn't have school books at the camp, so they have to get used to studying again."

"They were both good students. It won't take long for them to get back in the swing."

Grace considered sharing what Chiyo had told her about the camp, and then decided against it. Grace knew it would be uncomfortable for Makiko and Yoshi to reconnect with old friends if the others had any idea of the embarrassing and humiliating circumstances of the camp.

"Do you have needles and thread to make the *lei*?"

"Yes. We used to make them every year for May Day."

"Do you want to say hi to Vivian?" Mrs. Ozawa asked.

"No. I won't bother her now. Thank you for the flowers," Grace said, and she slipped out the side gate.

The house was empty when she got home. She heard voices next door, and realized her parents were over helping her aunt and uncle get settled. Grace got out the box of *lei* making tools, and sat down at the kitchen table. She spread out the flowers so they wouldn't crush each other, and began stringing the *lei*.

When she finished, she tied a small pink bow on it, and then put the box away. She carried the *lei* next door and walked into the house.

"Where's Chiyo?" she asked her aunt.

"In her room."

"That's beautiful," Lilly said. "Nice idea."

Chiyo was at her desk, studying.

Grace tiptoed up behind her and slipped the *lei* over her head. She leaned over and kissed her on the cheek. "*Aloha.* Welcome home."

Chiyo picked up the fragrant *lei* and held it to her nose. "Thank you, Gracie. I love you, too."

Sunday morning, Ken and Yoshi fixed breakfast, while the women sat in the living room discussing what to wear for lunch at the Rebacks'.

"They're very casual," Lilly said. "You don't have to try to impress them."

"I want to look my best," Naomi said. "The judge got us out of that hell, and I'll show my respect by dressing up."

Chiyo laughed. "You'd dress up to *go* to hell."

"Chiyo," Makiko said.

"Sorry."

"You'll like Dorothy," Grace said, changing the subject. "She's sweet. She and her mom both work with the Red Cross. There are so many divisions, and they've changed around, so I'm not sure where they're assigned right now."

The girls had eaten and changed, and were sitting in the living room when they heard, "Yoo-hoo."

Grace jumped up and opened the front door.

"Hi," Dorothy said. "Looks like you're ready."

"We sure are. Dorothy, these are my cousins, Naomi and Chiyo."

"I'm so happy to meet you," Dorothy said, "I'm even happier that you're finally home."

"Thank you," Chiyo said.

"We're glad to be here," Naomi told her.

"See you up there, Mom," Grace called down the hall.

"Okay," Lilly replied.

"This was so thoughtful of you," Naomi said as the four got into the car.

"Well, I knew you couldn't all fit into one car, and this seemed like the most logical solution."

When their parents arrived, the girls were all sitting on the patio, chatting with Dorothy. Sarah ushered the two couples out to the yard.

"Dorothy, this is Grace's Aunt Makiko and Uncle Yoshi."

Dorothy stood and greeted the girls' parents. "We've just been talking about your trip home. I hear it was longer than the trip to the mainland."

"In more ways than one," Yoshi said.

The judge came outside, carrying a tray of glasses filled with champagne. "Let's drink to our latest victory."

Sarah had set two tables: one for the girls and one for the parents. She brought plates of sandwiches out for each table and said, "Please, everyone...sit down."

"I've never had champagne before," Chiyo whispered to Grace.

Dorothy overheard her. "Somehow, I don't think it goes all that well with sandwiches."

Grace was still full from breakfast, but Naomi and Chiyo ate enthusiastically.

"These are delicious, Mrs. Reback," Naomi said.

"Thank you, dear."

"We had the most terrible food in the camp," she added.

"I imagine the whole experience was dreadful," Sarah said. "I don't know how I would have handled it, if it had happened to me."

"It's a blight on our nation," the judge said. "The idea the United States would treat people that way is unfathomable."

"Citizens," Yoshi said. "They're treating US *citizens* that way. I was born in this country. I served in the U.S. Army during the last war. I've lived here my whole life. And yet they put me and my family in a concentration camp. It's not only wrong, it's unconstitutional."

"You're absolutely right, Yoshi. It *is* unconstitutional; and it's prejudicial. Germans and Italians have not been treated the same way. What an affront to you, having risked your life for this country when you were called the last time."

Yoshi nodded.

"There are some who would like to do the same thing to the Japanese here," the judge said indignantly. "Thank heaven more reasonable minds have prevailed."

"Reasonable or expedient?" Ken asked. "Where would they send us? And who would work the fields or clean the houses, if the entire Japanese population of Hawaii were suddenly gone?"

The three men sat in silence.

"How is it you're so pro-Japanese, Judge?" Yoshi asked.

"I'm not pro-Japanese. I'm pro-law. In this country, we say that all men are created equal. Laws are written in accordance with that belief, and it's my job to make sure the laws are upheld. Without the law, we're nothing but savages."

"That's a bit strong, dear, don't you think?" Sarah said.

"I certainly do not."

"In California, it's against the law for a Japanese to marry a Caucasian," Yoshi said.

"And in the south, segregation is legal," the judge said. "Unfortunately, not all our laws are fair or just."

"What happens when you have to rule on an unjust law, Judge?" Lilly asked.

"That's a good question, Lilly. I'd like to think I'm impartial, and make my decision on the merits of the case. However, last time I checked I was human, and that might influence me some."

When they laughed, Grace relaxed. Although they were all in agreement, it seemed like the discussion had all the components of an explosion.

When they'd finished lunch, Sarah said, "Would anyone like a piece of pineapple upside down cake?"

"Yum," Grace said. "I would. Can I help?"

The others joined in her enthusiasm.

As curfew time approached, the families began saying their farewells.

"Judge, our family is indebted to you," Yoshi said. "Although I wish you no harm, I hope there will come a time when we might be able to repay the debt."

"Having met you, I feel sure you would have done the same for my family. Ken already has. Let's agree to call it even."

Yoshi and Makiko bowed deeply to the judge and his wife. "We hope to see you again soon."

As Dorothy drove the girls back home, she asked Naomi, "What was the worst thing about being in the camp? That is, if you don't mind me asking."

Naomi thought for a moment and then said, "The humiliation. We were treated like animals. Worse than animals. People value their animals and take good care of them. We were treated as if we were worthless. Whoever created those camps had no respect for us whatsoever."

"I'd be so angry," Dorothy said.

"At whom? President Roosevelt, for signing the order? The military, for singling out the Japanese? The people who built the barracks? The ones who stood in the guard towers with their rifles pointed at us? At the people of California, who sat back, watched it happen, and said nothing?" She shook her head. "When I left California, I was furious with all of them, but the more I thought about it on the ship, the more I realized that the anger was a waste of my energy. So, one day, I threw it overboard."

"You never told me that," Chiyo said. "None of it."

"I wasn't ever going to talk about it again."

"I'm sorry," Dorothy said. "I shouldn't have asked."

"That's okay. I'm sure other people will ask. I guess I should be ready to give them an answer."

Grace sat in the back seat listening to Naomi, amazed at the change in her cousin. She was not the same person who had left Hawaii the summer before.

"Is this why you changed your major?" Chiyo asked.

"What?" Grace said. "You didn't tell me you'd changed your major. I thought you were crazy about fashion design."

"I was. I suppose it's part of the reason. Things look different to me since we were at Manzanar." She turned to Grace. "I've transferred to pre-law."

"Oh, wow, that's a huge change," Grace said.

"I hope one day I can have a partnership with Dad."

"Have you talked to Daddy about that?" Chiyo asked.

"I have. He actually tried to talk me out of it. After a while, he realized I was completely serious. Now, he's excited about the possibilities it would present."

Grace shook her head. "Amazing." The war was bringing one change after another, and they weren't completely bad, after all.

CHAPTER 10

"Speak American?" Yoshi said. "The paper says now they're going to tell us what *language* we have to speak."

"Please, Yoshi, can't we just have a nice dinner?" Makiko pleaded.

The Kawakamis and the Fujitas were eating their evening meal together, as they often did.

"Not everyone here can speak English. What are they supposed to do, not talk?"

"Maybe they should learn English," Ken said.

"I believe the First Amendment to the Constitution guarantees us the right of free speech, not that the military is the least interested in the Constitution."

Grace had grown accustomed to her uncle challenging nearly every military order that was issued. And now, Naomi was beginning to echo his objections. Sometimes Grace worried that they might make trouble for the entire family.

"They're trying to promote unity, and diffuse some of the animosity from the war workers. Those folks from the mainland aren't used to hearing so many languages. It scares them," Ken said.

"They're trampling all over the constitution, and we're going along with it."

"You're not," Naomi said.

Yoshi smiled at her.

There was a noise on the porch, and then everyone heard, "Hey…anybody home?"

"Tom!" Grace cried, and ran to meet him.

Tom came in, hugged Grace, and then realized who was at the table.

"You're back!" He rushed to the table, shook hands with Yoshi, bowed to Makiko and then greeted Naomi and Chiyo with familiar pats. "The judge did it."

"He sure did," Yoshi agreed. "We'll be thanking him forever."

Lilly dished up a plate of supper, and handed it to Tom. "You have time to eat, don't you?"

"I'm off for two days."

What about Hiro, Grace wondered.

Of course, she didn't ask.

They all moved to make room for Tom at the table. "When did you get here?" he asked Yoshi.

His uncle filled him in on the details of their return.

"And everybody's back to school and all?"

"It's almost like we never left," Chiyo told him. "Except for all the changes here, that is."

"What's been the hardest thing for you?" Tom asked her.

"I started work last week."

"Work? Really? Where?"

"Dole Plantation," Chiyo said.

"Doing what?"

"Picking pineapples."

"The school board adopted a new policy for four-day school weeks, so students can help work in the fields four days a month," Lilly said.

"What is that like?" Tom asked Chiyo.

"Hard. And boring. And to make matters worse, the boys get paid more than the girls for doing the *exact* same work. I make forty-two cents an hour. Some lazy guy, who doesn't work half as hard, makes fifty-five."

Yoshi started to say something, but Makiko put her hand on his arm.

Tom gave her a resigned look. "*Shikata ga nai.*"

They were turning into their parents, Grace thought.

"What about you, Grace? Are you working, too?"

"No. I spend the extra day studying. I've doubled up on my classes, so I can graduate mid-term. The papers keep saying how badly they need manpower. I'll get a job in January."

"I'm at UH," Naomi told him. "I'm doing pre-law."

"Whoa, that's a big change."

"Speaking of changes," Naomi said, "there's barbed wire strung all along the beaches. When did that happen?"

"It's been weeks. The military put it up to deter invading forces," Tom told her.

"I still saw some folks out there on the beach."

"They left a few breaks in the wire, so people can get through. You can't keep the *kama'aina* from the water," he said. "Listen, why don't we all go to the beach tomorrow? We can take a lunch." He grinned at Grace. "Maybe Vivian can go with us."

"She'd like that, I think."

The girls agreed to make lunch, and Tom said he and Hiro would scout out a place to get through the barbed wire.

"You'll be careful," Makiko said.

"Yes," Tom told her. "And we'll come straight home, if there's an invasion."

"Tom!" Ken said.

"Sorry," he said to Makiko. "I'm used to talking like that at the barracks."

The next day was sunny and warm, like nearly every day in paradise. Hiro arrived at ten o'clock, and when the lunch was packed, they headed down to the beach. Hiro walked along side Grace, though not close enough to touch her.

"How have you been?" Grace asked him.

"Busy. They keep us working from dawn to dusk. The food is okay, and we sleep like logs, so we're fine. What about you?"

She told him about her new schedule, and her plan to start work in January.

"Where do you want to work?"

"I don't care, as long as I'm helping with the war effort. The papers are full of ads for jobs."

"It's too bad you can't work for the Navy. They pay really well."

"Why can't I work for the Navy?"

"You're kidding, right? Because you're Japanese. You'd never be hired by the military."

She felt both foolish and aggrieved.

"Don't worry. Local businesses are all hurting for help. Check out construction companies. With all the building going on, you could probably get something without any problem."

They talked easily, now. The shy boy her brother had brought home to meet the family was gone. Perhaps he had disappeared on patrol one night at the beginning of the war. The new Hiro had a confidence, an assuredness, that Grace found irresistible.

The beach was crowded. Servicemen on R&R, along with those stationed at Pearl Harbor, were all taking advantage of the beautiful weather and a few hours off. There were locals as well, a few of whom were surfing.

"Do you like to swim?" Hiro asked her. They'd set out mats on the sand. Vivian and Tom were already in the water.

"Not much. Richie was on the swim team at the university, and sometimes I'd go with him, but I'm not much of a swimmer."

"What about you girls?" Hiro asked Naomi and Chiyo.

Naomi stretched out on a mat. "I'm happy here."

"Me, too," Chiyo agreed. "You guys go ahead."

They waded in, and then kept walking into deeper water. Hiro swam, while Grace floated on her back. When she looked past the barbed wire on the beach and up at the mountains, it was so peaceful that she could almost forget about the war. She heard Vivian giggling at Tom, who was clowning in the waves.

"I think your brother likes Vivian," Hiro said. "He talks about her all the time."

Grace turned over so she could tread water with him. "I think she likes him, too."

"Can I tell him that?"

"Don't you think he can figure it out himself?"

"We Japanese boys aren't very smart about these things."

Grace wasn't sure how to respond to that.

"You know, there's a good chance we'll be able to enlist before long," Hiro said.

"Really?"

"Yes. I was hoping that if we do, you'd write me while I'm gone."

"Of course."

"I'm not a very good writer, but I'll try to send you one letter for every one I get from you."

"How many girls will hear that promise?"

He looked hurt.

"I'm teasing. I'm also tired. Let's go back."

They rested, and then ate the lunch the girls had packed. The sun was dipping toward the horizon, and a breeze was picking up when Vivian said, "I need to get home and study."

The other girls agreed, reluctantly. "We all do," Naomi said.

"This was nice," Tom said as they packed up their things. "Let's do it every week."

"Good idea," Vivian told him. "I'll just quit school."

Grace shot her a glance. She must really like him, if she'd even joke about that.

Thanksgiving was soon only days away. "Do you think we'll be able to get a turkey?" Chiyo asked her mother. The girls and their mothers were sitting in the Fujitas' front room after dinner.

"Send Naomi," Grace said. "The butcher will give her anything she wants."

Naomi laughed. "He's an old friend. It doesn't mean anything."

"I wish you'd start dating him," Grace said. "I'm sure we'd eat better if you did."

They did get a turkey for Thanksgiving, and Lilly prepared it as she always had. The house smelled heavenly to Grace, who set the table early in the afternoon.

"Do you suppose Tom will make it home?" she asked her mother.

"If he does, you'll have to add two places at the table. He never shows up without Hiro these days."

"I know," Grace said, a huge smile on her face.

"He's a nice young man," Lilly said. "And he's good looking, too."

Tom didn't make it for dinner, but he and Hiro turned up the next morning.

"We thought it would be fun to go to the zoo today," Tom said.

"Just the three of us?" Grace asked.

"No," her brother said. "Why don't you invite one of your friends to go with us?"

Grace thought a moment. "What about Margie?"

"Margie is busy," Tom said.

"What about Beatrice?"

Tom shook his head. "She's with Margie."

Grace laughed at him. "Okay, I'll call Vivian."

Although it was a beautiful day when they boarded the bus to the zoo, as they stood near the primate house, it started to rain. It rained nearly every week in Hawaii, so a squall was not unusual. They took shelter under a banyan tree, and waited for it to stop.

But it didn't. The tree soon proved to be insufficient cover for the amount of water coming down. They ran to the small café near the entrance and took refuge there. They ordered Cokes and watched as less optimistic patrons walked out of the gates.

"It'll stop soon," Tom predicted.

Finally, it did. Since so many people had left, they had the zoo practically to themselves. Once outside, Tom took Vivian's hand and went off in one direction, while Hiro led Grace in another.

"Did you two plan this?"

"Divide and conquer," he said.

They walked slowly, paying far less attention to the animals than to each other.

"Do you really think you'll enlist?" Grace asked.

"Yes."

"Do you ever think about the fighting? I mean, about someone shooting at you?"

"Sometimes."

"Doesn't it scare you?"

"It does."

"I couldn't do it."

"In a way, you already did."

She frowned at him. "How?"

He pulled her over to a bench, and they sat down. "You went out with your dad on the day of the attack. Weren't you scared?"

"Of course."

"But you went out anyway."

"I was with my dad."

"That wouldn't have made much difference if they had come back."

"It's not the same."

"Maybe not, but I still think it took a lot of guts."

"It wasn't as scary as when they took him away that night. I figured I was dead for sure when they drove off."

"And yet, you went out again."

"I had to run down the street to Vivian's."

"Alone."

"What choice did I have?"

"You could have called Mr. Ozawa to come get you."

"I never thought of that."

"You're braver than you think."

"Here you are," Tom said, as he and Vivian joined them.

"I need to get home. I've got a boatload of homework," Vivian said.

"You have three days," Hiro said.

"Yes, and I have four days' worth of work."

On the way back to the house, they agreed to go to the movies on Sunday afternoon.

"We probably won't have much more time off before Christmas," Tom told Grace when they were alone that night.

"Will you be home for Christmas?" she asked.

"Do you mean will Hiro be home?"

"That, too."

"I hope so. We won't know until the last minute. Hiro will be disappointed if we can't. He's completely stuck on you, Gracie."

"I'm glad. I'm keen on him, too."

To observe the anniversary of the Pearl Harbor attack, the territory held a war bond sale. People stood in long lines to purchase the bonds, doing all they could to support the war effort. Movie theaters played short films reminding citizens of the bombing and encouraging them to buy bonds to seek revenge on the "sneaky Japs."

The florists in Honolulu, who were mainly Japanese, closed their shops and spent the day placing flowers on the graves of those who perished on December 7th. Grace went with her father to Nuuanu Cemetery, and for the first time, walked among the graves, placing a small American flag on each.

"That was the most horrible day of my life," Ken said on the way home.

"Mom never talks about it," Grace said.

"It was too awful for words. The ones who didn't survive, and the ones who did, all suffered dreadfully. It must be impossible to speak of it."

"She threw away the uniform she wore that day. She couldn't get all the blood out of it."

"Or the memories."

As the semester drew to a close, Grace felt more and more pressure. She was determined to graduate with honors and worked harder than ever with the extra load.

"When are we going Christmas shopping?" Lilly asked Grace the week before the holiday.

"I have no time, Mom. Besides, with no tree, it doesn't even feel like Christmas."

"We can decorate the lemon tree."

"It's not the same."

"I know. Still, we have to do the best we can with what we have."

The weekend before Christmas, Tom and Hiro arrived with the most pathetic looking tree Grace had ever seen.

"We were clearing some land, and this was one of the casualties," Tom said. "I know it's a little sad, but with some lights and a few decorations, you can make it look beautiful."

"Thank you, Tom. I'll make it a masterpiece."

"We can't stay. We're actually picking up some supplies downtown. I'll try to get home next weekend. There's no chance for me to be here for Christmas."

She walked them out to their truck.

"I won't be off for Christmas, either," Hiro told her. "I'll be thinking about you, though. I'll see you on New Year's." He squeezed her hand, and jumped into the truck.

Grace and Chiyo had the little tree decorated in no time. When they were finished, there were more ornaments than there was tree. They stood back to admire their work.

"It's pretty funny looking," Chiyo said.

"It is. On the other hand, at least now we have someplace to put the gifts."

Chiyo looked at her. "Do you want anything special?"

"Not really. If I could have the impossible, I'd have Richie home."

"That would be a Christmas miracle."

"What about you, Chiyo?"

"I'm too old for Christmas. Surprises are for little kids."

However, that Christmas it was Chiyo who was the most surprised by her gift. Yoshi and Makiko waited until everyone else had finished opening their presents before handing Chiyo a large, beautifully wrapped box.

She frowned with confusion and squealed with happiness when she opened it.

"It's an Argus A," she cried. The 35mm camera looked so complex that Grace couldn't figure out where the shutter button was.

"Thank you," Chiyo told her parents, uncharacteristic tears in her eyes.

"We know how hard it was when you had to give up your camera. So, now you can start documenting our family events again," her father said.

"You're so talented, Chiyo, maybe you could get some pictures published in the newspaper," Naomi suggested.

"Of our family?"

"No. Scenic shots of Honolulu. The mountains or the ocean or whatever."

"You'll have to be careful about where you take pictures," Ken cautioned her. "The censors are monitoring all the film developers. They don't want us to take any photos of military installations or sensitive areas."

Yoshi grunted in disgust. "Do they think we're gathering information for the homeland?" He'd become increasingly critical of the repressive political climate, even though he wanted, and expected, the United States to win the war with Japan. Grace worried that he might voice his disapproval in public and be detained, or worse, sent back to the mainland.

"Who's hungry?" Lilly asked, taking the spotlight from her brother-in-law.

Grace liked Christmas, but she liked New Year's even better. To the Japanese, New Year's was the most important holiday on the calendar. They believed that the celebration of the New Year set the tone for prosperity in the coming months. Grandma and Makiko had always spent days preparing the special food called *osechi.* Grace's favorite was *ozoni,* rice cake soup and *kamaboko* or fish cakes. Normally, on the last day of December, all the temples rang bells 108 times at midnight. Since the temples had been closed, no bells would ring this year.

New Year's Day was for family. People travelled great distances to be home for the celebration. Grace knew it would be hard for the VVVs not to be home for New Year's, and hoped Tom and Hiro would be among the ones who were.

Naomi and Makiko began the preparations the day after Christmas. Grace wanted to help, but she had finals in January, and with her additional classes, she needed to spend every possible minute studying.

By curfew on New Year's Eve, Grace knew she wouldn't be seeing Hiro or Tom that day. She was disappointed, but made a conscious effort to act enthusiastic about celebrating without them.

"Come on, Grace, cheer up," Naomi said. "He'll come by tomorrow."

"Who?" Yoshi asked.

"Nobody," Grace said quickly.

Naomi flashed a huge smile at her father and said, "Hiro."

"Ah," Yoshi said.

"Hiro's a nice boy," Ken said absently

The girls laughed at their oblivious fathers.

Tom came home early the next morning. "I can only stay a little while. They're trying to make sure every guy gets a few minutes with his family." He stacked a plate with all the specially made food and grinned. "This looks as good as Grandma's."

He'd only been there an hour when they heard a truck rumbling outside. "That must be Hiro," he said.

Grace wanted to jump up and run to greet him, but didn't dare in front of her parents.

"Happy New Year," he said when Tom let him in.

"Happy New Year, Hiro," Ken said, amiably. "How are your parents?"

"Fine, thank you."

"Would you like something to eat?" Lilly offered.

"No, thanks. My mom's been stuffing me ever since I got here."

Tom looked at Grace. "Have you written a *haiku* this year?"

Writing the traditional seventeen syllable poems was another of Grace's favorite New Year traditions. *Haiku,* written by her family specifically for the New Year, celebrated the occasion, and often included the word "first", or references to the season.

"Yes."

"May we hear it?" her father asked.

She took a piece of paper from her pocket, and unfolded it. She looked at it for a few moments and then read:

"Winter's crashing waves
bring gifts of ocean seaweed
to rough, gnarled hands."

The room was silent until Ken said, "I think that may be one of your best."

Grace knew that many elderly Japanese believed seaweed was a curative for arthritis. She was delighted with her father's approval.

After the others read their poems, Tom said, "We've got to get back. The rest of the guys will be waiting for their turn."

Grace walked out to the truck with him and Hiro.

"I wrote a *haiku*," Hiro said quietly, "but it's just for you." He took out a small, intricately folded paper and handed it to her.

"Thank you."

"Read it later."

She slipped it carefully into her pocket.

"We'll see you as soon as we can," Tom said as he started the engine.

The rest of the afternoon dragged by. Grace felt the warm presence of Hiro's poem against her side all day. She saved the precious gift until after she'd gone to bed. Carefully, she opened the paper, taking note of how it was folded so she could redo it exactly. She leaned close to the light next to her bed and read:

"Winter's first sunset
a shooting star sears the sky
with brilliant light—you"

She read it again and again, savoring each word, and picturing the star as it split the peaceful, winter sky. Then she refolded the paper, turned off the light, and fell gently into contentment.

CHAPTER 11

Grace began making inquiries about jobs, at the same time she was studying for her finals. She met with resistance at many companies, and found that Hiro's prediction about her ancestry limiting where she would be hired was accurate.

She was studying at the kitchen table on a Friday afternoon when she heard, "Yoo-hoo."

"Dorothy, come in. What are you up to?"

"I was on my way home, and thought I'd come by for a visit. What are you doing?"

"Studying. What else?"

"Have you had any luck finding a job?"

"No. I can always work in the hotel or the fields, but I wanted to find a spot in an office, or maybe even a hospital."

"Well, Mother found out that they're looking for someone to work in the Red Cross office. Since you're in Junior Red Cross and you've worked in your dad's office, she thought you'd be a perfect fit. So, she talked to the director, Anne Palmer, and Miss Palmer said for you to call for an interview."

"Really? Oh my gosh, Dorothy. That's fantastic. Do you have the phone number?"

"Yes," she said, handing Grace a paper with a number on it. She smiled. "I think you've got a good chance at this."

"Will you thank your mother for me, please? I can't tell you how much I appreciate it."

"Of course." She glanced at her watch. "I've got to run. I'm in charge of dinner tonight, so I have to get to the market."

Grace walked her out to her car.

"You'll let us know about your interview, right?" Dorothy asked.

"Absolutely."

Grace called and made an appointment to see Miss Palmer on the Monday after her finals, and then wished she'd scheduled it sooner. With the interview looming, she found it hard to concentrate on her studies.

The next afternoon, her uncle came over, shaking a copy of the Star Bulletin. "Did you see this?" he asked them. Grace and her parents had just finished eating lunch.

Ken looked up. "I did."

"'Shall the Japanese be allowed to dominate Hawaii?' What kind of idiocy is this?"

An article in the paper that morning, reported that John Balch, former President of the Hawaii Telephone Company, had published a booklet about what he considered the "enormous threat" of the Japanese in Hawaii. Ken had read the article aloud to Grace and Lilly that morning. "This is really going to set Yoshi off," he'd predicted.

"This man is a racist, pure and simple," Yoshi went on. "He wants to evacuate one hundred thousand of us to the middle of the mainland. One hundred thousand! He's mad."

"It's not going to happen," Ken said.

"How do you know? You've already been arrested. We've already been put in a concentration camp. What makes you so sure it won't happen?"

"For one thing, it's impractical. Think of what it would cost: ships to the coast; feeding that many people for a ten day crossing; trains to the Midwest; building camps to hold everyone. It would cost a fortune."

Yoshi glowered at him. "They're capable of anything; money won't stop them. They're completely unconcerned about our welfare and will go to any length to control us or get rid of us. This idiot, Balch, says we're a menace to Hawaii. He makes it sound like we're an infestation of rats."

"I agree," Lilly said. Ken shot her a warning look. "I do. I think it agitates the people unnecessarily. The Filipinos here already hate the Japanese, because Japan invaded the Philippines; the Koreans hate the Japanese, because Japan subjugated Korea; and the *haoles* hate the Japanese, because they outnumber the whites and the white elite are afraid they'll be voted out of power. This sort of propaganda only makes Hawaii more volatile."

Grace was surprised to hear her mother support Yoshi. She was generally neutral when it came to politics.

"You're reacting exactly the way Balch wants," Ken said. "If you try to mount opposition to this, it will only confirm his assertion that we're dangerous and that something should be done about us."

"If we don't fight back, it looks like we're cowards."

"Better to lose face, than to lose our freedom," Ken said.

Yoshi's face contorted with anger. "You wouldn't say that if you'd been born here."

Ken stood and walked over to his brother-in-law. "Don't you *ever* question my loyalty to the United States. Ever!" He turned, walked out, and slammed the front door behind him.

Yoshi was utterly silent; then he stood and bowed gravely to Lilly. "I'm sorry," he said formally, and quickly left.

"Politics," Lilly said.

Grace finished her last final on January 22nd. The entire family celebrated with a dinner at the Fujitas'. Somehow, Tom and Hiro both managed to get time off. Grace hadn't seen Hiro since New Year's and was overjoyed that he was with them.

"Won't you miss graduating with your class?" he asked her.

"No, because I will graduate with them. The counselor said that I could participate in June. All the mid-year graduates will be able to, if they want."

"I'd like to be there," he told her.

"I'd like that, too."

Dorothy and her parents came by for dessert and gave Grace a delicate gold locket.

"It's beautiful," she said. "Could you help me?" she asked Dorothy.

"First, you have to put someone's picture in it."

Everyone looked at Hiro, who blushed fiercely.

"Here, let me help," Chiyo said. She aimed her camera at Hiro, and snapped the shutter.

"Maybe she doesn't want a picture of me."

"You'll do until someone else comes along," Tom told him.

"Your interview at the Red Cross is on Monday, isn't it?" Dorothy's mother asked Grace.

"Yes. And I'm really nervous."

"You don't need to be. Miss Palmer is very kind, and she's looking forward to meeting you. You'll do fine, I'm sure."

On Monday afternoon, Grace was at the Red Cross office attired in her best dress and shoes. She filled out the application the receptionist gave her, and then waited. A tall, attractive blonde woman came out of the private office and smiled at her. "Grace? I'm Anne Palmer. Please, come in."

The interview was over in an hour, and as Grace was leaving, Miss Palmer said, "Tomorrow at eight, then?"

"Yes, thank you," Grace told her. "I'll be here."

That night at dinner, she told her parents, "I'm sure I was hired because of Mrs. Reback's recommendation."

"Her recommendation wouldn't have meant much if you hadn't demonstrated your abilities by making the Honor Roll and working at the store," Ken assured her. "It wasn't Sarah who got the job, it was you."

"Still," Lilly said, "we owe her a great deal."

"We certainly do," Ken agreed. "However, Grace got this job on her own merits, and I want her to feel confident about that."

She started work the next morning. She was Miss Palmer's personal assistant and quickly learned that Anne did the work of three other people. Grace would somehow have to keep up. By the end of the day, she was exhausted.

"You'll get used to it," the receptionist, Irene, said when she was ready to leave. "Miss Palmer expects a lot of everyone, but no more than she does of herself. Believe me, you'll learn a lot working for her, and I wager you'll never be sorry you took this job."

Grace spent the first few days trying to understand the structure of the huge organization and the responsibilities of their office. Irene had worked there for several years, and Grace soon realized that if she had any questions, Irene would most likely have the answer. Anne was the head of all the divisions of the Red Cross in the Hawaiian Islands, which included not only local disaster services, but safety training, first aid stations, service to the military, international services, motor corps, and the canteen corps. There were more than twenty thousand volunteers who manned all the various sections, and more were joining every day.

By the end of the week, the wave of information was crashing down on Grace. "How am I ever going to keep up with all this?" she asked Irene. "How does Miss Palmer do it?"

"She inspires people. She leads by example, and she cares passionately about what she does. You will, too. That's how you'll do it."

The headlines in the paper the next morning said, "Army to accept AJAs for Combat Service." AJA, the acronym for Americans of Japanese Ancestry, was often used in periodicals in the islands. Ken sat at the kitchen table reading the article aloud to Lilly and Grace.

"It says they're looking for fifteen hundred volunteers from Hawaii."

"I doubt if that will be difficult," Lilly said. "All of Tom's friends are ready to go."

"Will Tom volunteer?" Grace asked, even though she already knew the answer.

"Yes," her father said. "He's been ready since the attack on Pearl Harbor."

Grace looked at her mother. Lilly turned away. And then it dawned on Grace: Tom and Richie could be fighting *against* each other.

"I need to get to work," Lilly said. "I'll see you later."

Ken followed her outside, and Grace could only imagine what he might be saying to comfort her mother. War was tearing her family to shreds.

She wasn't surprised to find Tom and Hiro at the house when she got home that evening.

"You heard, right?" Tom asked her.

"Are you going to join up?"

"Of course. It's what we've been waiting for."

She looked at Hiro, who nodded. For some reason, he didn't seem as enthusiastic as Tom.

"We're drafting a letter to headquarters to disband the VVV, so we can volunteer for service. It's strange. It coincides with our one year anniversary. We've already planned a big dinner dance to celebrate," Tom told her.

"We're still going to have the dance," Hiro said. "I was hoping that you'd go with me."

"I'd love to."

"It's on February 1st, and it's semi-formal," Tom said. "Do you think Vivian would like to go, too?"

"Of course she would."

The girls had only three days to shop for new dresses. Since Grace hadn't bought anything new for Christmas or the prom, Lilly said she could splurge on something special. On Friday, she and Vivian went to Liberty House, Grace's favorite department store on Fort Street.

"I'm so excited," Vivian said. "Do you think your brother likes me, or does he ask me out because it's convenient?"

"Hiro told me a while back that he likes you a lot."

"Honest?"

"That's what he said. Tom hasn't said anything, but that doesn't surprise me."

Grace watched as Vivian's face changed from sunny to somber. "I'm going to miss him."

"Me, too," Grace said. "Both of them."

Grace found a tea length, blue, dotted Swiss dress, with cap sleeves, a scoop neckline, and a full skirt. She chose white, open-toed high heels, and a small white hand bag to match. Vivian fell in love with a sleeveless, white sheath of delicate silk, and finally decided on sling back heels to match.

"I can wear this again if I go to the Senior Prom," Vivian said. "Except, of course, if Tom isn't here, I won't want to go."

"And if he is, you'll complain that he's already seen it."

"What if he's gone?"

"Let's not think about that," Grace said. "Let's think about the dance."

The evening of the party, Grace was sailing higher than a runaway kite. Hiro brought her a beautiful, white orchid corsage, even more lovely than the purple one Tom gave to Vivian. Ken let them take the car, which was now outfitted with dim-out lights, required by the military for night driving. The authorities had extended curfew until 10:00 pm, so the dance was scheduled to end at 9:30.

They sat at a table for eight in the large dining room of the South Seas restaurant in Waikiki. Grace recognized many of the VVVs, having met them during the past two years. A small band played background music while they ate dinner.

"Aren't you hungry?" Hiro asked her. "You've hardly eaten a thing."

She looked down at her plate. "I guess not," she said. "There's just so much going on. You know, this is my first *real* dance."

"I told you I'd take you out for real. If I have my way, this won't be the last time." He reached over, took her hand, and squeezed it. "Do you remember what you promised me?"

When he touched her, Grace's stomach tumbled. "That I'll write you."

"You won't forget."

"No, I won't forget."

"You two sound pretty serious over there," Tom said.

"We're talking about how nice Vivian looks tonight," Hiro said, before Grace could speak.

"Thank you," Vivian said. "So do you."

Tom put his arm around Vivian and drew her close to him. "Actually, you look beautiful."

"Like I told you," Hiro whispered to Grace, "he likes her."

The band played "String of Pearls," and "In the Mood," and other hits by Glenn Miller, Benny Goodman, and Cole Porter. Hiro wasn't much of a dancer, but Grace didn't mind in the least. She loved being in his arms and felt like a princess in the blue ball gown. She breathed in the aroma of his aftershave. "I like your cologne. What is it?"

"Old Spice. It's my dad's."

"He must smell good, too."

When the band took a break, everyone deserted the building. The patio, lit with hanging lanterns, offered couples a chance to be out in the fresh air. The area had been tented, so that the lights could not be seen from the street. It was warm, although cooler than it had been inside, even with so many people crowding around.

"Do you like your new job?" Hiro asked.

"Yes. There's so much to learn. I'm afraid that I'll never get it all down. I like Anne, and I don't want to disappoint her, so I'm trying to figure it out as fast as I can. I can't get over how much she accomplishes."

"I'm glad you found such a great place. Don't worry about disappointing your boss. I know you'll do a good job."

He smiled at her, and Grace flushed. She didn't want to smile, sure that if she did, joy would spread across her entire face, making her look like a clown. She didn't want to broadcast her feelings for him to the entire assembly.

He put his arm around her. "It'll be a while before we leave for the states. I'd like to see you again before then." After a moment, he added, "Actually, I'd like to see you a lot before then."

"I'd like that, too."

"Will your parents mind?"

"I don't think so."

"I'm going to miss you," he said. He started to say something else and then stopped himself. Instead, he led her back onto the dance floor. He held her tighter then, and perhaps just a little closer. She felt happiness bubble up inside.

She wished the night would never end.

On the way home, Hiro pulled her close, pressed his face against her hair and breathed in the scent of her perfume. "I'll never forget this evening," he whispered. "When I'm gone, this is what I'll think of every night."

"You'll be careful, won't you?"

"Absolutely. I'll be coming back before you know it."

"I'll be waiting."

Grace's family had supper at her cousins' house the next night. They'd barely begun to eat when Yoshi said, "So, Tom. What do you think of the Army's latest trick?"

"Trick?"

"Yes. They're running short of man power, so now all of a sudden the Japanese are fit for combat duty."

Tom frowned at him. "How is that a trick?"

"Logic would have AJAs used as translators here in the Pacific, instead of training *haoles* for the job. The Army needs to know what Japan is planning, and we could help with that. Instead, they propose to send all AJAs directly into combat."

"I'm proud to serve in any way I'm needed."

"Even after what they've done to us?"

"To us?"

"Yes. They arrested your father and kept him in jail for no good reason; they put my family in a concentration camp; they kicked you out of the HTG; they've frozen our bank accounts, closed our businesses, and refused to let us vote."

"I can't do anything about the past. What happened to the AJAs was horrible, but this is the chance I've been waiting for to serve my country."

"And fight against Richie?"

"Yoshi!" Makiko said.

Grace thought Tom might explode, or get up and leave. He didn't.

Tom sat quietly, looking at his uncle. After a long silence, he said, "I can only hope that by fighting, I'll help end the war. And, when it's over, Richie can come home. Do you think I'd be helping Richie by sitting it out?"

Grace saw the pride on her parents' faces.

Yoshi looked down momentarily, and then back at his nephew. "A succinct argument, worthy of a courtroom. Well said." He lifted his sake cup. "Here's to both of you coming home safely."

The military asked for fifteen hundred volunteers; ten thousand AJAs stepped forward to answer the call.

"I'm not surprised," Tom said. "We've been waiting for them to realize we're Americans, too."

"When will you have to leave?" Grace asked him.

"It won't be for a month or so. They have a lot of paperwork to deal with, plus physicals and all that. Meanwhile, I'll pretend like I'm on R&R. Too bad you're working."

"I'm not working at night. And the days are getting longer. The sad thing is, Vivian won't have a lot of spare time with all of her homework."

"She told me she's decided to flunk out this semester," he said, and laughed heartily at his own joke.

The four spent every minute they could manage together during the next six weeks. Tom and Hiro passed their physicals, along with most of the other VVV. They were fitted with uniforms and formed up into the 442nd Combat Unit. At the end of March, fifteen thousand islanders gathered on the grounds of the Iolani Palace to watch the induction, and bid farewell to the twenty-six hundred men leaving for boot camp. The men of the VVV were given the front rows of the assembly in recognition of their service over the previous year.

The night before Tom and Hiro were to leave, Grace and Hiro went out alone. He took her to dinner at the Royal Hawaiian Hotel. She hadn't been back since the summer.

"I hope it doesn't feel like you're going to work," he said as they were ushered into the dining room.

"Not at all. I was always in the kitchen, never out here. I always wondered what it was like on this side of the swinging doors."

After dinner, as they walked along the beach, Hiro held her hand. The sun was sitting on the distant horizon like a huge orange on a giant blue platter. They took their shoes off, and walked at the feathery edge of the waves.

"I'm going to miss you," Hiro said. "It doesn't seem fair that just when we've started dating, I have to leave."

She squeezed his hand. She was much more comfortable with him since the night of the dinner-dance. "Promise me that you'll be careful, Hiro. Promise me that you and Tom will watch out for each other."

"I promise. And, you won't forget to write me, will you." It wasn't a question.

"I won't forget."

She wondered what it would be like to leave everyone, and everything, behind. It was like what happened to Chiyo, though in her case, the family was together. This was very different. Hiro was going to war.

141

He stopped suddenly, and put his arms around her waist. He leaned over until there were only inches between their faces. He kissed her gently. He held her and looked at her with dark, intense eyes. "Every night, I'll dream of coming home to you."

She wound her arms around his neck, and kissed him. She had no idea there was such passion inside her, a fierce, yearning passion, which ignored the barriers of her upbringing.

He kissed her again and again, pulling her down to the sand.

She pushed him away gently. "I can't go home looking a mess."

"Tom might kill me before we ever leave."

She stood, brushing the sand from her skirt. "Let's go find some shave ice." When he took her hand again she said, "Come home safely, Hiro. I'll be waiting for you."

The next day Grace's entire family joined thousands of others who lined the street leading to Honolulu Harbor.

"Those duffle bags look like they weigh more than the men," Lilly said, as they watched the volunteers march by carrying their brand new, army issue packs, the size of small children.

"There they are," Grace cried, spying her brother and Hiro.

They all waved.

"Write me," Hiro yelled to her.

"I will," she cried.

I will.

CHAPTER 12

Japanese-owned businesses were slowly reopening, but since Ken could not get goods for Kawakami's, their store remained closed. Island services like house cleaning, gardening, and harvesting had suffered badly due to attitudes toward Japanese workers. Citizens gradually rehired their former employees, which eased the economic hardships in Asian households.

President Roosevelt announced that civil courts and local authorities in Hawaii could resume most of the functions that had been taken over by the military. Yoshi reopened his law practice and was busy helping island Japanese with legal problems both related, and unrelated, to the war.

The political situation was often the main topic of conversation when the Kawakamis and the Fujitas were together. Makiko had made chicken *karaage*, Japanese fried chicken, and invited Grace's family to join them one night for dinner. A much welcomed breeze blew through the open doors and windows as they sat down to the table.

"With Habeas Corpus still suspended," Yoshi said to Ken, "I can't do much for anyone who's been arrested. It's been more than a year since the military took over. I don't understand what the problem is. It's such a clear violation of our civil rights."

Chiyo rolled her eyes at Grace, who grinned back. Lilly gave them a warning glance. Yoshi and Ken missed it all.

"What sort of cases are you handling?" Ken asked.

"Mainly wills and estates. Even though people don't have much, they want to make sure if something happens, their children are protected." He paused a moment, then added, "And name changes."

"Name changes?" Grace repeated.

"Yes. Hundreds of Japanese are filing petitions to Anglicize their last names."

"Like someone couldn't tell they're Japanese by looking at them." Chiyo said.

"It just shows how desperate people are," Yoshi told her.

"Why do they need a will all of a sudden?" Chiyo asked. "Do they think there will be an invasion?" Her voice had an edge Grace hadn't heard in weeks.

Yoshi patted his daughter's hand. "I doubt that there will be an invasion. But coming so close to disaster makes people see things differently. This is when they take care of business they've let slide in the past."

Chiyo didn't say anything else. Grace wasn't sure her cousin was entirely convinced. Perhaps the experience at Manzanar left her wary of simple reassurances.

The girls cleaned up the kitchen after dinner and then decided to go for an ice cream cone.

"Don't forget your masks," Yoshi said as they were about to leave.

"Oh, Daddy," Chiyo said.

His stern look stopped any further protest.

"I hate this thing," Chiyo complained, as the three cousins walked away from the house. They'd all buckled on the ugly belts which held the cumbersome masks. "If they don't think the Japanese are coming back, why do we have to drag these around all over the place?"

"Think of it as an insurance policy," Naomi said. "Most of the time you don't need it. When you do, it's a life saver."

Grace frowned at her. "If your life insurance policy pays off, you're dead."

"Okay, bad analogy. You get what I mean."

"We do," Grace said. "How are your classes going? You haven't said much about them."

"Fine, I guess. It's weird, though. So many of the guys have enlisted, that the classes are small, and the students are mostly women."

"Are you going to take any classes this summer?"

"Yes. I have a whole semester to make up for, because of that godforsaken Manzanar."

"Have you heard from anyone at the camp?"

"No."

Grace waited for an explanation. There was none. "I thought you had some good friends there."

"I did."

"Haven't you written to them?"

"No."

Grace glanced at Chiyo who looked away.

"Why not?"

Naomi looked away, too, as if going to some invisible place with her sister. "How can I? What would I say? I'm free, they're not. I can't imagine telling them about being here and going to school, or the movies, or shopping, or the beach. It would only make them feel worse."

"It seems to me that losing a friendship would be worse. If you left and never thought about them again, that would be worse."

"I *do* think about them, all the time."

"But Naomi, *they* don't know that. The government has turned its back on them. It must seem like you have, too."

"I never thought of it that way."

Grace looked at Chiyo. "What about you? Have you written to any of your friends there?"

Chiyo shook her head. "I feel guilty just thinking about them. I wouldn't know what to say."

"It doesn't matter what you say. Tell them about the gas masks or blackout or curfew; tell them about meat from the butcher, or classes being mostly girls; tell them about barbed wire on the beaches, or working in the pineapple fields. Or, tell them funny things like people painting their windows black. Most of all, tell them you haven't forgotten them."

"Have you been thinking about this?" Naomi asked.

"No. Those are things I hear Anne say at work. It's what she tells people when they write to friends overseas. Some people have trouble writing their own family members."

"We should send care packages," Chiyo said to Naomi. "Remember how hard it was to get anything really nice there."

"You have to keep in mind that new Defense Rule," Grace said.

"What now?" Chiyo asked.

"It says you can't send certain things like food, candy, chewing gum or tobacco, not that you'd send tobacco. Oh, and shoes. You can't send shoes."

"Why?"

"Because all those things have to be shipped here, and they're in such short supply. The military doesn't want us to turn around and send them somewhere else."

"Everything here is shipped here," Naomi said.

Chiyo laughed. "Except pineapples."

"Just think of all the things you would have liked when you were at Manzanar and send some of those," Grace said. "I know your friends will be grateful you thought of them."

Dorothy's parents invited the Kawakamis and Fujitas for dinner on Easter Sunday. The morning before, Sarah dropped by Grace's house to say they had to cancel.

"Dorothy is sick; really sick, I'm afraid." she said. "I'd hate for anyone else to catch it. So, I think we'd better call off dinner tomorrow."

"What's she got?" Lilly asked.

Grace and her mother had been dying eggs, and were finishing cleaning up.

"Fever, sore throat, stiff neck," Sarah said.

"Is she nauseated?"

"Yes. And she has a wretched headache."

Lilly sat down at the kitchen table and indicated for Sarah join her. "I don't want to alarm you, Sarah, but this could be quite serious. There's been an outbreak of polio in Hawaii. In fact, we have three patients at Queens right now. If I were you, I'd call your doctor right away."

"Oh, Lord, Lilly, do you think she could have polio?"

"It's possible. The best thing is to call the doctor as soon as you get home."

Sarah stood to leave.

"Let me know if I can do anything," Lilly said. "Anything at all."

As soon as Sarah left, Grace asked, "Do you really think Dorothy has polio?" She could hardly get the words out of her mouth.

"I can't say that for sure, but it sounds like it. She has all the symptoms."

"I thought only little kids got polio."

"Children get it more frequently than adults. President Roosevelt had polio as an adult. It's rarely mentioned, but it does happen."

"Are you taking care of those kids you told Sarah about?"

"As a matter of fact, I am."

"Are they going to be okay?"

"I don't know, Grace. One of them is pretty sick. She's so tiny. She's only four. Her name is Shirley. I can't tell you…" She stopped without finishing the sentence.

Lilly went into Tom's room, where she had stored things in the nearly unused closet. She came back carrying a small, yellow paperback book.

"What's that?"

"It's about the treatment of polio. It was written by a nurse in Australia called Sister Kenny. Her clinic was nowhere near any major hospitals, so when these cases started showing up, she developed a treatment on her own. It was very successful, but it hasn't been welcomed in the mainstream medical community."

"How did you hear about her?"

"One of the nurses I've been working with, Wilma Martin, came up from Brisbane before the war started. She told me she'd trained with Sister Kenny. We talked a lot about it at the time, and she gave me this book last year. According to this book, the results of Sister Kenny's methods are much better than the orthodox treatment we're using here."

"Then why doesn't everybody use it?"

"Trying to get a doctor to accept a new treatment, particularly one that was developed by a nurse, is nearly impossible. Doctors don't like being told anything by a woman, much less a foreigner. They've been challenging her and fighting her ever since they heard about the treatment."

"Do you think she's right?"

"Wilma certainly does. She saw it work on dozens of cases."

"What are you going to do?"

"I'm going to read this book again and be ready to tell the Rebacks about it if Dorothy does have polio."

The judge came by late that afternoon. "I'm on my way home to get a few things for Sarah," he told them. "She wanted me to thank you for your advice, Lilly. If it hadn't been for you, it might have been days before Dorothy was diagnosed."

"I'm so sorry, James. Sarah must be frightened to death," Ken said.

"It's torture watching Dorothy suffer. She's in excruciating pain."

Lilly picked the book up off the end table. "This is about a new, completely unorthodox treatment of polio. One of our nurses at Queen's gave it to me. She knows Sister Kenny personally and trained under her in Australia."

The judge looked confused. "You mean there's a treatment other than those horrid casts and braces?"

"Yes. In fact, it's exactly the opposite. Sister Kenny applies hot, wet compresses to her patients' limbs, every two hours during the acute stage, which can last several days. Then, she uses gentle stretching and strengthening exercises. It contradicts everything we've been doing in the states for years. The book details all the differences. If I were you, I'd want to consider it."

He took it from her. "Do you think it works?"

"Wilma says she saw it work time and time again. I'm sure she'd be happy to talk to you about it, if you'd like."

The judge flipped through the book, pausing to consider some of the photographs. "Is anyone at Queen's using this method?"

Lilly shook her head. "No. But Wilma can teach me, and I'd be willing to help her treat Dorothy. You and Sarah will need to decide if that's what you want."

The judge sat down heavily. "How can we possibly know which way is the best?"

"Take the book. Read it. I'll call Wilma and see if she can come to the hospital later." She patted his arm. "We'll do everything we can to help, James."

He stood. "I appreciate this, Lilly. How can I thank you?"

She put her hand gently on his arm. "There's no need."

After the judge left, Lilly called Wilma, who agreed to meet them at the hospital that evening. "Even if the Rebacks decide against it," Lilly told Wilma, "I'd like you to explain it to them."

When Lilly got off the phone, Grace said, "Mom, could you catch polio from Dorothy?"

"It's possible, but extremely unlikely. Wilma and I have been treating polio patients for weeks. We use every precaution to make sure we don't catch infectious diseases." She put her arm around Grace. "You mustn't worry. I've treated patients with very serious illnesses in the past, and I've never, ever been infected."

"Will the doctors at Queen's allow you to use such a radical treatment?" Ken asked.

"They won't like it," she admitted. "The Rebacks may have a fight on their hands. I'm sure they'd have to sign a form releasing the hospital of any liability for the outcome. Ultimately, I think they'll agree to let us use Sister Kenny's method if that's what her parents want."

"Tell us more about the treatment," Ken said.

"According to Sister Kenny, the critical period is the acute state, right at the beginning, when the muscles are spasming. She discovered that the hot compresses relaxed the muscles, and prevented them from contracting. When that stage passed, she used specific exercises to strengthen and 'reeducate' the affected muscles, so they worked properly again."

"Every two hours?"

"Yes. Twenty-four hours a day, for as long as the acute stage lasts."

"How will you do that, Mom?"

"Wilma will teach me, and we'll trade off. We could train Sarah too, and any other nurses who want to help."

"What's the other treatment?" Grace asked.

"Patients are put in casts or braces, and not allowed to move at all, sometimes for as long as six months."

"Lord," Ken said. "What a horrid prospect."

"Kenny insists that keeping the body immobilized robs a patient of proper care, and all but guarantees that the muscles will atrophy and become useless."

"Which is why children end up crippled," Ken said.

"Yes. That's what she believes."

"And you do, too?" Grace asked.

"Yes."

They ate dinner with the Fujitas, and then Lilly changed into her uniform.

"If we start treatment tonight, there's no telling when I'll be home again."

"Aunt Lilly," Naomi said, as she was ready to leave, "if you need someone else to help out, I could learn how to do the treatments, too. I'd be honored to help."

"That's very gracious of you, Naomi, not to mention brave. You know, you'd be taking a risk."

"I'm serious. We owe their family so much. If you're treating Dorothy every two hours, you'll be exhausted in no time."

"Yes, you're right. It'll be challenging. We just might accept your offer. That is, if the Rebacks want to take a chance on this protocol."

"Tell Dorothy hello for all of us," Makiko said.

"I certainly will."

Late that night, Grace sat with her father, listening to "Ed Sullivan," a musical variety show on the radio. Lilly had not returned from the hospital, nor had she called.

"Do you think the Rebacks decided to try the Kenny treatment?" Grace asked.

"It seems like it, since your mom hasn't come home. I think I would, that is, if you had polio. It sounds much more hopeful than the other treatment."

"Could Dorothy die?"

"If the virus attacked her lungs I suppose she could. I don't think dying is the biggest threat. I've heard of far more people being paralyzed than dying," Ken said.

"I wonder if Dorothy is scared."

"How could she *not* be? Having no control over your body must be terrifying."

Grace remembered waking up screaming, weeks before, with a charley horse in her leg. How it would feel if your whole body were doing that?

Lilly didn't come home that night, but she was there by dinner time on Easter Sunday.

"How is Dorothy?" Grace asked.

Lilly poured herself a cup of tea. She shook her head sadly. "She's in a lot of pain. The hot compresses are the only thing that seem to help her." She took a sip of tea, and laid her head against the back of the chair. "Wilma and Sarah are with her right now. They insisted that I come home for a break."

"How did the doctors handle the Rebacks' decision about the treatment?" Ken asked.

"A couple of them were in agreement; a couple were indifferent; and one said he'd make sure this would end my nursing career."

"You're kidding," Ken said.

She shook her head. "He was furious. At least he kept it between us, and not in front of Dorothy's parents."

"If you get the results you expect, he won't have a leg to stand on," Ken said.

Lilly laughed. "Was that intentional?"

He grinned at her.

"I'm going to lie down for a bit. Wilma has been up two days straight, and she plans to stay there through the night. She wants me to get some sleep, and come in fresh in the morning."

"What about Sarah?"

"She won't leave. They made a bed up for her in a small office down the hall from Dorothy's room, but I don't think she's even been in there."

Just then, Makiko knocked at the door. "Dinner's ready," she said.

While the two families had supper, Lilly gave the Fujitas the news about Dorothy.

"Would you like me to go with you tomorrow?" Naomi asked.

"Wilma has a friend who is already familiar with the treatment. She's coming in tomorrow. But the Rebacks wanted me to tell you how much it meant to them that you offered.

They were extremely touched. At the same time, they didn't want you to be exposed unnecessarily."

The next morning, Grace woke up early. She heard her parents talking in the kitchen. She put on a robe and joined them. Her mother was already dressed in her uniform.

"It's only six," Grace said. "Are you going to the hospital already?"

"Yes. Wilma needs to have break."

"Can I drive you?" Grace asked.

"If you'd like."

Grace hurried into her room and changed. Her father fixed them eggs and toast, and they ate quickly. The morning sun was creeping up the back side of the Pali, turning the overcast sky golden pink. Grace drove down the street toward the hospital, wondering how long it would be before she could see her friend again.

"Will you tell Dorothy hello for me?"

"Of course."

The streets were deserted, and they arrived at the hospital in less than five minutes. Her mother could easily have walked, but Grace felt that by driving her, she was at least helping a little bit.

She pulled into the parking lot and up to the entrance. When she stopped, she noticed a couple sitting on a bench near the door. The woman was sobbing.

"Oh, God," Lilly said.

"What?"

"Those are Shirley's parents."

Lilly got out of the car, and rushed over to them.

The woman looked up at her. "She's gone," she cried. "Shirley's gone."

Lilly sat down next to her, and wrapped her arms around the woman. "I'm so sorry."

And then, the man began to cry…loud, heart-tearing sobs, that pierced the morning like an air raid siren.

"She was so little. Why?" he wailed.

The woman looked at Lilly. "I wish we'd listened to Miss Wilma. Maybe Shirley would have gotten better if we'd tried…"

"You mustn't blame yourself," Lilly soothed. "We can't know for sure if that would have made any difference at all."

"We should have tried," she said, and began weeping again.

Grace felt their inexorable pain crawling toward the car. She leaned over, closed the door, and started for home. She didn't think she could stand to hear any more.

Every day that next week, Grace waited to hear the news, hoping that Sister Kenny's treatment would bring Dorothy through the crisis. Her mother came home only twice. Both times she was exhausted, and went straight to bed. Both times, Grace drove her to the hospital the next day. Neither time did Grace ask about Shirley.

By the end of the second week, the acute state had passed, and Dorothy was out of isolation. Lilly came home on Friday night, more tired than Grace had ever seen her.

"Now the real work starts," Lilly said. "We have to exercise her limbs to reeducate the muscles, and reestablish normal nerve conduction. Dorothy has to work even harder: she has to learn to walk again."

"Will that be every two hours as well?" Ken asked.

"No. At this point, her body needs lots of rest. We'll only work with her twice a day."

"When can she come home?" Grace asked.

"I'm afraid it will be a while," Lilly said. "The good news is, it looks like she'll be coming home without any braces."

Grace got her first letter from Tom the next week. She'd written to both him and Hiro, and told them about Dorothy.

Tom's letter was brief.

Please tell Dorothy that I'm thinking of her. I'm sure Mom will do everything humanly possible to help her get well. I can't tell you where we are, however, you can be sure it's nothing like home. The food is pretty good, the days are long, and I sleep like a log, whatever that means. I miss you all. Please tell Vivian that I'll write to her soon. Hiro says hello.

She didn't hear from Hiro for another three days. She saved the letter that finally came, until after she'd climbed into bed that night. She opened it slowly and carefully.

Dear Grace,
I know Tom has already written you, and told you as much as he could about this place. It took us forever to get here and to be honest, it's not so great. I miss home. I don't know what the future holds, so all I can write about is the past. I think about all the things we did together and how fun it was, being with you. I know this isn't much of a letter. I'll do better next time. Meanwhile, this is why I took so long to answer:

Winds whisper softly
dark breezes sway giant trees
the moon lights my way

I miss you like crazy. Hiro

She read the letter again and again, until her eyes would not stay open. Then, she tucked it under her pillow, turned out the light, and imagined herself in her blue dress, dancing with Hiro under a starry sky. They danced and danced, right into her dreams.

When Dorothy was released from the hospital during the second week of June, Sarah invited the families over to visit.

"She gets tired easily, but she's missed you all so much. She says she can't wait any longer to see you," Sarah told Lilly.

"We won't stay," Lilly assured her. "We certainly don't want her to relapse."

Dorothy was lying on a lounge chair on the patio when they arrived. Grace was shocked to see how thin and pale she looked. She started to stand up, but Lilly stopped her.

"Stay right where you are," she said.

"I'm perfectly fine," Dorothy insisted. "I want everyone to see that."

"We know," Lilly said. "But let's not overdo it."

"You sound exactly like a nurse I know," Dorothy said.

Grace, Naomi, and Chiyo, pulled their chairs over next to Dorothy's, and were soon listening to the details of Dorothy's ordeal from her side of the bed.

"She sounds strong," Makiko said to Sarah. "You must be so relieved."

"Relieved and grateful. I'm convinced she would never have recovered like this, if it hadn't been for Lilly."

"It wasn't me, it was Sister Kenny."

"It was your willingness to take a chance, knowing that at least some of the doctors you work with would disapprove. You put your career on the line. We can never thank you enough."

The judge came out from the kitchen, carrying a tray of glasses filled with champagne. "We have yet another reason to celebrate. This is getting to be a habit."

"Or a tradition," Ken said.

When they each had a glass, the judge raised his. "Here's to friends and family, both near and far. Here's to our health, our happiness, and our safety." He nodded to Ken and Lilly, and then took a first sip.

CHAPTER 13

"That dress is perfect for you," Vivian said, as Grace turned one way and then the other, carefully assessing the simple purple and white cotton dress in the mirror.

"Do you think it looks too childish?" Grace asked. She knew her father would approve, but Grace wanted to look older, not younger.

"Not at all."

"I still like the blue one better," Chiyo said.

The three girls were shopping together for graduation dresses, but had spent the better part of the day looking for an outfit for Vivian. Grace now felt rushed to make a decision.

"Come on, Grace," Vivian said. "At this rate we'll be late for the movie." Vivian gave her a little shove toward the dressing room.

"Well, if you hadn't taken so long," Grace said, turning yet one more time.

Vivian looked at her with impatience.

"Oh, all right," Grace said.

After she changed, she paid for the dress, and the three girls walked to the theater, where a long line had already formed for *Springtime in the Rockies*.

"I can't believe graduation is only a week away," Chiyo said. "It doesn't seem possible."

"Have you decided what you're going to do yet?" Vivian asked her.

Chiyo shook her head. "My mom wants me to go to university. My dad thinks I should get a job. If I could find a really good job like Grace has, it would be easy." She stopped, and then added in a whisper, "I don't want to work in the fields or clean houses."

"I don't blame you," Vivian said. She looked at Grace. "Does Mrs. Reback have any more friends?"

"I think you should go to school," Grace said.

"You sound just like my mother."

"Say," Vivian said, "I've been meaning to ask you, have you seen Dorothy?"

"No. Since Paul is home, I haven't wanted to bother her. They have little enough time together; I'm sure he's been worried sick about her, and needs to see that she's really okay."

"I'll bet she's glad to have him home. Not only so she can see him, but because it means he isn't in the line of fire."

They reached the front of the line, paid the girl in the ticket booth, and squeezed their way into the lobby.

Grace pointed toward the candy counter. "I'm going to get some Milk Duds."

Chiyo shook her head. "Popcorn for me."

"Bit-O-Honey," Vivian said.

As they walked down the row to their seats, Grace felt her sandals sticking to the dirty floor. She didn't want to put the new dress down, so she balanced the bag in her lap as she and Chiyo shared their candy and popcorn. Juggling everything, she nearly dropped the candy box on the floor. "We didn't plan this very well."

The lights dimmed and a newsreel came on, showing scenes of fighting in the Pacific. Grace closed her eyes, but couldn't block out the sound of heavy artillery guns, which shook the theater as if the explosions were right outside. "Our brave men and women continue to push back the sneaky Japs," the narrator said. "A hospital ship loaded with U.S. Army nurses arrives in Port Moresby, to care for troops wounded in the furious fight for New Guinea. Across the Coral Sea we find a group of Japanese soldiers captured off Guadalcanal. These POWs are lucky: their American counterparts are not treated as well by the enemy."

Her eyes flew open, and she scanned the face of each prisoner, hoping that Richie might be one of them. If he were, she'd know he was out of the fighting. However, nearly every POW walked with his head bowed in shame, so she couldn't make out any of their features.

"Are you looking for Richie?" Chiyo whispered.

"Yes."

"Me, too."

Grace wasn't sure whether she was disappointed or relieved that he wasn't there.

They walked home by way of the high school, where the army had parked a tank on the front lawn, near one of the many trenches that volunteers had dug after the bombing.

"Do you suppose they'll move that thing on graduation day?" Vivian asked. "It won't add much to our class picture."

"I think we should all sit on it, just so we don't forget what was happening this year," Chiyo said.

"I'd prefer to forget," Grace said.

When they reached Vivian's house, she invited them in.

"No, thanks," Grace said. "I need to write some letters."

"I told Mom I'd help her with the laundry," Chiyo said.

Grace and Chiyo met Naomi walking out of their house with a very handsome young man. She smiled at the girls. "Frank, this is my sister, Chiyo, and my cousin, Grace." She looked at the girls as though she'd just won a huge prize. "This is Lieutenant Frank Berry."

"Hello ladies," he said.

"We're going to dinner and then dancing," Naomi said. "I'll see you later."

They watched as the couple walked down the street.

"How does she manage it?" Chiyo asked. "She always finds the best looking guys."

"Will your parents mind that he's Caucasian?"

"I think they've given up worrying about what she does. Between UCLA, Manzanar, UH, and the war, she's beyond their control. Since she's decided to do law, Daddy thinks she can do no wrong. Naomi is Naomi."

"Just like Richie is Richie," Grace said. "Speaking of brothers, I need to go write some letters. I'll see you later."

To reduce the weight of overseas mail, the military encouraged citizens to use wafer-thin stationery, known as onion skin. Grace loved the way it crackled when she filled the page with writing. She used a lined sheet underneath the transparent paper, so that the lines of writing were straight and evenly spaced. The ink pen scratched on the page as she wrote.

She addressed the first letter to Tom. He was much easier to write to, and she let herself tell him all about her days without any restraint. She chattered on about work, family, and her friends. She told him about her new dress for graduation, about Paul being home on leave and ended as she usually did, with a funny story.

Then she made herself a cup of tea, and considered her letter to Hiro. She knew Tom would share her letter with him, and she didn't want to repeat the same news. She didn't imagine that Hiro ever shared her letters with Tom, however, since theirs were growing more personal and private.

You've been gone for seventy-six days. For some reason, that sounds better than saying you've been gone for eleven weeks. Actually, I don't think it's the time that makes it seem so hard—I think it's the distance. You're half a world away. Since I've never been there, I can't even imagine what it's like.

Chiyo and Vivian and I went to the movies today. A newsreel played first, like always these days. The report was about nurses arriving in the war zone, ready to take care of soldiers who had been wounded at the front. There were U.S. Army nurses as well as Australian sisters. I wonder if any of them knew Sister Kenny.

Dorothy is doing so well. Paul is home on leave, and they went to windward side for a little R&R together. Her doctor says she should be able to return to most of her normal activities by the end of the month. What an amazing recovery. Mom is now her hero.

I've been looking for a book of *haiku* to send you. So many people burned anything Japanese after the war started, that it hasn't been easy. Anne told me about a small, used book store in Kailua, but I haven't been able to get over there. Maybe I can make it after graduation.

Be sure to let me know if you want me to send you anything else. I'm reading *Crazy Horse,* and will send it to you as soon as I'm done. I am only buying paperback books, since they weigh so much less than the hardbound. The army likes it better that way, even if the Post Office might prefer the latter.

Graduation is next week. I don't feel very excited about it, I'm afraid. School seems like a lifetime ago. I don't see many of my friends any more...everyone is so busy. Vivian is working at the drug store full time this summer, and part time again in the fall, when she starts at UH. I wish I could go too, but working is the best thing right now. I'll wait and go with you when you come home.

This letter is so long, it seems like I've written a book. I hope you are still seeing me in my blue dress every night. I'm here, you know, just waiting for you to come back.

The orange moon rides
heavily on the mountain
while cloud curtains wait

I'm waiting too.

Grace

She was confident that nothing in the letter would interest the censors. They looked for hidden secrets, not veiled emotions.

The families ate dinner together the next evening.

"Did you have fun last night?" Grace asked Naomi.

"It was the cat's meow," she said. Naomi had begun using the slang that peppered Tom's speech. "We went to the most posh restaurant, and then to a club for dancing and drinks."

"Drinks?" her mother repeated.

"Soft drinks, Mom."

"What does the Lieutenant do?" Yoshi asked.

"I'm not sure. He's so evasive when I ask him about it, that I think maybe he's in some branch of intelligence." She smiled in the special way they all knew so well. "I'll get it out of him eventually."

"That could get him in trouble," Makiko warned.

"I didn't say I was going to tell anyone else. It's more of a personal challenge."

Grace noticed Ken shake his head. Naomi always pushed the limits.

"Are we going out to dinner after graduation?" Chiyo asked.

"Absolutely," her father said. "Your Uncle Ken and I have already made the arrangements."

"Arrangements where?" Grace asked.

"You'll have to wait and see," he said mysteriously.

The strains of the recessional had barely faded when the two families left the school and headed away from the downtown area. Chiyo and Grace went with Naomi in Yoshi's car while the others went with Ken.

"Do you know where we're going?" Chiyo asked her sister.

"Didn't I tell you that secrets are safe with me?" Naomi said. "You'll see soon enough."

They hadn't driven for long, when Grace realized they were going to the Rebacks' house. When they arrived, they found it decorated with crepe paper, balloons, and Christmas tree lights.

Dorothy and Paul came out of the front door, when the cars pulled into the driveway.

"Surprise!" Dorothy cried.

She had regained her rosy cheeks and bouncy demeanor, with only a slight hint of weakness from her recent ordeal.

"Paul!" Ken said. He shook hands with the young man. "It's so good to see you. I don't think you've met the rest of our family." He made the introductions, just as James and Sarah appeared.

"Come in, come in," the judge told them. "Congratulations," he said, putting one arm around Grace and the other around Chiyo. He led them out to the patio, which was festooned with strings of confetti and even more balloons. Tiki torches lined the edge of the patio, and burned brilliantly in the early evening dusk.

"Who wants champagne?" he asked.

"How do you manage to get champagne?" Yoshi asked. "Not that I'm complaining, but alcohol is so hard to come by these days."

James chuckled. "It's no mystery. We have a long history in our family of celebrating with champagne. I had two cases when the war started. It'll have to end pretty soon, though, or we'll be drinking pineapple juice."

He opened two bottles with a flourish, and poured a glass for each of them. He raised his, and beamed at Grace and Chiyo. "Here's to yet another success for our family."

Grace warmed with pleasure, when she heard him refer to her family as his. What an extraordinary man he was.

Sarah had prepared a buffet with island favorites, including pulled pork, rice balls, fresh pineapple, and shaved coconut. "I was lucky at the butcher this week," she told Lilly. "We could have ended up with beef liver or veal kidneys."

"Uck," Grace said.

"You don't like veal kidneys?" James teased.

She looked at him with suspicion. "Do you?"

He laughed. "No."

A soft breeze blew up from the valley, bringing the scent of frangipani and plumeria.

The only thing that would make it more perfect, were if the boys were there: all three of them.

"How was your graduation?" Anne asked Grace on Monday morning. Irene was running errands, and the two women were alone in the office.

"It was beautiful. In fact, it was perfect. Except my brothers weren't there."

"Brothers? You have more than one?"

Too late, Grace remembered that she hadn't told Anne about Richie. She was uncomfortable that her brother was probably fighting for the enemy, and she rarely mentioned him. Her inadvertent use of the plural word gave her no option.

"Yes. My brother Richie," she began and then stopped. "My grandfather died in June of 1941. My grandmother insisted on taking his ashes back to Japan, and my father didn't want her to go alone. Richie said he'd go with her. And then, after they got there, all shipping was halted."

"They're stuck there," Anne finished for her.

"Yes."

Anne was quiet only a moment, before letting out a sharp gasp. "He was drafted?"

"That's what my father thinks. He was born here, but he has dual citizenship. Daddy says the government there would consider him a Japanese citizen, and he'd be conscripted by the army."

"Does he speak Japanese?"

"Yes. We all went to Saturday school."

Anne shook her head. "This must be awful for your parents. Not knowing is always the worst."

"I think you're right. They don't talk much about him." Grace fought the tears.

"I wish there were something I could do. Since he's a Japanese citizen, the military wouldn't give us any information about him. We'll have to wait and hope for the best. When the time comes, I'll do all I can to help get him back home."

Grace felt comforted when Anne said "we'll" have to wait. She liked knowing that Anne was in their corner.

Naomi was taking summer classes, yet still found time to volunteer at the USO, the United Service Organization. The USO had locations throughout the United States and its territories, and provided servicemen a little piece of home wherever they were stationed. Soldiers could go there to read, play cards, write letters, or simply talk. Local women volunteered to provide sympathetic company and dance partners for the frequently held parties.

"Come with me tonight," Naomi said to Grace and Chiyo the following Saturday. "It's fun. You meet some really nice guys, and some of them are pretty good dancers."

It didn't sound fun to Grace. It sounded strange and awkward. "I don't know."

"Don't try to use the 'I have to study' excuse," Naomi told her.

"What about the 'I don't have anything to wear' excuse?"

"That one won't work either. You can borrow something of mine."

"What about the 'I don't know how to dance' excuse?"

Naomi couldn't suppress a laugh. "So, you'll go?"

Grace said, "I suppose so."

Chiyo looked trapped. "I guess."

"Great! We'll leave at about six. Frank said he could borrow a car."

"Frank?" Grace and Chiyo said at the same time.

"Of course."

"I thought you were supposed to be there for guys who don't have any girlfriends."

"That's why we're taking you." She grinned with such pleasure, that Grace had to laugh.

Frank and Naomi chattered happily all the way to the dance, while Grace and Chiyo sat nervously in the back seat.

"What if nobody asks me to dance?" Chiyo said softly. "It will be so embarrassing."

She had no cause for concern. All three girls were asked to dance again and again. Grace was afraid that soldiers might be reluctant to dance with Japanese girls, but there were Chinese girls and Korean girls there as well. Nobody seemed to make any distinctions. One handsome sailor asked Chiyo to dance nearly every other number.

"His name is Oliver," she told Grace. "He's from Boston. He told me his family has a fishing boat."

Just as she finished speaking, Oliver joined them. "May I have this dance?" he asked, his smile revealing beautiful white teeth.

Chiyo stood. "Oliver, this is my cousin, Grace."

"Hi, Grace. Nice to meet you."

"You, too."

A soldier approached Grace. "How about a dance, sugar?"

His familiarity made her uncomfortable, although she wasn't exactly sure why. He was very good looking; tall, blond and blue-eyed. She wanted to say no, but she didn't want to make a scene.

She stood. "Okay," she said, with little enthusiasm.

He led her out to the floor, and put his arms around her. When he drew her close, the foul stench of liquor on his breath nearly made her gag.

"You're a cute little thing. You live around here?"

She started to say she lived in California, and then thought better of it. "Not far."

"How's about us spending a little private time together?" he whispered.

Grace knew they didn't serve alcohol at the USO clubs, and this was the reason why.

"My father won't allow me to date," she said simply.

"He wouldn't have to know," he said, pulling her closer.

She pushed at him, and tried to turn away.

"Hey!" he said, grabbing her arm.

Frank was beside her before she took another step. "Is there a problem here?"

"What's it to you?" the soldier said belligerently.

"This is my sister," he told the man. He took Grace's hand. "We were on our way to get a Coke."

The soldier took a menacing step toward Frank.

Frank looked at him sternly. "Not a good idea, buddy."

A second soldier came up and put his arm around the first one's shoulder. "Time to go, Walter." He looked at Grace. "He just lost his best friend. He's actually a nice guy." He turned Walter around, and maneuvered him out of the club.

"Sorry, Grace. Are you okay?"

Naomi came over with two sodas. "What's wrong?"

"Nothing," Grace said quickly.

"Your cousin just got a dose of drunk soldier."

"They aren't supposed to let them in here if they're drunk."

"Sometimes they bring in their own booze in a flask."

"Let's forget it," Grace said. She was ready to leave.

"How about a dance?" Frank asked her.

Grace shook her head no.

"I think that's a good idea," Naomi said. "It's sort of like getting back on a horse after you get bucked off."

Grace frowned at her, but Frank took her hand, and led her out to the dance floor.

"Naomi tells me you work for Anne Palmer."

"Yes. Do you know her?"

"Sure do. She's a great gal. Hard worker, too. I'll bet she keeps you hopping."

"That's an understatement."

"Our section works pretty closely with the Red Cross," he said, without further explanation.

He was a good dancer, and Grace was glad he'd asked her. She didn't want the incident with the soldier to be the final memory of the evening.

"You two looked pretty good dancing out there," Naomi said. "I think I'd better keep my eye on you, Grace," she added as she put her arm through Frank's.

"Her heart is at boot camp in the states," Chiyo said.

Grace felt her face flush, but didn't bother to argue. Her heart *was* at boot camp in the states.

A letter from Tom the following week gave the family their first look at life for the AJAs. Lilly read it out loud.

"We went out on bivouac last week, and they gave us a good workout. My pack weighs as much as a large sack of rice, and it got heavier every day. I'm sure some of the weight was because of the dirt I was carrying around. The dust stuck to us like one finger *poi*. The food was pretty good, considering the circumstances. On the other hand, the only time we stopped was when we ate, so that might have made it taste better.

I met up with Margie's brother, Sam, who says he knows Grace. He is a funny guy. He's always cracking jokes. The boys from the states call us islanders 'buddhaboys'; we call them 'kanakaheads', since we're sure if a cocoanut fell on one of those empty noggins, that's what we'd hear. We don't get along all that well. I guess we'll have to learn.

I know that you can't send us any food, but I sure wish you could. I miss Mom's cooking. All the guys here miss the food from home. We talk about food a lot. Everybody has their favorite meal. When we have free time, that's what we usually gab about. Tonight we're going to see a movie. I think it's a comedy, but I'm not sure. Thanks for the letters and the books. Hope everybody is okay. Say hi to Viv, and Dorothy, and everybody else. Tom."

"That's the longest letter he's written yet," Grace said. "He must *really* be missing home."

"Most of those boys have never been away from home before, much less away from Hawaii. I bet they're all homesick. Poor kids," Lilly said.

"Do you suppose there's a USO near his camp?" Grace asked.

"Probably. It's possible they might not welcome Japanese boys, even if they are soldiers," Ken said.

"It's not fair. Our boys are risking their lives just like any of the others. Why do they keep discriminating against us?" Grace asked.

"If we knew the answer to that question, we could stop a lot of misery in this world," her father said. "I'm afraid there's something in human nature that looks for a scapegoat."

Life improved for all islanders in mid-July when blackout regulations were relaxed to allow lights on until ten PM, with the exception of rooms facing the sea. At last, residents could once again let the refreshing ocean breezes blow through their homes, to cool them down at night.

"It's such a pleasure to have fresh air at night," Lilly said. "It seems almost like normal again." She opened the window in Grace's bedroom with a smile on her face that Grace hadn't seen in a very long time.

What was normal? How could anything be normal again until Tom and Richie came home?

Naomi came over the next Saturday, smiling happily, and waving a letter at Grace. "You were right. This is from my friend, Eleanor. You know, at Manzanar. She says she thought I'd forgotten all about her."

"Oh, Naomi, that's great. How is she doing there?"

"I asked her to tell me that when I wrote. She says that the heat is unbearable. They can't stand to be in the houses during the day, but there's no place out of the sun to go where they can cool off. Her father put up a blanket on poles to make some shade outside their front door, but even with that, everyone is miserable. She says that meals in the mess hall are like eating in hell."

"The whole thing sounds like hell. I don't think I could stand it," Grace said.

"She doesn't have much choice, does she?"

"I suppose not." She thought a moment. "Didn't you say that the older kids could leave to go to college?"

"Yes, provided they can get accepted somewhere, find a place to live, and pay for their tuition. Most people there have no money. Remember, not many of them are working, and bank accounts were frozen. Coming up with tuition plus room and board is pretty hard."

"Then how do any of them leave?" Grace asked.

"There are a few organizations that are arranging for families to house students in towns near campuses where Japanese students are welcome. Mostly, it's done through churches like the Friends. Older kids can actually leave during harvest time, too, if they're willing to do backbreaking work in the fields. Some of the boys went to Idaho to pick potatoes, and the people there weren't very nice to them. It wasn't like that everywhere…some people were very kind."

"They're mean because we're Japanese," Grace said.

"And Japan started the war."

"The government started it, we didn't." She felt like the argument went around in circles, and yet the Japanese always ended up getting the blame.

"What they've done to us is so wrong, not only morally, but constitutionally, as well. I *know* there will be lawsuits about it in the future."

"Is that what Uncle Yoshi thinks?"

"Absolutely." She looked at her watch. "Oh, it's late. I've got to run. Frank is picking me up in half an hour."

"Where are you going?"

"We're off to dinner first, and then we're going dancing at the officers' club."

"Have fun."

"We always do."

Anne was depending on Grace more and more as the summer progressed, and their office became increasingly busy. New volunteers joined the Red Cross every week, and had to be processed and attached to an appropriate unit. Goods, such as rolled bandages, knitted caps and socks, as well as donated books and food items, needed to be packaged and shipped.

"Did the new uniforms for the Gray Ladies arrive?" Anne asked Grace. She was referring to the women who worked in hospitals, directly with soldiers who were sick or wounded.

"Yes," Grace told her. "I called Mrs. Wallace, and she'll be by to pick them up this afternoon."

"Perfect. Thank you." She picked up a file of papers from her desk. "I've got a meeting at the hospital at Pearl. There's something going on there that will involve us. I'll talk to you about it later."

When Anne returned she called Grace into her office. She handed her a post card which had "United States Armed Forces" printed at the top. Below, there were blanks to fill in, next to the headings: Name, Rank, and Serial Number. Then, a check off list, which included options like:

1) I am a POW
2) I am fine
3) I was injured and am hospitalized
4) I am ill and being cared for

"Up until now, the military hasn't had many Japanese POWs. Their military code requires that they fight to the death.

Now that the tide has turned, some Japanese soldiers have seen the futility of their efforts, and have begun surrendering. Others have been captured. The Geneva Convention states that all POWs must be allowed to notify their family of their situation. Notifications are handled through the International Red Cross."

"Can they write on these?" Grace asked, handing her back the card. "Like a personal message of some sort?"

"Yes, although all the cards pass by censors, like everything else. They'll come through our office before going on to IRC. There are already a few POWs here. Eventually, the majority will be sent to the states; those who are badly injured or seriously ill will stay here until they can travel. Of course, they'll all be questioned carefully. Anyway, our job is to make sure the cards are complete, and filed with IRC in a timely manner."

"It must be pretty scary to be a POW in a foreign hospital, to be injured and not speak your enemy's language." Grace shook her head. "How does the military ever get men to go into battle? I would *not* be able to do it."

"It may seem impossible, but look at all the young men who do. War makes heroes of people in many ways. None of us know what we're capable of until we're put to the test. And that means in both positive and negative ways."

Grace didn't have a brave bone in her body, of that she was quite sure.

In August, the military closed Waikiki beach to all servicemen, in an attempt to curb the spread of Dengue Fever.

"What's Dengue Fever?" Grace asked her mother, after seeing the headlines in the Sunday paper.

"It's pronounced den-gee. It's a mosquito borne illness that's extremely painful. It starts with a high fever, and progresses with headache, nausea, and terrible joint and muscle pain."

"Do you have any patients who've got it?"

"Yes. Several."

Grace felt a familiar anxiety. "Could you catch it?"

"Only from a mosquito. Your Dad is probably more likely to get it than I am, since he's outside all the time."

"Mosquitoes don't like me," Ken said. "I have sour blood."

"It's not funny, Daddy."

"When you can't do anything about a situation, the only thing left is to laugh about it. You mustn't worry, Grace. It won't help."

"How can I not worry? First, Grandpa died, then we were bombed, and you were arrested, Richie left, Tom left, and then Dorothy got polio."

"Your mother and I are here, and we're okay," her father said. "Believe me, worrying won't help anything, and it won't change anything. All we can do is the best we can do. After that, *shikata ga nai.*"

CHAPTER 14

"I miss *Obon*," Chiyo said. She and Grace and Naomi were walking downtown and had just passed their local temple, now long closed and deserted. Thick vines grew over the walls, and made the grounds look like a setting for a horror movie.

"I wonder if Grandma is well enough to celebrate in Japan," Grace said.

"I wonder if she's even alive," Naomi said.

Both the other girls gasped.

"Well, we haven't heard anything, and it's been over two years. Who knows what's happened to her."

"How could we have heard anything, with the shipping embargo and the war?" Grace asked her. Sometimes, Naomi made Grace want to scream.

"Doesn't the Red Cross do that sort of thing? Notify people when family members die?"

Chiyo stopped. "I do not want to talk about this."

Naomi and Grace stopped, too.

"You started it." Naomi said.

"I only said I missed *Obon*. I miss speaking Japanese. I miss *being* Japanese. I haven't had a *kimono* on in two years. It's practically against the law to be me!"

Grace was surprised by her cousin's vehemence. "Gosh, Chiyo, you could certainly put on your *kimono* if you want to."

"And go where, exactly?"

"I don't know. Where would you like to go?"

"To *Obon*," Chiyo said. "Or to Japanese school."

"Ugh," Naomi said. "Only you."

"I have an idea," Grace said. "Let's ask your mom to make *Obon* for us. The food I mean. We'll invite the Rebacks. We can all wear *yukata* and tell them about our *bon* traditions."

"Do you think they'd like that?" Chiyo asked.

"I do."

"You know, I bet they would," Naomi said.

Makiko was resistant that evening when they suggested the idea during supper, but Ken thought it was terrific. "We've gone there to eat so many times and never once asked them here. I think it's about time we returned their kindness."

"What about the *yukata*? Do you think that's too...Japanese?" Chiyo asked.

"No more Japanese than *Obon*," he said. "We're carrying on a tradition, not supporting the Japanese war effort. Why shouldn't we be able to celebrate our customs in our own home?"

"Could I invite Anne?" Grace asked.

"Why not?" Lilly said.

"Could I invite Frank?" Naomi asked.

Yoshi looked dubious. "That's a little different. He's part of the military. I think that might be a bad idea."

"He grew up in Japan, Daddy. He practically *is* Japanese. I think he'd like it."

Yoshi looked at Ken, who nodded. "Okay," he said, although he didn't sound enthusiastic.

"Why don't you call Sarah, and see if they have plans next Sunday," Ken said to Lilly. Then, he looked at his sister. "Will that give you enough time?"

Makiko paused. "Without Mom, it'll be hard."

"Chiyo and I can help," Naomi said.

"And I can help," Lilly said.

"Me, too," Grace added.

"Okay. We'll do the best we can," Makiko said.

A quick phone call and explanation to Sarah confirmed that the Rebacks were available, and happy to join them.

"I'll see Frank tomorrow," Naomi said, "and find out if he can come."

"I'm pretty sure Anne's schedule is clear that day," Grace said. She looked at Chiyo. "You've started quite a ball rolling. I hope your *yukata* still fits."

"I'm in trouble if I can't wear a *yukata*."

Both Anne and Frank accepted their invitations eagerly.

"I hope I can get all the meat we need," Makiko said to Lilly the next evening.

"We'll send Naomi," Lilly laughed.

"We can all go to a different market and see what we end up with," Naomi said. "We're bound to get what we need that way."

And, they did. By the morning of their *Obon* party, Makiko and the other women had nearly completed the preparations. They were all in the Fujitas' kitchen finishing up the last of the food.

"This looks exactly like Grandma's," Chiyo exclaimed. She surveyed the table laden with all her favorite dishes and smiled. "Thank you, Mom."

"You're welcome," Makiko said.

"She's right, Makiko. Your mother would be proud of you if she could see all this."

"I hope everyone enjoys it," Makiko said.

"They'll love it," Yoshi said. He'd just come in the back door.

Of course, he was right.

"Mrs. Fujita," Frank said, picking up a stick of *kushi katsu*, "I haven't tasted anything this good since I was a kid in Japan."

Makiko smiled and bowed slightly to him. "Thank you."

Sarah also picked one up. "Now what is this again?"

"It's breaded, deep fried pork," Lilly told her.

"I like this one," Dorothy said. "*Gyoza*, right?"

"Yes. That one is mushroom," Chiyo told her. "The others are chicken."

Dorothy took a bite. "Mushroom dumplings. Yum."

The women had also prepared shrimp sushi, Spam *musubi*, and *kuri-manju*, a bean paste based dessert.

"Makiko, could I get the recipe for the *gyoza*?" Anne asked.

Makiko laughed. "There are no recipes. I mean none that are written down. Everyone who makes it does it a little differently. It's handed down through the family. We do it by touch, and smell, taste, look, and feel. You could come over and watch me one day, if you'd like. It would be easy enough to teach you."

"Could I come, too?" Dorothy asked. "I love these."

"Yes, of course." Makiko looked pleased. "I'd be happy to teach you both."

Dorothy sat down next to Grace. "I love your *kimono*."

"Actually it isn't a *kimono*, it's a *yukata*. It's a little different. First, it's made of cotton. It's lighter and more informal. It's mainly for summer."

"I never realized," Dorothy said.

"What about the *bon* dance. Tell us about that," the judge said.

Chiyo explained about the *Obon* Festival, and detailed the dance at the end. "The very last thing is the lantern lighting. That's when the family members put lanterns in the stream, to guide the spirits of the dead back to their resting place."

"It's a beautiful ceremony," Grace told him. "It's my favorite part."

"Well, I for one, will be attending *Obon* with you, as soon as this miserable war is over," the judge said.

And Grace felt quite sure he would.

That night she wrote Tom, and told him about their *Obon* party.

It wasn't like the real *Obon,* but the food was delicious, Anne and Frank were impressed, and Chiyo was so happy to wear her *yukata.* The war has affected her differently than it has me, more deeply, more personally, if that's possible. She says she misses being Japanese. Isn't that something?

She wrote Hiro last and closed, as they both did now, with a *haiku.*

Tiny golden lights
lanterns floating in a stream
bid Grandpa farewell

When Grace arrived at work the next morning, Anne was already in the office, poring over a report at her desk.

"What's up today?" Grace asked her.

"I'm supposed to get this finished and returned to IRC right away. I'm not sure what's going on, but something big is in the works."

"What do you want me to do?"

"Go through those request forms, and see what needs to be ordered. I think there are some calls you could return. You know the drill."

"This is no drill," Grace quipped. "This is the real McCoy."

Anne laughed at her.

Anne became increasingly distracted and secretive over the next several days. Grace knew that something very unusual was coming and grew more and more curious about what it might be. Still, Anne was closed-lipped, and Grace knew better than to ask.

Frank and Naomi asked Grace and Chiyo to go with them to the USO dance the Saturday after school started again.

"I have to study," Chiyo complained.

"So do I," Naomi said. "But we need to do our part for the war effort."

"Right," Grace laughed. "I'm *sure* that's the reason you're going."

"Come on. It'll be fun."

Chiyo looked at Grace for help. "You know how much work I have to do. Tell her."

"Let's go for a couple of hours. And then I'll come home with you when you're ready."

They were dressed and ready to go when Frank arrived at five o'clock that afternoon. "I don't know which one of you is the prettiest," he said as he walked them out to the car.

"I am, of course," Naomi said, and Grace couldn't help but agree.

"Look who's here, Chiyo," Naomi said when they entered the club.

They'd barely taken three steps into the room before Oliver was at Chiyo's side.

"Would you like to dance?" he asked her.

Grace took the small purse her cousin was carrying. "I don't think he can wait."

Oliver looked embarrassed. "I've been here every week hoping you'd come back."

Chiyo smiled sweetly at him.

Naomi gave them a little shove toward the dance floor. "Go on. She doesn't have much time. She has to study."

Oliver frowned, and Chiyo shook her head. "Let's dance."

Naomi laughed. "You're going to have to find someone else to go home early with you," she said to Grace. "I think Chiyo's here for the duration."

They found a table where Grace and Naomi sat while Frank went to get them drinks.

"Chiyo definitely has an admirer," Naomi said.

Grace looked out at the couple on the floor. "He's cute, and he's every bit as shy as she is."

Later, Grace was alone at the table, when she felt a tap on her shoulder. She looked up and recognized Walter.

Oh, no, she thought.

He looked down at the floor and then back at her. "I understand I owe you an apology."

It was painful to see how uncomfortable he was.

"I don't remember much about that night, but my buddy assured me I was way out of line."

"Would you like to sit down?"

He looked unsure. "Is it okay?"

"Yes."

He sat, keeping a careful distance from her.

"Your friend said that you'd been having a tough time."

It seemed to take all his energy to speak. "I'd just lost my best friend. Saw him get his..." he stopped. "He died right in front of me," he said finally.

"I'm so sorry. I can't imagine how awful that must have been."

"It's still hard to believe."

They sat for a time in silence.

"Is everything okay here?" Frank asked. He stood next to Grace, his voice edged with concern.

"Yes. We're fine," Grace assured him.

The young man stood and extended his hand. "Walter Avery. I'm here to apologize to the young lady. Do I owe you one, too?"

"No. I think I understand. You take care of yourself, soldier."

"Thank you, sir."

He sat back down again. "I shouldn't have been drinking that night. I probably shouldn't have been out at all. I just didn't know what else to do." He paused. "I still don't."

Grace had no idea what to say. Sadness oozed from him and hung in the air like cold, grey fog.

"What was his name?"

"Joey. Joseph Graham. Sometimes I called him Cracker." He chuckled. "He hated that."

"Did you know him for long?"

"Since the first grade. We went all through school together and joined up together."

"Best friends."

"It was my idea. Joining up." The long pause was excruciating. "So, I guess it's my fault he's dead."

"Do you think Joey would say that?"

He looked at her with surprise. "I don't know. I never thought about it."

She was quiet for a moment and then said, "If you didn't pull the trigger yourself, then I don't think you killed him." She looked at him with gentle eyes. "It isn't your fault. It's the war. The war killed him, not you."

He looked at her intently, as if she'd reached inside him and touched his heart. "I wonder what he *would* say."

"He'd probably tell you he didn't blame you. He'd probably tell you to live the best life you can and ask you never to forget him."

"Are you some sort of doctor or nurse?"

"No. I work for the Red Cross."

"I'll bet you're good at your job. You're easy to talk to."

"That's nice to hear. Thank you."

"I don't want to take up your whole evening. I only wanted to tell you how sorry I am that I was rude to you."

"It's okay, Walter. I understand now."

"Thank you," he said, standing.

She looked up into his sad eyes. "Come again when you feel more like dancing. Take care of yourself. That's what Joey would want."

His eyes filmed over with tears. He nodded, turned quickly, and was soon lost in the crowd.

She danced with several boys that night, but Walter's sad eyes never left her. How many others had watched their best friends die? How many more casualties would she meet, whose invisible wounds were still bleeding?

On Monday, Anne had one visitor after another in her office, each one closing the door when they went in. Three naval officers were with her for over an hour and gave Grace a cautionary glance when they left.

"What the heck is going on?" Irene asked her late in the afternoon.

"I have absolutely no idea."

Grace was nearly bursting with curiosity by the end of the day. She was ready to leave without a hint about what was afoot, when Anne came out to her desk. Irene had left early to take a deposit to the bank.

"Can I have a word before you leave?"

Anne led her back into the inner office and closed the door again. She sat down behind her desk and leaned forward. "What I'm about to tell you is to be held in strictest confidence." She stopped, and Grace realized she expected a reply.

"I understand. Of course, I won't say anything to anyone."

"Good. I'm sure you suspected that all this commotion has been leading up to something important, and it is. Tomorrow we're going to have a special visitor, and it is imperative that the highest possible security is maintained." She stopped again, and Grace waited.

"Mrs. Roosevelt has been on a trip here in the Pacific, and tomorrow, she will be landing in Hawaii."

Grace's mouth dropped open anticipating what was coming next.

"She's going to be visiting the boys in the hospitals, as well as some of the local military installations. And," she paused dramatically, "she wants to meet some of our Red Cross volunteers."

"Us?" Grace squeaked.

"Yes. Although we're not volunteers, we'll definitely be with them."

"Which volunteers? There are so many. How can you deicide?"

"You certainly grasped that challenge quickly. Of course, it wasn't easy. In the end, I chose a cross section: a division of the Gray Ladies, the Motor Corps, and then one volunteer from each of the other thirteen divisions."

"Have you told them yet?"

"They think they're attending a luncheon."

"When will you tell them?"

"After they've all arrived and before she gets there."

"Will we be able to talk to her?"

"No. You'll be introduced, but that will be all."

"That will be enough."

"Here's what I need: I need you to be right beside me, but invisible. If something needs to happen quickly, I don't want to have to look for you, I want you there. However, I don't want anyone to notice you. Can you do that?"

"I can."

Anne stood. "I knew I could depend on you."

"Should I wear anything special?"

"Just your uniform. You'll feel right at home. Mrs. Roosevelt has worn a Red Cross uniform every day during this entire trip."

"Really?"

"Yes. She thinks it makes it more comfortable for the boys to talk to her."

"Can I tell my family about it afterwards?"

"Of course. I imagine they'll be delighted."

"That's for sure."

Grace walked home feeling so excited that she could have jumped out of her skin. She wondered how she would get through the next twenty-four hours without anyone noticing. She was glad no one was at the house when she got there. She spent half an hour making sure her uniform was clean, ironed, and in good repair.

She couldn't help looking at the clock all evening, wishing the time would pass more quickly.

"Are you nervous about something?" Lilly asked. "You seem jumpy."

"No, I'm just tired. I didn't sleep well last night. Maybe I'll go to bed and read for a while."

Her father frowned. "It's seven-thirty."

"It's a good book."

However, she wasn't the least tired, and the time passed almost as slowly as the horrible night when the war started.

She walked to work early. Anne was already there. "Are you excited?" Grace asked.

"Yes. A little nervous, too. I want everything to go smoothly."

"I'm sure it will. Everything you plan goes well."

The meeting was scheduled to take place at the Naval Hospital at Aiea, where many of the Gray Ladies worked. All of the volunteers, dressed in pristine uniforms, were assembled when Grace and Anne arrived. Grace recognized a few of the women; Anne knew them all. Anne greeted them warmly, asking a few of them questions about family members, especially when they were in the service. Then she asked them all to be seated.

"I have a special assignment for you today, and that is to represent all of our Red Cross volunteers by meeting the President's wife, Mrs. Eleanor Roosevelt."

At first there was a stunned silence, and then everyone began talking. Anne allowed the initial shock to die down before speaking again. "I had a very difficult time deciding whom to select for this honor. Hundreds of our volunteers have distinguished themselves with their dedicated service. However, I decided that since Mrs. Roosevelt has been visiting the wounded, the obvious division would be the Gray Ladies, who treat them, and the Motor Pool, who transport them."

Grace watched, as one woman after another smiled at her own good fortune.

"In addition," Anne continued, "there is one representative here from each of the other divisions. There won't be time for you to be introduced individually. I'm sure you will understand and respect both her position and her privacy by not speaking unless she addresses you personally."

She looked over at the Military Liaison who stood by the door. "Is there anything else?" she asked him.

"The photographs."

"Ah, yes. The First Lady's photographer will be taking pictures during the meeting, and afterward he will probably want a group shot. If so, you'll be instructed how and where to assemble. Please do so as quickly and quietly as possible. I've been told that we will be given copies of the pictures, so you will each have one of your own. Now, are there any questions?"

After a pause one of the Gray Ladies raised her hand.

"Yes, Clara."

"It's not a question. I just wanted to thank you for giving each of us this extraordinary opportunity."

The others began clapping.

"You all deserve it," Anne said. "I'm proud of you."

Half an hour passed and then another. Anne talked quietly to various women in the group, while Grace stood near the Liaison, who didn't say a word. Finally, there were three sharp raps on the door.

"Miss Palmer?" he said, with a nod toward the door.

Anne looked up, and immediately started toward the front of the room. "This is it, ladies."

The door opened, and two naval officers entered, followed by the First Lady and several other people, including a photographer.

"Mrs. Roosevelt," the first officer said, "this is Anne Palmer, the Director of the American Red Cross here in Hawaii."

Anne nodded her head. "It's a pleasure to meet you, Mrs. Roosevelt."

"I'm delighted. As you can see," she said, glancing down at the uniform she wore, "I'm a big fan of the Red Cross."

"Thank you," Anne said. "It's an honor to have your support."

Grace stood to the side, and slightly behind Anne, as she'd been instructed. She could barely see the President's wife, but could hear her clearly. Suddenly, Mrs. Roosevelt stepped past Anne and looked directly at Grace. "And who is this young lady?"

Anne turned. "This is my assistant, Grace Kawakami."

"Hello, Grace," she said, and then in a conspiratorial voice asked, "have you been waiting long?"

Grace glanced at Anne, who nodded her head.

"No, Ma'am, not too long for you."

Mrs. Roosevelt patted her on her arm.

"Now, who are the others here?" she asked Anne.

"These are the Gray Ladies, the Motor Corps, and one representative from each of the Red Cross divisions on Oahu."

The First Lady smiled broadly at the assembly.

"Did you want to say a few words?" the officer in charge asked.

"Yes, if I could."

The others stepped aside, and Mrs. Roosevelt spoke in a clear, high voice. "The American Red Cross is one of our country's greatest assets. The President and I are grateful to all of you, and your fellow volunteers, for the countless hours you have given in service. Every day I hear from our boys in uniform, about how they or their families have been helped by the ARC. You may not always be acknowledged, but trust me when I say, you are always appreciated."

There was no mistaking the sincerity in her voice, and Grace smiled as proudly as the other women in the room.

"How many of you have family members in the armed forces?" Mrs. Roosevelt asked.

Most of the women raised a hand.

Mrs. Roosevelt said, "So do I. We all want our boys and girls to get the best care, and that's exactly what the Red Cross provides. Please accept thanks from my husband, myself, and the entire country." She looked over at the ranking officer. "What's next, pictures?"

"If you'd like."

"Let's go outside," she suggested.

The photographer had already chosen a spot outside on the patio, and he gave the group directions on how to line up.

"Let's have Miss Palmer here by me," Mrs. Roosevelt said. She looked around. "And Grace as well."

Grace shot an uncertain glance at Anne, who indicated for her to join them. So, she walked to the front of the group, and stood next to the First Lady. She wasn't sure if she was nervous or anxious or excited or scared, but she was sure that the sound of her pounding of her heart could rival native drums on a distant island.

When the photographer was finished, Mrs. Roosevelt said, "Good. That's done. Now we can talk."

She spoke to each woman, including Grace, asking about their family, and thanking them again for their service. When she'd finished, she looked at the officer. "What's next?"

"The hospital," he said.

She turned back to the group. "Goodbye, ladies. If you're ever in Washington, DC, please come by for a visit."

They were all laughing as she walked off with her entourage.

Grace was beside herself that night at dinner, as she told the family about her day.

"She actually said your name?" Chiyo asked.

"Yes. She won't remember it tomorrow, but she said it today."

"You're practically a celebrity," Naomi said. "Wait until they hear about this at the USO."

"Please don't make a big deal out of it," Grace said. "It's not like I accomplished anything."

"You met the President's wife," Naomi argued. "I think that's a pretty big deal."

"She's right," Yoshi said. "Not many people have that opportunity." Her uncle reached over and ruffled her hair. "Enjoy the notoriety. It won't last long."

She wrote to Hiro that night.

You'll never guess what happened today: I met Mrs. Eleanor Roosevelt. I had my picture taken standing right next to her! She was visiting the troops in the Pacific and made a stop here. She looks like somebody's grandmother, and she has a way of speaking that makes you want to listen to every word. I bet those boys she visited in the hospital felt better as soon as she spoke to them. The photographer said we'd all get a copy of the picture. I'll show it to you when you get home.

Then she closed with:

Brittle orange leaves
cling desperately to branches
autumn but not here

The next day the newspapers were full of stories about the First Lady's visit to Oahu. Grace pored over the articles, and studied all the photos of the President's wife. She felt an appreciation for the First Lady that she'd never had before. She carefully cut out each story to show Hiro and her brothers when they returned home.

"You really met Mrs. Roosevelt?" Frank said when she saw him again.

"Yes."

"What's she like?"

Grace thought a moment. "I think the most unusual thing about her was that she seemed like everybody else, like one of us. Friendly, plain, and down to earth, like someone you could tell your troubles to, and she'd understand."

Frank chuckled. "Did she invite you to the White House?"

"As a matter of fact, she did."

"Can I go with you?" Naomi asked.

"You bet," Grace said. "You drive."

Even Dorothy heard the news, and called her. "You really met her?"

"How did you know?"

"I saw Chiyo downtown. She's so proud."

"It's not like I *did* anything."

"Maybe not. But you're in an exclusive club. I don't know another person who's met the President or his wife."

"Between you and me, it was pretty exciting."

"I would think so. Did you tell Hiro?"

"Yes. I haven't heard back from him yet. I'm sure he'll have some interesting comment about it. He's always teasing me."

"So, when are we going to get together? How about a movie this weekend?"

"I'd like that. Something particular?"

"I think *Coney Island* is playing. Why don't you see if Naomi and Chiyo and Vivian want to go, too?"

"Sounds like fun. I'll talk to them, and let you know."

She hadn't seen Vivian in some time, so she walked down to her friend's house.

"Hi," she said when Vivian came to the door. "What are you doing?"

"Studying. Come on in. My parents are shopping, and I could use a break."

Grace followed Vivian into her room, where she noticed a letter from Tom on the bed. She pointed to it. "How is my brother?" she asked.

"Okay, I guess."

"What's that supposed to mean?"

"I'm not sure. I think there's something he's worried about, even though he hasn't said what it is."

"Do you think he's sick or hurt?"

"No, it isn't like that. It's subtle. I don't think he's hiding anything. Maybe he doesn't even know. Maybe I'm crazy. He just keeps asking me not to forget him."

Grace felt a chill. "Hiro says the same thing when he writes."

"Maybe they're all afraid we'll forget them because they're so far away. It must feel like they're on another planet."

"Maybe he doesn't hear from us enough. I'll write him tonight."

"Don't tell him I said anything."

"No, I won't."

"I wish we could send him the sweets he likes so much."

"I know. That would cheer him up." Grace was quiet for a while and then said, "Maybe we can."

"How? The censors check everything."

"Maybe Naomi's friend, Ellie, would help us. We could send her something she wants, and instead of paying us, she could use the money to put together a care package for Tom."

"That's a terrific idea. Do you think she'd do it?"

"I don't see why not. I'll ask Naomi to write to her and ask. Meanwhile, how would you like to go to the movies on Saturday? Dorothy wants to get all the girls together to see *Coney Island*."

"Betty Grable is in that. I love her. Yes, I want to go."

"Good. Then it's a date. Now I have to ask Naomi and Chiyo."

"Naomi won't go without Frank. They're tighter than a frozen faucet."

"He's a nice guy. It's so strange to hear him speak Japanese. If you close your eyes, you can't tell he isn't one of us."

"I know," she said. She paused and then added, "I hate to do it, but I'd better get back to my books. I'll plan on Saturday."

Naomi and Chiyo agreed to join them. When Grace asked about Ellie helping with a care package, Naomi was eager to involve her friend. "Ellie loves to knit. I'll send her some yarn and tell her what we'd like her to put in Tom's package. I know she'll do it. One of the awful things about camp was having nothing to do that mattered. This will be like a gift to *her*."

Grace didn't tell anyone what Vivian said about Tom. Whatever it was, it sounded private and somehow ominous. She'd do whatever she could to improve his circumstances and his outlook. She'd have to trust Tom to figure out the rest.

CHAPTER 15

"The kids at McKinley High have started another war bond drive," Vivian said. She and Grace were having a rare lunch together downtown.

"Didn't they already raise enough for that one hundred and fifty bed hospital?"

"Yes, and that wasn't very long ago, either."

Grace shook her head. "How much money can people afford?"

"I guess they want to give all they possibly can to end the war, even when it means more sacrifices than they're already making."

"Have you heard anything from my brother?"

"I have. He says the 100th Battalion shipped out. Margie's brother, Sam, is in that group."

"I don't suppose he could say where they were going."

"Somewhere in Europe. They won't send our boys to fight in the Pacific. I guess they think people will get confused about who the enemy is." She laughed and looked around them before leaning over close to Grace. "They don't seem to think it's difficult for the *haoles* to tell who the enemy is in Germany. What's the difference?"

"You're right. I never thought of it that way."

"It's because they *think* of us as the enemy, no matter what side we're on."

"Oh, Vivian, that's not true."

"But it seems like it. Why else would they put thousands of us in camps in the states?"

"My mom says they are afraid of us taking over."

"And doing what? Making whites eat more rice?"

They both giggled.

"What do you hear from Hiro?"

Grace smiled wistfully. "He's so sweet. He writes beautiful *haiku*. I told him he should have been an English major instead of a math major."

"His mom is a teacher. Maybe he gets it from her."

"Do you know her?" Grace asked, surprised.

"No. But my dad does. So anyway, what does 'sweet Hiro' have to say?"

"He says the officers are pushing them to the limit. Fortunately, they're beginning to get along better with the mainland boys."

"They'd better. They'll need to trust each other and depend on each other once they go into battle."

"You're beginning to sound like a psychologist already."

"It's just stuff I hear at school. There's a lot of war talk, even in classes."

"We can't get away from it no matter where we go."

They finished their lunch and left the restaurant. The street was packed with people, all searching for a place to eat.

"Good thing we came early," Grace said. "Every place is so crowded these days."

"Between the military and the thousands of war workers, there's no place left for the *kama'ainas*."

"You know what my grandmother would say."

"*Shikata ga nai*," they said at the same time.

"We sound like a couple of old women," Vivian said.

"Okay, old lady, don't forget we're going to the movies tomorrow."

"I won't. I've got to run. I'll see you then."

"Bye."

Grace walked to her office quickly, taking back streets in order to avoid the crowds.

"Did you have a nice lunch?" Anne asked.

"Yes."

"I have a meeting at Civil Defense. Would you go through these POW cards, make sure they're complete, and then get them ready to send?"

"Sure."

"See you later," Anne called, as she closed the door.

Grace went through the cards slowly, thinking about the twenty-two young men whose lives now depended on their enemy. It must be terrifying, especially if you were wounded and had no way to communicate with a doctor or nurse.

Yasuaki Takaguchi, Private; Hirano Kawahara, Private; Yutaka Kimura, Private. In fact, they were all privates. They were probably all Tom's age, or Richie's. Was Richie a POW somewhere? She hoped so. She hoped he was out of the fighting.

The following week Anne received a note from Washington, D.C.

I enjoyed my visit in Hawaii, and appreciate all the work you and your organization are doing on behalf of our country. Best wishes to you and your staff for your continued service to the United States.

Eleanor Roosevelt.

"This is really something. Do you suppose she wrote everyone she visited?" Grace asked.

"I don't know. It could be that her staff writes these notes. Still it's a nice gesture, and it must make other people feel just as good as it has us."

"Let's write her back."

Anne looked at her, surprised.

"Let's write her back and tell her how much her stopover meant to us. I heard everyone talking that day after she left. Some of them sounded like it was the biggest event of their lives. It made them want to work even harder."

Anne considered it. "I think that's a great idea. Write it from your own point of view. Tell her what you told me."

"Really?"

"Yes. You know, she encourages people to write to her in her daily newspaper column. I'll look it over, and then you can send it out on our letterhead. Since she works so hard to relate to the average citizen, I think a letter from you might mean a lot to her."

"Can I think about it until tomorrow? I want to get it just right."

"Of course."

Grace reflected on various things she could tell the First Lady, none of which seemed important enough to bother her with. She looked at some of the articles Mrs. Roosevelt had written that Anne had saved and realized that she often wrote about ways people could best serve the war effort. So, telling her what she'd said to Anne was probably the best idea.

The next day, she showed Anne her draft.

Dear Mrs. Roosevelt,

Your recent visit to us in Hawaii was an event that will never be forgotten. After you left our brief meeting, the volunteers were so excited. I overheard many of the women say how much you inspired them and how you made them want to work even harder for the war effort. Thank you for your support of the Red Cross. Even with your busy schedule, you were able to make us feel like an important part of the home front battle.

Sincerely yours,

Grace Kawakami, Assistant to Anne Palmer

"Nicely done, Grace. You said it well. I'm sure that Mrs. Roosevelt will appreciate hearing from you."

Grace couldn't imagine that Mrs. Roosevelt would be very impressed. Now that she'd written the letter, it seemed childish and naïve. The woman's husband was the President of the United States. What would she care about a *hapa-haole* girl in Hawaii? Still, she typed it on the ARC stationery, put it in the mail, and didn't tell anyone about it.

She promised Naomi she'd go to the USO dance that weekend, and although she would have preferred to stay home and read, she went. Oliver was there as always, and whisked Chiyo away to the dance floor the minute they arrived. Frank and Naomi followed as soon as they'd settled in at a table.

Grace could almost sense that Walter was there, even though she didn't see him. Within minutes of their arrival, he stood beside her at the table. She looked into his eyes and found not the sadness, but a new, solemn look of resignation.

"Hi," he said. "I hoped we could have a dance."

She stood. "I'd like that."

He was an unconventional, though not awkward dancer, and she soon fell into the pattern of his unique style.

"I wanted to thank you."

"Oh? For what?"

"For what you said about Joey. It helped me a lot. When I stopped dwelling on what I felt and considered how he would have felt, things got better."

"I'm glad. I'm sure it wasn't easy. My brothers are both..." she hesitated, not sure how to say it, "are both overseas. I don't know how I'd stand it if anything happened to them."

"Are they with the 442nd?"

"Tom is. I'm not sure about Richie." She did not want to tell Walter that Richie might be fighting with the enemy. "Who are you with?"

"I'm at Fort Shafter. It's temporary. My platoon was hit pretty bad, and they're trying to get the rest of us reassigned. I'm a radio operator, and I've been helping them reconfigure some equipment."

He walked her back to the table where Chiyo and Oliver joined them. Grace made the introductions.

"Where are you stationed?" Walter asked Oliver.

"Pearl. I'm in maintenance. LSTs mostly."

"Seen any action?"

"No. I got here after the Seventh."

"Where are you from?"

"Boston. You?"

"Ohio. A little town called Canton."

When Frank and Naomi joined them, Walter and Oliver both stood. "Good evening sir," Oliver said.

"At ease, gentlemen. We're all friends here."

Oliver and Walter waited to sit until Naomi had taken a chair.

"You two look great out there," Grace said to Naomi.

"You didn't look so bad yourself," Naomi said. "You're a pretty good dancer, Walter."

"Thank you, ma'am."

Grace could see he was uncomfortable. She looked at him and said, "If you're not going to ask me to dance again, someone else will."

He smiled and stood. "Shall we?"

The evening passed far more quickly than Grace had anticipated, and they were soon saying good night. On the way home in the car, Chiyo was quiet.

Naomi turned to the back seat. "What's up with you? Cat got your tongue?"

She didn't speak for a minute, and then said, "Do you think Mom and Dad would mind if I went out with Oliver?"

"Isn't that what you're doing already?"

"It's not the same. I mean a real date."

"Do you mean because he's not Japanese?"

"Yes."

"Frank's not Japanese."

"I'm *hapa*," Frank said, and they all laughed.

"No, I don't think so. They might, if it weren't for Aunt Lilly."

Naomi was wrong. Their father minded very much.

"No," Yoshi said. "It's bad enough that Naomi is dating a *haole*. Find one of your own kind."

"That's not fair," Chiyo complained.

She and Grace were setting the table for Sunday supper.

"She's not asking to marry him," Makiko said softly. "I don't see the problem."

"You don't?" He sounded shocked. "It will lead to nothing good."

Grace wanted to tell him what a nice guy Oliver was, but thought it best not to get into the middle of it.

"Maybe if we met him. She could invite him over," Makiko suggested.

Chiyo looked at Grace as if pleading for help.

Yoshi didn't say anything for quite a while. Finally he said, "I'll think about it."

On November 15th, the governor's office instituted a mandatory forty-eight hour work week. Although it didn't affect everyone, most war workers were now expected to work six days out of seven.

"What about us?" Grace asked Anne the following day.

"I'm not quite sure. I think we'll continue with five days for a while, and see if our work load warrants changing it. We've been getting things done so far with no problem, so if six days isn't necessary, I don't see the reason."

Lilly had to work the new schedule at the hospital, and Ken found another part time job, which kept him busier than ever. Grace came home every day to an empty house. It reminded her regularly of how much she missed Tom and Richie. She wrote Tom more often now, although she didn't see anything in his letters to her that explained Vivian's concern.

Dear Grace,

Now that you're such close friends with the President's wife, the guys here would like to see if you could get a few things changed. First, the weather. It doesn't suit our delicate nature. Second, the food. We'd like our own cook from home who knows how to fix our favorite dishes. Third, we'd all like to get a little more time off, so we can see the country around here. And last, we'd all like to meet her, too, so please ask her if she could come by for tea one afternoon. Seriously, I'm proud of you. I'll bet she was impressed with your letter. You've always been a good writer. Take care of yourself. I miss you. Hiro does, too. He talks about you constantly. Aloha, Tom

Grace welcomed one of the changes she noticed at about that time: radio stations, which had played patriotic music and military marches for months and months, were gradually returning to the familiar Hawaiian music she loved. Of course, none of the Japanese stations had returned, which was not surprising. Citizens were still expected to speak in English, and Japanese women were not supposed to wear *kimono* in public, but hearing the melodic, traditional island songs again was comforting.

Sarah and the judge invited the Kawakamis and the Fujitas for Thanksgiving dinner. Lilly often had to work on holidays, but she managed to trade her shift with another nurse from the mainland, who had no family in the islands.

"The butcher said if I was there when the store opened, I should be able to get a turkey," Sarah told Lilly. "If not, we'll have something less traditional." She had dropped by Grace's house, on her way home from her afternoon shift at the canteen.

"It doesn't matter what we have, as long as we're together," Lilly said.

"Will Paul be home?" Grace asked.

"No. The Enterprise was here week before last, and Dorothy had an entire day with him. The ship is out again now, and I don't know when he'll be back."

"How is Dorothy?"

Sarah smiled. "Fine. She has a surprise for you."

"What? Tell me."

"No. I'll let her tell you. It's very exciting news."

Grace had no idea what kind of surprise her friend might have for her.

"What do you suppose it could be?" Grace asked her mother after Sarah left.

"Maybe she got a new job. Didn't you say she'd been looking?"

"Yes, she was. But the new rules say we can't leave a job without permission from the Office of Civil Defense, and that takes weeks."

"I'd forgotten. Well then, I have no idea."

"Maybe she and Paul got a house."

"Probably not. With the housing shortage, there's practically nothing available."

Grace shook her head. "I guess we'll just have to wait."

The instant she saw Dorothy, the wait was over.

"You're going to have a baby!" Grace cried.

Dorothy had answered the door on Thanksgiving wearing a bright pink smock. She smiled with delight. "Yes. Isn't it wonderful?"

The Kawakamis and the Fujitas crowded into the house, hugging Dorothy and congratulating her.

"When are you due?" Lilly asked.

"Around the end of March."

"How are you feeling? Do you notice any weakness or difficulty moving?"

"No, thanks to you."

"You worked hard to get strong again," Lilly told her.

Sarah came in from the kitchen. "Isn't it exciting?" she said, putting her arm around Dorothy and kissing the top of her head. "I can't wait."

"What does Paul think about it?" Ken asked.

"He's ready to go out and buy a baseball and glove," Dorothy said.

"What if it's a girl?" Makiko asked.

"He doesn't care. He'll teach either one to play baseball. It's his favorite sport."

The judge came in from the kitchen, wearing a faded red apron. "I put the bird back in the oven; it doesn't look quite done." He shook hands with Ken and Yoshi. "I guess I'm going to be a grandfather before you two. I'd like her to be an attorney, but I suppose we'll have to wait a while to see if she has the aptitude for it."

Naomi laughed. "You'd better have twins if you want to keep everybody happy."

Dorothy's eyes widened. "Twins?"

"Do twins run in the family?" Lilly asked.

Sarah shook her head. "No, thank goodness."

"Well, it's easier to have one at a time," Lilly said. "You'll find one will keep you busy enough."

"And me, too," Sarah said.

They had opened the table in the dining room to its full length, and set it with beautiful china, crystal and white linens.

"It looks so pretty," Lilly said. "I love a beautiful table."

"Thank you," Sarah said. "My mother left me all those things. We don't use them very often, but I always get them out for the holidays."

The dinner was delicious. Sarah had prepared a traditional Thanksgiving meal, and everyone ate turkey until they were stuffed.

"I've got pie," Sarah said as she cleared the table.

Yoshi moaned. "You're kidding. Dessert? On top of all that?"

"We can wait a bit," the judge said. "Why don't we sit out on the patio for a while? It's still mild outside."

They enjoyed the rest of the evening, along with their pie, out on the patio overlooking the valley. Lights from the few houses down below shone like stars in an otherwise dark sky. Grace realized that those houses couldn't be seen from the ocean, so they didn't have to worry about the blackout.

When they got home that night, Grace wrote Hiro.

Dorothy is going to have a baby! We're all so excited. I feel like I'm going to be an auntie. I'll have to brush up on my babysitting, so I can help her out once in a while. Paul wants a boy, and the judge wants a girl, so someone is going to be disappointed. It's amazing to think that only nine months ago she was in the hospital with polio. We sat out on the patio at the Rebacks' after dinner. It would have been perfect if only you'd been there. Since they live on a hill above a valley that is nowhere near the ocean, they have more freedom when it comes to blackout.

Sparkling lights glimmer
Fireflies in the valley
No blackout below

Thinking of you. Grace

Honolulu was jammed with Marines. The Second Division had returned from Guadalcanal for R&R. The USO was busier than ever, and Grace, Naomi, and Chiyo were going out two or three nights a week. Frank continued to borrow a car from one friend or another, so they rarely had to walk.

"It sure would be nice to have a new dress," Naomi said one afternoon, as they waited for Frank to pick them up.

"Who's got the money?" Chiyo asked.

"Or the time?" Grace added.

"I suppose I could make one," Naomi said, responding to neither of them.

"I haven't made anything in ages," Grace said. "I have an idea. Let's all make a new outfit for Christmas."

Naomi and Chiyo looked at each other. "In our spare time?" Naomi asked.

"Come on, it'll be fun. It'd only take a day."

"It would take a day for Naomi to decide on a pattern," Chiyo said.

Just then, Frank pulled up in front. They walked out to meet him.

"You ladies look lovely," he said when he greeted them. "Are those new outfits?"

"You've got to be kidding," Naomi said.

The USO was crowded, just like everywhere else in town. Oliver was already there, and took Chiyo off the moment he spotted her.

"That boy is in love," Frank said as they searched for a place to sit.

"Oh, don't let my father hear you say that. Chiyo's been telling him they're just friends."

Frank shook his head. "He's in love."

"I think she is, too," Grace said.

The three of them crowded around a table meant for two. They'd barely sat down when a tall, handsome Marine approached them.

"Anybody care to dance?" he asked.

Frank took Naomi's hand. "This young lady is with me."

The marine turned his attention to Grace, who stood. "Sure."

The floor was so packed that they could barely move.

"This reminds me of the Mad Hatter's tea party," he said, and when she frowned at him he quoted, "'No room, no room.'"

Grace laughed. "I don't know many guys who are that familiar with 'Alice in Wonderland'."

"I have a little sister, and that was her favorite book. I used to read it to her all the time."

"Where are you from?"

"Montana. My name is Nick Carmichael. I haven't been this close to a girl in months, so I should at least know your name as well."

"Grace Kawakami."

"You're Japanese?"

"My father is Japanese and my mother is Caucasian."

He considered what she told him. "Well, they say this is the melting pot."

Grace thought she saw Walter at the edge of the dance floor, but quickly lost sight of him.

"Do you come here often?" Nick asked her.

"A couple of nights a week. My cousin's boyfriend brings us."

The music stopped. "How about another?"

"Sure."

It was hard to know whether he was a good dancer or not since they had so little room to move, but they stayed on the floor for three more numbers. Then, he took her back to the table.

"I shouldn't monopolize all your time," he told her. "I'll be back, if that's okay."

"I'd like that."

She hadn't been at the table long, before a young sailor approached her. "Could I please have a dance?"

"Sure."

He was shy and awkward, and a terrible dancer. Grace stuck it out for two dances before she told him she wanted to get something to drink.

"I'll get it. You sit. Coke?"

"That would be great."

She sat down, and was soon joined by Chiyo and Oliver.

"It sure is hot in here," Chiyo said, fanning herself with a dance program.

The sailor returned with the drinks. "Hey, Ollie. Didn't know you were here."

Oliver put out his hand. "Hi, Bobby. You movin' in?"

Bobby dropped his head. "Nah."

"Chiyo, Grace, this is my buddy, Bobby Hardin. We work together at Pearl."

"Where are you from?" Chiyo asked him.

"Seattle."

Grace spent the rest of the evening trying to get more than two word answers from him. His shyness was so complete, it was painful for them all. Yet he seemed content to sit and wait when one of the other boys asked her to dance. Chiyo and Oliver spent more time at the table than usual, Grace thought perhaps to make things easier for Bobby. And then, at the end of the evening he suddenly found his voice.

"Will you be here next week?" he asked Grace. His eyes were riveted on her face.

"I'm not sure."

"I hope so. I'll be here. I'll look for you."

"Okay. Well then, maybe I'll see you."

On the way home, Chiyo was the quiet one. Grace looked at her and asked, "What's going on?"

"Oliver wants to take me out for dinner. Not that it's such a great deal when you consider how long you have to stand in line to get a table anywhere."

"Mom won't mind," Naomi said. "I'll talk to Daddy."

"Will you?"

"Sure. Give me a couple of days."

Grace nudged Chiyo. "She can work miracles."

After she went to bed that night, Grace finished reading *The Human Comedy*, the book by William Saroyan, which had recently been made into a movie. She'd decided to donate it to The Junior Civilian Defense Corps, the group spearheading a program called "Read a Book—Give a Book", where islanders donated books they'd read, to be sent to boys in the military.

Those who participated were asked to write their name and a message of some sort on the flyleaf.

Grace wasn't sure what to write. Suggestions were a note of encouragement for the soldier who would get the book; a comment about the story; something personal about her or about Hawaii; a bit about the Red Cross, or the work she was doing. After an hour of consideration, she decided on, "I hope this book gives you a break from your work. I thought it was very enjoyable."

The following night, air raid sirens began to wail minutes after blackout was announced. Grace was in the shower. She had to get out with shampoo still in her hair.

"Hurry up, Grace," Ken told her.

"I'm hurrying, although I don't know why. We haven't had a single bomb since the attack two years ago. I'm sure it's a false alarm like all the rest."

Ken put an arm around her as they went out to their small bomb shelter. "You've become pretty casual about this. A big change from the first night of the war."

"If they'd come back, I'm sure it would be a different story."

Some of the alarms had lasted hours and tried the patience of the residents. There were never any explanations or justification for the drills. Some people had begun to ignore them and carried on as usual, which frustrated and angered the military. They insisted that everyone needed to take cover.

The drill lasted only forty-five minutes before the all clear sounded.

"See," Grace said to her father as they climbed out of the shelter.

Lilly laughed. "I trust you're not disappointed."

"No. Just cold and wet."

"Go get rinsed off. I'll make tea."

She crawled into bed with a hot cup of tea, warm at last.

The next day a letter arrived from Tom.

Dear Grace,

The most amazing thing happened today. I got a huge care package from someone at Manzanar named Ellie. It was full of candy, and books, and newspapers; socks, canned meat, tea, and cigarettes. And not only for me. A bunch of the guys got to share. I'm not sure how this Ellie got my name, but I'm thinking it might have been from Naomi or Chiyo. Be sure to tell me as soon as possible. It's the new camp mystery. Aloha, Tom.

Grace couldn't wait to share his letter with her cousins, so she ran next door and right into a huge argument.

"I don't like it," Yoshi was saying as she walked in the door. "There's no telling where he'll take her."

Grace knew immediately that they were talking about Oliver.

"He won't be able to take her off the island," Naomi said as Grace walked through the room, trying to be invisible.

"Why can't she ask him to come here for dinner?"

"Would you welcome him?"

"More than I would if he took her out."

"Okay. Let's see what Oliver has to say about it."

Naomi joined Chiyo and Grace in Chiyo's room. "Success," she said. "Just ask him to come here for dinner."

"Here?"

"Sure. Once Daddy meets him, things will be fine."

"I guess I don't have much choice."

"What's up?" Naomi asked, turning her attention to Grace.

"Look," Grace said, waving Tom's letter at her.

Naomi read it and smiled. "Well done, Ellie. I'll write to her, and tell her what a hit she made with Tom's unit."

"Please thank her for us. And tell her if there's anything she wants from here, to let me know."

"We can send her a care package for Christmas," Naomi said.

"We'd better get it in the mail, or it won't get there before Easter."

Chiyo invited Oliver for dinner the following week, and to her complete surprise and utter dismay, he accepted.

"What if Daddy is nasty to him?" she moaned.

"He won't dare be in front of all of us," Naomi said. "Maybe I'll ask Frank, too. That should help."

They decided to make it their Christmas dinner. Lilly prepared a ham, and Makiko prepared a chicken. The girls set the table with all of Lilly's good china on a bright red tablecloth. Even though there was no tree, they'd hung decorations and stockings, and the house looked very festive.

When Oliver arrived, Chiyo flitted around like a firefly, offering him tea, and *kakimochi,* and a place to sit.

"So, what is it that you do?" Yoshi asked him.

Oliver looked at Frank for support.

"He could tell you," Frank said, with a laugh, "but then he'd have to kill you."

Yoshi's look told everyone he was not amused.

Grace watched Chiyo squirm with discomfort.

"I work on LSTs," Oliver said. "That's pretty much it."

"And where are you from?"

"Boston. My father has a fishing boat there."

"Oh? My father was a fisherman," Yoshi said with a broad smile. "Tell me about your boat."

And, that was all it took.

CHAPTER 16

The headline in the Star-Bulletin read: "Battle for Italy Expected Hourly." Ken sat at the kitchen table with the paper held high, completely engrossed in the article.

"Tom said Margie's brother, Sam, is with that group," Grace told him.

It was a few moments before her father registered what she'd said. "I don't envy them."

"There's a rumor at the hospital that a huge contingent is leaving for the Marshalls," Lilly said. "You'd think that some of the doctors are taking truth serum, the way they talk."

"Anybody who reads the paper and looks at a map could guess what they're going to do half the time," Ken said.

Grace thought of Richie and wondered where he might be. Was he safe? Was he scared? Was he still alive? She wondered if her parents talked about him when they were alone.

Christmas had passed, and 1944 had begun without any word from Tom or Hiro. Grace worried about them, even though they were still in training. She'd read about soldiers who had died in training accidents. For some reason, it was worse than dying in battle: a tragic waste of a life.

Anne was scheduled to go on a three island tour, to review the Red Cross units on Hawaii, Maui, and Kauai. Grace would be in charge while she was gone.

"Are you sure I'm ready for this?" she asked Anne the next day at work. "I've only been here a year."

"You'll be fine. Everyone knows I'll be away. If anything major comes up and you can't handle it, you can call headquarters on the big island. I'll be back in a week."

"I'll do my best," she promised.

She was grateful that Anne had decided that working six days a week was not necessary for them, but she felt guilty seeing how many people, including her mother, were regularly working the extra hours. She considered getting a second job somewhere, but Lilly talked her out of it.

Grace was looking forward to her nineteenth birthday. She, Chiyo, Naomi, and Vivian were all going up to Dorothy's for a small luncheon to celebrate. However, this birthday party would have a different twist. The girls decided to surprise Dorothy with a baby shower, letting her think that the party was for Grace. They would go for lunch, and then Lilly, Makiko, and several of Dorothy's other friends would arrive for cake, punch, and the shower.

The day of the party, Naomi drove them all up to Dorothy's. Grace was delighted with the chance to dress up. They'd even worn hats and high heels.

"We may as well dress to the nines," Naomi told them. "How often do we get a chance to get dolled up?"

Dorothy was on the patio when they arrived, fast asleep.

"She's tired all the time, now," Sarah told the girls.

"Should we let her sleep?" Grace whispered.

"No. She's been looking forward to seeing you for days. Go ahead and wake her up."

They went out onto the patio, where the table had been set with pink and white linens. Sarah spoke softly to Dorothy, touching her tenderly on the arm. She opened her eyes slowly and looked around.

"You're here. Is it that late already?"

"It is," Naomi said. "And you look adorable, so you've had enough beauty sleep."

Dorothy sat up and then prepared to stand. She had to make three attempts before she was able to get up. She laughed. "My center of gravity is *way* off." She looked around. "So, how is everybody?"

They all started talking at once, asking each other questions and catching up.

When they'd finished their lunch, Dorothy said, "Isn't it time for Grace to open gifts?"

"Yes," Naomi said. "Chiyo, come help me bring the presents out here."

The two sisters went into the house and returned shortly, followed by Lilly, Makiko, and ten other friends, all carrying stacks of gifts.

"Surprise!" Naomi said. "It's a birthday party for your little one."

Dorothy began laughing and crying at the same time. "I don't believe it. I had no idea."

"It can't be too hard to surprise someone who's sleeping all the time," Grace said.

"Grace," Lilly said.

"It's true," Dorothy admitted. "I fall asleep every time I sit down."

"I'd like to tell you it'll get better after the baby comes, but in truth, it probably won't," Lilly said. "Still, with built in help, you'll manage very well."

By the time they all left, Dorothy was back on the lounge chair, asleep again. Next to her, the unwrapped gifts were stacked on the table, one after another tiny outfit in green or yellow or white, nestled in soft white tissue. One blue bow had slipped down, and was crushed under Dorothy's hip.

"When she wakes up, she'll realize how many thank you notes she has to write, and she'll be exhausted all over again," Sarah said, as she walked everyone out.

On the way home in the car, Chiyo looked back at the Rebacks' house. "I'd like to have a baby," she said wistfully.

"Whose?" Vivian asked.

"As if we didn't know," Naomi said.

"Be careful," Grace warned her.

"Don't worry," Chiyo said. "That day is a long way off."

Naomi turned to look at her sister, "Is there something you're not telling us?"

"Maybe."

Naomi glanced back at Grace. "I guess there's more than dancing going on at the USO."

Anne had been back from her trip only a few days, when she called Grace into her office. "Several people have told me what a great job you did while I was gone. I knew you could handle it, but it's nice to be recognized."

"Thank you. Nothing much happened out of the ordinary."

"No presidential visits?"

"No. But Mrs. Roosevelt called, and we had a nice, long chat."

"I hope you told her hello for me."

Chiyo went to a movie with Oliver on Friday, and they spent the next evening wrapped in each other's arms at the USO dance. The other men knew that when Oliver was there, it was no use asking her to dance.

"It looks like they're pretty serious," Naomi said, watching the pair. "I don't know what they're dreaming up, but my dad is barely used to them dating, so I hope it isn't marriage."

"They've only known each other six months." Frank said.

"I've heard of it happening in six days," Naomi told him.

Grace shook her head. "I can't imagine."

"Imagine what?" Chiyo said. Her eyes were bright, and her face was flushed. She looked from one to the other. "Imagine what?" she repeated.

"Imagine what it's going to be like when the war is over," Grace said quickly.

"Well, I'll tell you this much: if I never have to wait in a line again, I'll be happy," Chiyo said. "What about you?" she asked Frank.

"I'll be glad to go places when and where I want, without papers or curfews. You?" he said, looking at Naomi.

"I'll be happy when Daddy and Uncle Ken can work again. Their real jobs," she added. Then she looked at Grace.

"I just want the boys to come home."

She learned the next day about one who wouldn't.

Dear Grace,

I know I told you that Margie's brother, Sam, was with the 100th when they shipped out. We heard yesterday that he was killed in action last week. We didn't get any details other than the fighting had been heavy, and there were lots of casualties. We'll probably hear about more of our friends before long. I don't see how training can prepare us for battle. I'm not sure how I will face enemy fire, and not turn tail and run. Don't tell anybody I said that—it sounds so cowardly. Grandmother would disown me. I have to admit I'm scared, though. Say a little prayer for me, would you? Tom

This must be what Vivian was talking about. She wished she could think of something to tell him that would help. She knew that she would be terrified if she were in his situation and had no idea how to encourage him.

At the end of February, there was an article in the paper about the 100th Battalion being taken out of action after forty straight days of battle.

"Have you talked to Margie at all?" Grace asked Vivian.

"No. I sent her a card, but I haven't called her. I don't know what to say."

They were on their way downtown together, to see the Mickey Rooney movie, *The Human Comedy*.

"A bunch of our friends are in the 100th, you know: Kaz Yanaga; Jimmy Mitsuoka; Shigeh Hayakawa, and Eddie Watanabe. I'm sure there are others."

"Chiyo and Naomi know a lot of them, too."

"Maybe wars would end faster if the old men had to fight them instead of the young men."

"Why do they need to fight, anyway? What is it they want?"

"Who?" Vivian asked.

"The Japanese."

"More land, I guess. Or power. I don't know. We're just trying to stop them. Hitler, too. He has to be stopped. Have you heard those stories about the camps over there?"

"Yes. The guys at the USO talk about the war constantly. I try not to listen. It's too upsetting."

"You should pay attention, Grace. Tom is going to be sent there."

"I know. But it's hard to think about it. It's depressing."

"You're writing him though, right?"

"Of course."

"What does Hiro have to say?"

"Not much, other than what Tom says."

"Does he still write haiku for you?"

"Yes."

"That's so romantic. It's like a love letter."

Grace thought about the beautiful poems Hiro had written. She'd saved them all, of course. In a way, they were love letters, a way of him exposing his tender self to her.

"I hope he likes mine as much as I like his."

"I'm sure he does. You've always written exceptional haiku."

"Thank you. I've always liked haiku, probably because my father used to read them to me when I was little."

The line at the theater stretched down the street and around the block.

"I hope it's worth it," Vivian said, as they joined the waiting crowd.

"If it's anywhere near as good as the book, it'll be great."

When it was over, they agreed it was.

On Monday, Anne was reading the newspaper when Grace arrived at the office.

"Look at this. The students at McKinley have raised enough in war bonds to buy a Liberator Bomber. That's over three hundred thousand dollars! That's amazing."

"They're a determined bunch of kids."

"They get to name the plane. They decided on 'Madame Pele.' That's the perfect name for a bomber, considering it rains down fire."

Grace shuddered, remembering their own rain of fire on December 7th. She hoped she would never have to go through that nightmare again.

That night, a letter from Hiro was waiting for her when she got home. She was curious, but preferred to read his letters in solitude, after she got in bed at night. She took it into her room and put it on her pillow. Then, she put on a pot of water for tea and looked in the refrigerator to see what she could start for dinner.

When her parents arrived home, she had supper ready. Lilly looked exhausted.

"Sit down, Mom. I'll get you a cup of tea."

"Thank you," Lilly said, collapsing on the couch. "I had a tough day."

"I'm sorry. Here," she said, and handed her mother the cup of tea. "Maybe this will help."

Lilly fell asleep on the couch, having barely touched her tea.

"Let her be," Ken said. He helped Grace dish up supper. "She probably needs sleep more than food right now."

She was still sleeping when Grace went to bed.

Dear Grace,

I wish I had something exciting to report, but I don't. We've been busy as usual with training. On our time off, we play cards and read. One of the guys is trying to teach me to play the ukulele. I'm all thumbs, so it sounds pretty bad. Tom hasn't been himself lately. He took Sam's death pretty hard, and doesn't join in with the rest of us much these days. I'm sure he'll pull out of it, but you might want to tell everyone to write him more often. You don't need to give them any details. He wouldn't like that. I read the book you sent. Thank you. I like your idea of us going to UH together when I get home. That's something to look forward to.

The moon shines brightly
trapped high on distant mountains
dressed in winter's white

I miss you more than I can say. Hiro

Frank couldn't get a car that Saturday, so the group had to walk to the USO dance. When they arrived, Oliver had already staked out a table for them.

"I thought you were never going to get here," he said.

"Sorry," Chiyo told him.

He took her by the hand. "You'll just have to stay later," he said, and she laughed.

Walter came up to Grace. "Would you like to dance?"

"Sure."

The table was eventually taken over by five other servicemen, since it was abandoned for so long. Bobby asked Grace for several dances, as did three other men she'd met in the past. When the evening was over, Chiyo and Oliver were nowhere to be found.

"Did you see them walk out?" Naomi asked Grace.

"No."

"Well, we can't leave without her," she said. She looked at Frank. "Would you take a look down the street, and see if you can find them? We'll wait here."

Walter and Bobby stayed with Naomi and Grace. Frank returned in five minutes.

"Not a sign of them anywhere."

Ten minutes later, the pair came running around the corner from the direction of the beach.

"Sorry," Chiyo told them.

The grin on her face told Grace she was not all that sorry.

"Where have you *been*?" Naomi asked, annoyed.

"We went for a walk," Oliver said. "I'm sorry. I should have been watching the time."

Grace thought they both looked guilty, and at the same time, pleased with themselves.

"We have to go," Frank said. "I found a ride for us."

"I'll call you," Oliver told Chiyo.

"Okay," she said.

Chiyo was humming to herself all the way home. When they got out of the car in front of their houses, Frank walked them up to the porch. He put his hand on Chiyo's arm. "I hope you aren't thinking of doing anything foolish," he said quietly. "Things won't go well for Oliver if you do. The Navy expects him to act like a gentleman."

Chiyo looked down.

"Do you understand?"

"Yes."

Grace heard the brief conversation just before she went into her own house and wondered what Frank meant. Was he talking about marriage? Interracial marriage? Or maybe something less honorable. Or was he simply talking about Chiyo being so young? Or was he concerned about her parents' disapproval? Whatever it was, Frank was obviously concerned.

Dorothy called the following week. "The doctor says it won't be long now."

"Are you nervous?" Grace asked her.

"A little. I only hope it doesn't decide to come in the middle of the night."

"You'd better call us, so we can come and visit."

"Don't worry. Your mom will hear about it the minute she gets to work. My folks will make sure of that."

"I'm glad you're going to Queen's, and not the Naval Hospital."

Dorothy laughed. "It's like a second home."

"Do you still want to come for dinner for St. Patrick's Day?"

"Yes, of course. I think my parents are going to the McHenry's. They can drop me off on their way there."

"All right, then. We'll see you on Friday night."

"I've never quite understood St. Patrick's Day," Ken said to Dorothy after her parents had dropped her off for dinner.

"Oh, Ken," Lilly said. "I've explained it a hundred times. My mother was Irish, and it was her father's favorite holiday. Even more than Christmas."

"The Irish are Catholics, and you're a Protestant."

"They're not all Catholic."

"St. Patrick was."

"Ken."

Grace and Dorothy laughed.

"It's an excuse for the Irish men to get drunk," Ken said quietly to the girls.

When they sat down at the table, Dorothy looked mournfully at her plate of corned beef and cabbage. "It smells so good, but I feel full just looking at it. It seems like there's no extra room inside me these days, even for food."

Lilly smiled at her. "That's going to change very soon."

"I hope so," Dorothy said, taking her first bite. "Oh, it's yummy." Her appetite didn't falter through the entire meal.

"We'll do the dishes, Mom," Grace said when they'd finished. "You rest."

"I think it would be better if Dorothy rested. You and I can do the dishes."

"I'm not an invalid," Dorothy protested. "I can help."

Lilly put the leftover food away, while Grace washed the dishes and Dorothy dried. As they were finishing, Dorothy cried out in surprise.

"What's wrong, dear?" Lilly asked her.

Dorothy looked down at her feet, now in the middle of a puddle of clear fluid. Her cheeks flushed red with embarrassment. "I peed," she said in a strained, choked voice.

Lilly took her hand and patted it gently. "I don't think so. I think maybe your water broke." She guided her to a kitchen chair. "Do you have any pain?"

"Yes. I've been having contractions on and off for days. The doctor said it was normal."

"It is. At this point though, things have changed. Do you have a phone number for the McHenry's?"

"Yes. It's in my purse."

"I'll get it," Grace said.

They tried the number, which was busy.

"Are you okay?" Grace asked. "Do you need anything?"

"I'm fine."

Lilly tried the number again. "It's still busy."

Dorothy groaned. Lilly put her hand on her belly. "You're having a contraction. Try to relax and not fight it."

"Shall I try the number again?" Grace asked.

"Yes."

"Still busy," she reported.

Dorothy moaned again.

"Good heavens," Lilly said. "Three minutes!" She looked at Dorothy. "Do you have any idea how long your mom was in labor with you?"

"Yes. Two hours. She talks about it all the time."

Lilly cleared her throat. "Okay. Ken, you need to get the car. Grace, I need you to go get Uncle Yoshi. Dorothy, write down the McHenry's address."

"I don't know it," Dorothy said with alarm.

Lilly grabbed the phone book and handed it to her, along with a pen and a tablet. "Look it up."

The Fujitas all came back with Grace.

"What can we do?" Yoshi asked.

"I need you to drive to the McHenry's house, and tell James and Sarah that Dorothy is in labor. Their phone has been busy, and we can't wait any longer. Her contractions are already three minutes apart. Ken and I are taking her to Queen's."

Ken opened the front door. "I'm ready out here."

Dorothy cried out and gripped Lilly's hand.

When the contraction ended, Lilly put her arm around the girl. "We need to get to the hospital, sweetheart. Ken and I are going to help you out to the car."

Lilly got into the back seat with Dorothy, and Grace sat in the front with her father. They pulled away from the curb, just as Yoshi drove off with Chiyo and Naomi.

"This is going to be tricky with the blackout," Ken said quietly to Grace. "So, help me keep a close watch."

"Okay."

"Oh!" Dorothy cried. "That hurts!"

"I know, sweetheart," Lilly soothed. "It won't be long."

She was quiet for a bit, and then started grunting.

"Two minutes, Ken. Go through the lights. Nobody is out this late."

"Okay." He nudged Grace. "Watch the cross streets. Yell if you see anything."

He raced west on King Street, slowing at the intersections just long enough to make sure no one was approaching.

"Oooohhh," Dorothy cried. She bore down.

"Don't push, Dorothy. If you can help it, don't push."

Just then, a police siren wailed behind them.

"Daddy!" Grace cried.

"Don't stop, Ken!"

"Hold on, everybody," he said. He went two more blocks, and veered into the Emergency Room driveway at the hospital. He drove right up to the door and slammed on the brakes. The police car screeched to a halt right behind them.

"Stop where you are!" an officer yelled.

Lilly opened her door before Ken even had time to react. She stepped out, her hands above her head. "We need help," she said loudly and slowly. "I'm a nurse. We have a woman here about to give birth. I need your help!"

The two officers approached the car.

Two nurses came out of the emergency room entrance. "Lilly?" one said.

"Mavis. Thank God. I need a gurney, stat! I've got a full term, pregnant woman, at less than a minute apart."

Dorothy was screaming, "It's coming!"

They lifted her onto the gurney, and rushed her inside.

"Go park. I'll see you inside," Lilly yelled at Ken.

By the time they found a place for the car, parked and hurried back to the emergency room, no one was in sight.

"Where is everybody?" Grace asked her father.

An attendant came around the corner. "They're trying to get her up to a delivery room," he said. "I'm not sure they're going to make it."

"Should we wait here?" Ken asked.

"It's probably best. Are you her father?"

"No. Her parents are on the way."

"Then this is the best place to wait. It's the only entrance open at this hour."

Ten minutes later, the judge and Sarah came rushing through the door.

"Where is she?" Sarah cried.

"Up in delivery. Lilly is with her," Ken told them.

"Thank God!" the judge said.

Just then, Yoshi, Naomi and Chiyo burst in.

"Where is she?" Naomi asked.

"Upstairs," Grace said.

The judge shook Ken's hand. "We're in your debt again," he said.

"Not at all."

The two policemen came out of the elevator and walked up to the group.

"Who's the race car driver?" one asked harshly.

"Is there a problem, officer? I'm Judge James Reback," he told them, handing the first one his business card.

Ken joined them. "I was driving. I know it looked reckless, but we were careful to watch for cross traffic."

"They were trying to get my daughter here before she had the baby," the judge explained. "If there is any sort of fine, I'm happy to pay it."

"No fine, Judge," the officer said, respectfully. He looked at Ken again. "Next time, try to leave a little sooner."

With that, the officers turned and left.

"I thought they were going to arrest you," Chiyo said.

Everyone laughed except Grace. For her, Ken getting arrested was no joke.

An hour later, Lilly came out of the elevator with a huge smile lighting up her face. "Congratulations. It's a girl. Mother and daughter are both doing well."

"Can we see her?" Sarah asked.

"In a few minutes. A nurse will come get you."

"Lilly, we can't thank you enough," Sarah said.

The judge gave her a hug. "She's absolutely right. We owe you so much."

"You're more than welcome," Lilly told them.

"Who does the baby look like?" Grace asked.

"What's her name?" Naomi added.

"I think it's time for us to go," Lilly told the girls. "We'll talk about it when we get home."

"I'll call you tomorrow," Sarah said to Lilly.

"Congratulations again. I know you're going to love being a grandma."

When they got home, Makiko had hot tea and dessert waiting for them. "So, boy or girl?" she asked the minute they walked in.

"Girl," Lilly said. "Six pounds, four ounces; nineteen inches. We *barely* made it in time."

"And what is her name?"

"Dorothy wasn't sure. She has time to think about it. She'll probably be in the hospital for five or six days."

"Why?" Chiyo asked. "Is something wrong with her?"

"No, that's normal. It gives her a chance to get her strength back, and get used to being a mommy."

"Can we go see her?"

"Of course. Just not tomorrow. She'll be exhausted."

"A baby girl," Chiyo said dreamily.

Grace looked at her, and wondered why that seemed so wonderful to her. Maybe because she hadn't heard Dorothy in the car on the way to the hospital.

That night after she went to bed, Grace wrote Hiro.

We had the most exciting adventure tonight, racing Dorothy to the hospital after blackout. She was ready to have the baby, and we barely got her there in time. She had a little girl. She hasn't decided on a name yet. Boy, it was quite an education in that car. It doesn't make me want to have a baby any time soon. My mom says you forget the pain, but I'll never forget that car ride.

Chiyo has fallen for Oliver. She is being very vague about their plans. Frank thinks they're up to something that won't go over well. I like Oliver, and he seems like a great guy. Still, they haven't known each other very long.

I'm busy at work. We've had more people to process through S.I., where you'll remember my father spent time. Some are fine, but many have problems and need help from people in my mom's profession. I think of you every day and dream of you coming home.

Silvery ribbons
of rain wrapping up winter
as a gift for spring

Grace

Dorothy came home a week later with baby Rebecca. Grace and the family all went up to the Rebacks' to visit and see the newborn.

"She's so tiny," Naomi said. "Aren't you nervous?"

"Why?" Dorothy asked.

"I don't know. I'd be afraid of doing something wrong, of hurting her."

Dorothy shook her head. "No. The nurse told me she wouldn't break unless I dropped her." She laughed. "I think we're going to do just fine." She looked at her daughter with a loving smile. "I'm going to call her Becca."

Everyone agreed that the name was perfect and that Becca was not only a beauty, but more than likely a gifted child and well-suited to a life as a baseball-playing lawyer.

They didn't stay long. Lilly said Dorothy still needed plenty of rest.

"Will you come for Easter?" Sarah asked.

Both families agreed they would.

On Easter Sunday, they were together on the Rebacks' patio once again, enjoying each other and a sumptuous meal. Baby Becca's Easter basket was three times as big as she was, and filled with wash cloths, receiving blankets, diapers, stuffed animals, powder, lotion, shampoo and a baseball and mitt.

"It looks like being an only child is the way to go," Naomi said.

Makiko gave her a disapproving look.

"First born at the very least," Dorothy agreed. She laughed. "I've been spoiled, and I recommend it."

But Dorothy didn't act spoiled, and Grace seriously doubted that she was. Her concern for others and her generosity were not qualities Grace associated with someone who was spoiled.

"I can't wait until she's old enough for an Easter egg hunt, or to sit on Santa's lap, or take tap dancing lessons," Dorothy said.

"Don't wish her life away," her mother said. "I guarantee it will go faster than you think possible. Trust me. Enjoy her while she's little."

"Your mom is right. Enjoy every day with her. Before you know it, she'll be graduating from high school," Lilly said with a wistful smile.

"I hope you'll let us babysit," Chiyo said. "I love babies."

"Since when?" Naomi asked.

"Since forever."

"I'll take all the help I can get," Dorothy said.

"You can count on me, too," Grace said.

"We could start a business," Ken said. "The Kawakami-Fujita Babysitting Service: newborns a specialty."

Chiyo looked at the baby. "I'm in. Especially if they're all as cute as Becca."

The judge picked up his granddaughter. "There will never be another baby as cute as Becca."

CHAPTER 17

"They're having a May Day dance at the USO," Chiyo said, her words riding a wave of excitement. "I think we should all make *leis*."

The girls were helping set the table for a barbeque supper at the Fujitas'. Chiyo had just talked to Oliver on the phone, and Grace was amused at her usually reserved cousin, who reminded Grace of a six-week-old puppy.

"Come on, it'll be fun," Chiyo begged. "There are plenty of plumeria blooming, and it's easy. We've made them lots of times before."

"When was the last time any of us wore a *lei*?" Grace asked sadly.

"Actually, I had one not so long ago," Chiyo said. She smiled at Grace.

"I like the idea," Grace said. "We could ask them to post something on the bulletin board at the club so other girls could make them, too. I can stop on my way home from work and talk to one of the hostesses."

"If we're going to make leis, we should go all out and get new outfits," Naomi said.

Grace laughed. "Any excuse for a new outfit."

"That's not true. We've talked about it for months, but we haven't done anything about it. I'd even be willing to *make* something."

"You?" Chiyo said.

"Be nice," Grace told her.

"I bet Mom and Aunt Lilly would help," Naomi said.

"You expect Aunt Lilly to use her one day off to help you make a dress?" Chiyo asked in astonishment.

"I don't *expect* anything. I think they'd *like* to help."

"Help what?" Lilly said as she came into the house, carrying a bowl of potato salad.

"Help us make dresses," Naomi said.

"Oh? Dresses for what?"

"A dance at the USO," Naomi said, and then told her about Chiyo's idea, as well as her own.

"That sounds like fun," Lilly said.

Just then, Makiko came in from the back yard, where Yoshi and Ken were cooking the meat. Naomi told her about the plan.

"I'd love to help, too. Keep in mind there's not much time. It's only three weeks away. You girls will have to go shopping for patterns and fabric right away."

The cousins agreed to meet Monday at noon to shop for supplies. Grace knew that she and Chiyo would have no problem making decisions about patterns and fabric, but she doubted that Naomi would be able to make her choices during a short lunch hour.

And of course, she was right.

"I don't know," Naomi said, "I like the blue, but the green stripe would be so perfect with that pattern."

Grace and Chiyo had already chosen patterns and fabric, and paid for them as well. The two stood holding their purchases, waiting for Naomi to make up her mind.

"I've got to get back to work," Grace finally said. She shifted impatiently from one foot to another. "Do you need me?"

"No, no. You go on. This may take me a while."

"Surprise, surprise," Chiyo said.

Naomi made a face at her. "You can go, too."

"Fine. I'll see you later."

"Don't be mad," Grace said as she followed Chiyo out the shop door.

"She never thinks about anyone but herself," Chiyo complained.

"Don't let her spoil your fun. You got beautiful fabric, and I think that pattern is perfect for you. Oliver is going to love it."

"Do you really think so?"

"I'm sure of it."

The evening of the dance, the three girls were proudly wearing their new outfits, taking pictures in the Fujitas' living room. Grace had on a gauzy blue dress with a sweetheart neckline and a full skirt. She wore a *lei* of pink and white plumeria. Chiyo's dress was soft, apple green cotton with a scoop neck, cap sleeves, and a circular skirt. Her *lei* was yellow plumeria and pikaki. Naomi wore a sleeveless yellow sheath, with a square neckline, and an organza overskirt. Somewhere, she had found purple Vanda orchids for her *lei*.

"You girls look beautiful," Lilly said. "I'm proud of all of you. Those dresses couldn't be more perfect."

"We could never have finished them without your help, Aunt Lilly," Chiyo told her.

"That's for sure," Makiko agreed.

"Just another successful team effort," Lilly told them.

Frank let out a long, low wolf whistle when he arrived. "Wow!" He made a motion with his hand indicating for the girls to turn around. "You girls are knock-outs. You're going to make every other gal at the dance jealous."

"Will you take a picture of us?" Naomi asked Chiyo as she took Frank's arm.

"Of course," Chiyo said, having long since forgotten her frustration with her sister.

Nearly every girl at the dance was wearing a *lei* and the air was filled with the fragrance of island flowers. Grace closed her eyes, imagining a perfect evening, with Richie and Tom safe at home, and Hiro's arms around her. An idyllic dream.

"Would you like to wake up and dance?" Walter asked. He stood next to her, an impish grin on his handsome face.

"I was thinking about my brothers," she said. She could feel the rush of blood to her face.

"Is that all?"

She dropped her eyes.

"So then, you have someone special?"

"Yes."

They walked out to the dance floor, and he put his arms around her. "If anything should ever happen between you two, you know, if it doesn't work out, I hope you'll let me know."

Grace was surprised. She'd known Walter now for months, but had never imagined he'd be interested in her. He was very sweet and very handsome; she thought she would probably enjoy going out with him, if things were different. But she was Hiro's girlfriend.

"I'll do that."

The evening flew by. Naomi had warned Chiyo several times not to disappear again, and Grace noticed she and Oliver had been conspicuously present all night. When they announced last dance, Chiyo and Oliver were the first couple on the floor. They swayed with each other, eyes closed, as if they were characters in their own, private storybook.

At the end of the dance, Chiyo took off her *lei* and put it over Oliver's head. Then she kissed him. Grace saw him mouth the words "I love you." They were both smiling with a private joy as they left the club.

"Can we drop you, Ollie?" Frank asked.

"No, thanks. I'll get a ride with Bobby and a couple of his buddies." He took Chiyo's hand one last time. "I'll call you."

Grace saw the look of love that passed between them, and felt an inexplicable chill. Yoshi had accepted their relationship and seemed to like Oliver. Chiyo was happy; Oliver was devoted. The only uncertainty in their lives, in all of their lives, was the war. What would the war bring?

There was a short, cryptic letter from Tom the following week. Lilly read it aloud at the dinner table.

"We're packing up, and you know what that means. Time for us to join the 100th. Can't say I'm looking forward to it. I'll do my duty, but I doubt that I'll like it. Some of the guys seem well-suited for this, but I've come to realize that I'm not one of them. You won't have reason to be ashamed of me, so don't worry. I'll write again as soon as we're on solid ground."

"The 100th has seen a lot of action," Ken said. "I don't wonder he's not looking forward to it, I wouldn't be either."

The papers had been saying that the 100th was in Italy, so Grace assumed that was where Tom and Hiro were headed. She wished they had waited a while to join up, so they could have been in the group of interpreters who worked well behind the front lines. She knew that casualties had been growing on the European front and worried that Tom's reluctance might somehow make him more vulnerable.

Islanders were ecstatic when blackout restrictions were lifted in May, although cars were still required to have coverings on lights. Other than that, life improved dramatically.

Dorothy was particularly happy. "It will be so much easier to make a bottle for the baby in the middle of the night. At two o'clock in the morning I invariably get burned, spill the milk, or drop something on my foot in the dark."

Lilly said there were far fewer injured patients arriving in the emergency room. Since the blackout had been ordered, dozens of people had tripped and fallen on their way to the bathroom in the dark.

Legal challenges against the remnants of Martial Law continued; the people of Hawaii wanted the right of Habeas Corpus returned.

Grace was busier than ever at work, and yet Anne was still unwilling to add another eight hours to their week. "As long as we're keeping up," she insisted, "I see no reason for it." Grace was grateful to have both days off for the weekend, since so many people, including Lilly, still did not.

"Are you coming with us to the dance tonight?" Naomi called to Grace. They were each hanging wet laundry on the clotheslines in their back yards.

"I guess so. I don't have anything else planned."

"Frank borrowed a car, so we'll get to ride in style."

"I assume Chiyo's going."

"Yes. Something isn't quite right, though. She hasn't heard from Oliver all week."

"Uh, oh. Is that red hot affair cooling down?"

"Not on her part."

Oliver wasn't at the dance. Neither was Bobby. And, nobody seemed to know where they were.

"Maybe they shipped out," Grace suggested.

"He's not on a ship. He's stationed at Pearl. Why would they send him anywhere else?" Chiyo asked. She was jumpy and agitated.

Toward the end of the evening, she danced with a couple of friends, but spent most of her time asking other sailors if they knew where Oliver was. She never once took her eyes off the door.

She didn't hear from him again the following week, either.

"Maybe he's sick," Grace told her, trying to be helpful.

"For two weeks?"

They were on their way to the Saturday dance again the next weekend. Chiyo was anxious and unable to hold still. According to Naomi, she wasn't sleeping well, and had nearly failed a test because she couldn't concentrate.

"Somebody has to know *something*," Naomi said.

"That doesn't mean they'll tell her," Frank warned.

"What do you mean?" Chiyo asked, her tone challenging.

"Just that. Something may have happened that they can't talk about."

Grace wondered if *he* knew something he couldn't talk about.

They scoured the room when they got to the dance, but Oliver was not there. Chiyo sat dejectedly at the table, the Coke in front of her untouched. Suddenly she jumped up. "Bobby!"

The young man approached them. He had an ugly gash on the side of his face, and his right arm was in a cast and sling.

"What happened?"

"There was an accident."

"Where's Oliver?"

"He's in the hospital. He's hurt bad, Chiyo."

"Oh, no!"

Bobby looked down at his feet.

"I want to see him. Frank, please, will you take me?"

"They won't let you, Chiyo. It's on base. They won't let you in," Bobby said.

"Frank," she pleaded. "Can't you help?"

Frank shook his head. "I doubt it."

Chiyo looked as close to tears as Grace had ever seen her. "Please, Frank. Please ask."

"I'll see what I can do. You have to understand that the Navy doesn't like civilians on base, and particularly not Japanese civilians. That's just the way it is."

Bobby sat down next to Chiyo. His eyes were dull and his voice, somber. "I'm so sorry." Grace wasn't sure what looked more painful, the obvious wound on his face, or the hidden one in his heart.

"Tell me what happened," Chiyo said.

"I don't know. There was a huge explosion. We were working; all of a sudden, people were flying through the air, and the whole place was on fire. I thought it was the Japs." He looked uncomfortable. "Sorry."

"Go on. What about Oliver?"

"I didn't see him again for a couple of days. He got burned really bad."

Chiyo grabbed his arm. "Is he awake? Can he talk?"

Bobby shook his head. "They've got him pretty drugged up."

Grace looked at Frank. "Do you think the Red Cross could get her in?"

"It wouldn't hurt to ask."

On Monday, she told Anne about Oliver.

"Do you think there's *any* way we could get her in to see him?" Grace asked.

Anne looked doubtful. "I can ask. I wouldn't hold your breath, Grace. It's highly unlikely they'd let anyone in, much less a Japanese girl."

"Poor Chiyo. And poor Oliver. He has no family here."

Anne looked at her impatiently. "Just like every other sailor in that hospital," she chastened.

"Of course. You're right. I'm sorry."

"I have a meeting at Pearl tomorrow. I'll see what I can do. Don't say anything to anyone about this. If we do manage to get her in, the fewer people who know about it, the better."

Anne had news on Wednesday. "The commander said he'd give me a pass to take her in. He checked on Oliver personally before I left." Her sad eyes told Grace what she didn't want to know. "The reason he's making an exception, is that they don't think he'll survive."

Grace gasped.

"Do you think your cousin can handle that? He's badly burned, and according to the nurse, barely alive."

Grace paused only a moment. "She'll handle it. She's *samurai*."

"You'll need to warn her, Grace. It isn't going to be easy. It won't help if she falls apart in front of him."

"I'll make sure she understands."

"As soon as she's ready, I'll call the commander and arrange a time. They'll send a car here for us."

"Thank you, Anne. I know you went out on a limb for this. My family appreciates it very much."

"I hope you feel the same way afterwards."

All afternoon, Grace considered how she should tell Chiyo about Oliver. The doctor was only allowing her to visit him because Oliver was dying. How, exactly, do you say that? Grace walked home, her feet dragging slowly through sands of sadness.

Chiyo was studying in the dining room when Grace let herself into the Fujita's house.

"Hi," Chiyo said. "Did Anne find out anything today?'

"Yes." She sat down at the table next to her cousin. "The news isn't good, Chiyo. In fact, it couldn't be much worse."

Chiyo sat up straight, her back as rigid as their grandmother's. "Tell me."

"The doctor said he's…he's not going to make it."

Chiyo's eyes closed. "Can I see him?"

"Yes, but only for a few minutes."

Her cousin opened her eyes again. "When?"

"As soon as you're ready."

"I'm ready."

"Do you want me to go with you?"

"No. I'd like to see him alone."

The two families ate dinner together that night. Grace told them about Oliver's grave condition, and the arrangement Anne was making for Chiyo to see him.

"It won't be easy," Lilly said. "Burn victims are in horrid pain; they're usually sedated. If his face was burned, he may not be able to see you, or even to speak."

"Thank you for telling me. I know it will be hard, but I have to see him." She was quiet for a moment. "He asked me to marry him, and I want to give him my answer."

"What is your answer?" her father asked.

"My answer is yes."

No one spoke for several moments. Then, Yoshi reached for Chiyo's hand. "He's a fine young man. I'd be happy to welcome him into our family."

The visit was scheduled for Thursday afternoon. Yoshi brought Chiyo to Anne's office.

"I appreciate your doing this," Yoshi told Anne.

"I hope it isn't too much for her," she said.

They were gone for two, interminable hours. When they returned, Chiyo looked hollow-eyed, yet somehow peaceful.

"Are you okay?" Grace asked her.

"Yes. He didn't look as bad as I expected. He wasn't awake and he didn't move at all, but I told him I love him, and that we can get married as soon as he's better."

Grace glanced at Anne.

"He's not going to get better, Chiyo."

"I know. But I didn't want to tell him that."

Three days later the commander called Anne. She spoke briefly to him, and then called Grace into her office.

"I'm sorry to have to tell you this. Oliver died this morning."

Grace closed her eyes. "Poor Chiyo."

"Yes." She was quiet for a bit. "Do you want me to tell her?"

"No. I'll do it."

"He'll be buried at Nuuanu."

"We'll probably have some sort of ceremony for the family. Thank you, Anne."

She spent the rest of the afternoon sorting through papers that she didn't actually see. She walked home slowly, dreading what was to come. She was relieved to find Makiko at their house.

"What's happened? Is it Oliver?"

"Yes. He died this morning."

"Chiyo's been expecting it."

"Even so, do you think she's ready to hear it?"

"I don't know if you're ever ready for someone you love to die. Shall I tell her?"

"Do you think it would be easier that way?"

"Maybe."

Grace was surprised when Chiyo came over after dinner, dry-eyed and composed. "I want to thank you. I appreciate everything you and Anne did to make it possible for me to see him. I'm so glad I got to tell him I loved him."

"I'm so sorry, Chiyo. I wish it hadn't turned out this way."

"You might not say that if you'd seen him." She paused. "The nurse told me that if he'd lived, he would have pain and surgeries the rest of his life. He might have been blind or deaf. He probably wouldn't have been able to work. I would have married him, of course, if he'd still wanted to. But I would have hated watching him suffer."

Grace hugged her. "He'd be so proud of you, Chiyo. He was very special. I know that none of us will ever forget him."

"No, I won't either."

Chiyo returned to school and continued her normal activities. But she didn't want to go to the dance the next weekend, which Grace thought perfectly understandable.

"I'm so sorry about Oliver," Frank told Chiyo when he came to pick up Naomi and Grace. "He was a fine sailor and certainly was crazy about you."

"Thank you, Frank."

Once they were at the dance, Naomi said, "I need to go to the powder room. I'll be with you in a minute."

Frank and Grace found a table and sat down together.

Grace was glad to have a moment alone with him. "I've been wondering, did you know? About Oliver and the accident?"

"I knew about the accident. I suspected he'd been hurt when he wasn't here the first week."

"But you didn't tell us."

"No."

"Because of security?"

"Partly that. Partly because I thought Chiyo might need time to get used to the idea. When she found out what happened, it wasn't such a shock. She already suspected something was wrong. Did I do the right thing? I'm never sure about these things."

"Yes, I think that was the best thing to do."

"I hope that's the last time I have to make that decision."

Of course, it wouldn't be.

War headlines highlighted the newspaper on June 8th: "Invasion! German Defenses Hammered." And under that: "Americans, British, and Canadians Land in France." The articles detailed an enormous campaign in Europe, involving thousands of troops.

"With any luck, this is the beginning of the end," Ken said as he finished reading the paper. "We've lost enough lives to the war."

But that afternoon, two American planes collided over Honolulu and crashed in the *Kalihi-Kai* district, killing ten civilians, and injuring fifteen. Some of the injured were taken to Queen's Hospital.

"It was like December 7th all over again," Lilly told Grace and Ken that night. "But these were our planes, which makes it even worse."

"Did anyone die?" Grace asked.

"All the men in the planes died. The navy hasn't yet said how many."

"Everybody you took care of, lived, right?"

"Yes." She looked closely at her daughter. "You know Grace, that won't always be the case. I can't save everyone I take care of. I certainly try to, but it just isn't possible. So, don't kid yourself about me having special powers. I'll always do my very best, but I'm not a magician."

Her mother's words made Grace feel like a child. "I know. I just feel better when you're helping people than I do when anybody else is. You've saved a lot of lives already, like Dorothy's."

Lilly hugged her. "I helped care for Dorothy...it wasn't only me. I don't want you to have unrealistic expectations."

Grace still believed her mother had magical powers. She *had* saved Dorothy. And she might even have saved Oliver, if she'd had the chance.

The newscast on the radio that night was all about the Normandy invasion. They reported that thousands of allied troops were fighting in France, trying to push the Germans back. Hundreds had been killed and even more wounded. Grace finally went into her room to get away from it. She couldn't stand thinking that Richie, Tom, and Hiro could be fighting in similar circumstances.

Talk of the invasion monopolized the conversations at the USO dance the next weekend.

"Our guys are doing a hell of a job over there," Walter told Grace. "Oh, sorry about that. I'm not around that many ladies, and my language shows it."

"That's okay."

They were dancing to a Glenn Miller tune. They had danced together so often that Grace now anticipated his every twist and turn.

"Whatever happened about your transfer?" she asked.

"It looks like I'll be here for a while. I guess the CO likes my work, so he put in a requisition to keep me on base."

"Are you happy about not leaving?"

"I'm happy about not leaving you."

She looked up at him. "Walter, you know..."

"I do know," he interrupted her. "But you can't blame me for dreaming."

"I just don't want any misunderstandings."

"Don't worry, I understand."

Frank and Naomi were at the table when they walked back.

"How is Chiyo doing?" Walter asked Naomi.

"She doesn't say much. She's been studying for finals. I'm not sure how well she'll do, since she's so distracted. Not that I blame her. It was all such a shock. Still, I never see her cry, and I never hear her complain."

Grace almost expected her to say, "She's *samurai*," though, of course, she didn't. You didn't say that in public these days.

"Please give her my sympathies," Walter said.

"Thank you, I will," Naomi told him.

The USO wasn't the same without Chiyo and Oliver. Grace kept looking for them on the dance floor. It was a shock each time she realized that she would never see them dance together again.

"So many people gone," she said to Walter when Naomi and Frank went for drinks.

"Way too many."

"Do you think it's almost over?"

"Do you want an honest answer?"

"Maybe not."

"In that case, yes, I think it's almost over."

CHAPTER 18

Dear Grace,

We've landed at last, here in the land of ravioli. We're on the move, and I couldn't tell you where we are, even if I knew. Spirits are generally high, since many of the guys genuinely want to get into the fight. I'll do whatever I have to, but the truth is, I'd much rather be anywhere else. I was sorry to hear about Chiyo's friend. What a waste this damn war is. So many young men. And what will we have gained when it's all over? There's no choice, of course. We had to get into it. Even so, I think it's a terrible waste.

They tell us once we're camped, they'll give us a day off (not all at once, of course.) Tom and I will go into whatever town is nearby and take a look-see. This is pretty heady stuff for a bunch of island boys who have never been away from home before.

My folks sent me a copy of the Star, and I read about the plane crash over Kalihi. That must have been terrifying for everyone in the area. I hate to think of you being at home, yet still in danger. It's bad enough here, knowing that we need to watch out for things falling out of the sky. I want you to take good care of yourself. I expect to find you exactly the same when I get back again.

The endless ocean
Majestic, cerulean blue
Carries me away

Thinking of you and dreaming of home. Hiro

She read the *haiku* several times before she turned off the light. She loved the way he used words like cerulean and majestic. He expressed himself so beautifully on paper. She wondered if he would do the same in person. Probably not. That wasn't the way people really spoke. Except maybe Shakespeare. She closed her eyes and drifted into a dream with Hiro by her side, here at home again.

Since the school semester had ended, Chiyo, Vivian, and Naomi had more free time than Grace. They were all working part-time summer jobs, but were enjoying the break from their studies. The four girls began going to the movies together every Friday afternoon.

They were standing in line at the theater the following week, when Naomi started waving, and called out, "Walter, over here!"

Grace noticed him then, across the street, with a group of noisy soldiers.

"Hey," he shouted. He spoke briefly to his friends and came over to the girls.

"Hi there," he said.

"Where are you off to?" Naomi asked.

His friends were watching them, talking and laughing.

"We're headed over to the USO."

"Why don't you join us? This is supposed to be a good movie," Naomi said.

Walter looked at Grace, as if seeking her approval.

She nodded, somewhat hesitantly.

"I don't want to crash your party," he told them.

"Don't be silly," Naomi said. "Your friends are welcome, too." She waved at the others, but they started moving down the street, leaving Walter with the girls.

"Are you sure this is okay?" he asked Grace.

"Of course."

The movie was a disappointment. When it was over, Walter said, "Let's go get an ice cream. My treat."

Chiyo and Vivian said they were headed home, but Naomi said, "Yum. Let's go."

The three had barely rounded the corner, when Naomi ran into friends of hers from the university.

"Come with us, Naomi," one of them said. "We're going to Benson's."

Naomi looked at Grace. "You don't mind, do you?" and without waiting for a response, happily joined her friends.

Walter looked at her in surprise. "That was quick. Do you still want to get an ice cream?"

"You're not going to abandon me now, are you?"

"Not a chance."

They walked to the ice cream stand and stood in line.

"Tell me about yourself, Grace. What did you do before the war?"

"I was in high school when it started. I took an accelerated program so I could graduate early and get a job."

"And what about afterward? What will you do then?"

"I want to go back to school. I'd like to be a nurse. My mom is a nurse, a really good nurse. It probably sounds childish, but I'd like to be one, too."

"My mom is a nurse," he said, smiling. "I think it's a noble profession and a worthy goal."

After they bought their cones, they walked down toward the beach. Grace was uncomfortable being alone with him. At the dances, there were always others around. The USO was familiar and safe. This was somehow risky.

Walter seemed completely relaxed.

"What will you do after the war?" she asked, unable to stand the silence.

"I'd like to finish my education, too. I was studying architecture at Ohio State." He was quiet for a while. "It seems like such a long time ago."

"Sometimes it seems like we've always been at war."

He pointed toward the barbed wire that lined the beach. "I bet it's beautiful here without that."

"Yes. And it used to be peaceful. And," she paused, "easy going. Now everybody is in a hurry. They're always late because they have to wait in lines; they can't wait to get what they want, or get it fast enough."

"So, you'll be glad to see us all leave."

"Did I say that?"

"Sort of."

"I didn't mean to. I was just trying to tell you how much it's changed."

"You said your brothers are overseas. Where are they?"

Grace was taken off guard and uncertain how to answer. She wasn't prepared to talk about Richie. "My brother, Tom, is in Italy. He's with the 442nd."

"I hear they're quite an outfit, real fighters."

"Yes."

"And the others?"

"There's only one other. Richie. We're not sure where he is."

"Is he a POW?"

"He might be. We don't know."

He waited.

"It's a long story," she said finally.

"I've got time. I don't have to be back to base until tomorrow."

She had no idea how he would react to Richie's circumstances. Given that his best friend had been killed by the Japanese, he might not be very sympathetic. But he was waiting for an answer, and she had to say something.

"My grandfather died three years ago, and my grandmother insisted on taking his ashes back to Japan. It's an important tradition in our culture to be buried at home. My father didn't want her to go alone, so Richie went with her." She wished she didn't have to go on, but he was listening intently, knowing there was more. "They got stuck there. My grandmother was in the hospital, and Richie wouldn't leave her. My father is pretty sure he's been drafted."

"Wow, that's tough." And then, the wretchedness of it seemed to dawn on him. "Your brothers could end up fighting against each other."

"Yes. It could turn out that way."

"That must be pretty hard on your folks."

"On all of us."

"Yes. For you, too, of course."

"We have no idea where he is, whether he's okay, or what will happen when the war is over."

"Geez, that's really rotten. It must be pretty awful for him, too, having to fight against the United States."

"I hate to even think about it."

"I don't blame you. So let's not. Let's do something fun to take your mind off it."

"Like what?"

"Well, what about going to the zoo?"

"Now?"

"No, tomorrow. How about it? Shall we go to the zoo?"

"I guess so," she said. It came out so easily that it seemed like the only possible answer. It wasn't until late that night, after she was home and in bed that she realized he'd asked her out, and she had accepted.

Once wouldn't hurt, would it?

He came to the house the next day as they'd agreed. Lilly was at work, but Ken was home.

"Dad, this is Walter Avery. We met at the USO."

"Mr. Kawakami, it's nice to meet you."

She hadn't noticed how tall he was before, but he towered over her father.

"You, too, Walter. So, you're off to the zoo?"

"Yes, sir."

"Well, have a good time."

They walked to the zoo, which was only a mile away from her house. She told him about growing up in Hawaii, about her Japanese heritage, about Dorothy, and Anne. He told her about his family, his home town, his first girlfriend, and Joey. She couldn't believe how relaxed they were together. The conversation flowed so naturally, she had no time to be self-conscious or nervous.

"Joey and I decided to join up together. Everybody was going in, and I told him we should go, too. He wasn't too keen about it at first. After a while, he sort of liked the idea. We'd only been in a year when he got killed."

"I bet you miss him a lot."

"I do. You know it really helped when you asked me what he'd say. I'll never forget that."

"I'm glad that I could make a difference."

After the zoo, Walter suggested a walk on the beach. "Why don't we get some sandwiches and have a picnic?"

"Okay."

The line at the snack bar, like lines everywhere else, was long and slow.

"I hope they don't run out of food before we get there," Walter said.

There were only two girls working behind the counter, and although they seemed to be moving at a remarkable speed, the line still crept along like a snail through poi.

"It's so slow that a person could starve waiting."

"There aren't enough people on the island, to take care of all the people on the island," Grace said.

"I guess what you need is more island."

When they finally got their lunch, they walked down to the beach. Walter helped her through a break in the barbed wire, and they walked until they found some shade near a grove of palm trees.

"Do you miss home a lot?" she asked him as they unwrapped their sandwiches.

"Sometimes. Sometimes it's not so bad. Hawaii is a nice place. It sure has better weather than Ohio. The trip over here was quite a shock. It took forever. I'd never been far from home before, never even seen the ocean."

She laughed.

"What's so funny?"

"I've lived by the ocean my whole life. I don't think there's been a single day of my life when I *didn't* see the ocean."

"I think I'll miss it when I'm home again." He took off his shoes and socks, and ran his bare feet through the warm sand. "Yep, I'm going to miss this."

When they'd finished eating, he rolled his pant legs up. "Let's see how warm the water is." He stood and pulled her to her feet, but didn't let go of her hand as they walked down to the water. Once again, it felt so natural to Grace that she didn't resist.

They darted in and out of the water, daring the waves to hit them higher and higher. But playing with water is like playing with fire. A huge wave caught them off guard, and knocked them off their feet. Walter jumped up, lifted Grace from the surf, and carried her to the dry sand. All the while, she was laughing like a child.

"Where did that one come from?" she sputtered. She was wet to her waist and covered with sand.

"Beats me. But it looks like growing up by the ocean, doesn't mean you're immune to its tricks."

"The ocean is a mystery. Even the natives can be fooled. I'm pretty sure that nobody understands it."

"Well, I've learned never to turn my back on it. You might say I learned it the hard way."

"Why is it that lessons are always painful?"

He settled back on the sand. "That's a good question. I don't really know. Why do you think?"

She considered it. "Maybe because otherwise, we wouldn't remember them."

"Or maybe so we don't make the same mistake twice. And yet, some of the guys in my unit do just that. They don't seem to learn."

"Do you have any other good friends in your unit?"

"No. The guys are fine and all, but I don't know any of them very well."

"Are you afraid?"

"Afraid?"

"You know, of losing someone else?"

"Maybe." He stood. "Are you going to the dance tonight?" He was doing his best to brush the sand off his pant legs, and perhaps change the subject.

"Yes."

They started walking back along the beach.

"I hope you'll save me a dance or two."

"Of course."

He wanted more than a dance or two. Halfway through the evening, when Frank and Walter went to get drinks, Naomi said. "What's the deal? Are you two an item?"

"An item?"

"You haven't danced with anybody other than him all night."

"I danced with those two sailors," Grace protested.

Naomi gave her a sideways glance. "Don't get me wrong I like Walter. And you two look great together dancing. But he does seem a lot more attentive lately."

Grace felt self-conscious and uncomfortable. "Well, we're not an item."

"Pardon me for asking," Naomi said, but the grin on her face said she didn't believe a word that Grace said.

Grace tried to make herself available for other boys after that, yet Walter was either dancing with her, or waiting for her at the table. When she considered it, she had to admit that she enjoyed the attention as well as his company, particularly after getting to know him better that afternoon.

When the dance was over, Walter walked with her out to Frank's car.

"Can I call you?"

"I guess so," she said, suddenly feeling uncertain.

"I'll talk to you soon then."

She waved to him as she and Frank and Naomi drove away.

"So, you two are *not* an item?" Naomi asked.

"No, we're not."

"You could have fooled me. Pay attention, Grace. The boy's in love," Naomi said.

"Oh, for heaven's sake."

"Mark my words, he's a goner."

Grace went to bed feeling confused and guilty. She'd been interested in Hiro for months, had thought of no one else, had exchanged letters that bordered on love letters. And now, she'd said that Walter could call her; had spent practically an entire day alone with him.

What was wrong with her?

On Monday, a letter arrived from Tom. Lilly was dishing up dinner, and asked Ken to read it out loud.

"Hi everybody,

I'm writing from battlefield central. I've only got a couple of minutes. Things around here are hot and heavy. I'm trying to keep my head down and my rifle up. I've been hearing a lot of prayers lately, so I'm not the only nervous one. We do what we have to these days, no matter how we feel. I haven't had any mail for a long while. I assume it's because we're on the move so much. Still, a letter or two would be nice, so please write soon. Aloha, Tom"

"I write him twice a week," Grace said.

"Like he said, it's because he's moving around so much. Your letters will catch up to him, and he'll have a field day reading them," Ken assured her.

"Your father and I write him, and so do Makiko and the girls," Lilly said, setting plates of rice and chicken on the table.

"And Vivian," Grace added.

"He might have to take a day off to read them all," Ken said.

"I hope the uncles are writing to Richie," Grace said. When she saw the look on her mother's face, she added, "I'm sorry."

"It's okay. I hope they are, too."

"I wish this stupid war was over," Grace said. "I want them all home."

"I dream of it every night," Lilly said. "I want nothing more than all of us here where we belong."

"It must be the most common dream in the world," Ken said. "We all want our families home safe."

Grace walked down to Vivian's after dinner. She'd received a letter from Tom as well.

"He sounds depressed to me," Vivian said. "He hasn't gotten a letter from me in two weeks."

"Not from us, either."

"All we can do is keep writing."

"And pray it ends soon."

When Grace walked into the office on Thursday, Anne greeted her with a huge smile. "Did you see the paper this morning?"

"No. I overslept."

"Guess who's in town?"

"Who?"

"President Roosevelt! He's visiting the troops."

"Do we get to meet him?"

"No. I'm afraid seeing Mrs. Roosevelt is as far up the political ladder as we get to climb."

The afternoon paper was full of news about the President's visit, complete with photographs of him driving through the naval hospital grounds, and speaking to the men in uniform.

Walter called her that night, thrilled that he'd caught a glimpse of the President as his motorcade passed by.

"I wish I'd been there," Grace said.

"No complaints, please. You got to meet his wife."

"You're right."

"I heard about a new restaurant not far from your house. It's called The Willows. It's on a site called *Kapa'akea*." He said the word slowly, pronouncing each syllable carefully, as if he were talking to a four-year-old.

"I know where that is. It's on the other side of the stadium. The *Alii* used to have picnics there."

"*Alii?*"

"The Hawaiian royalty."

"Ah. Well, they've got a lunch room there now, and some of the guys say it's pretty keen. I thought maybe we could try it out on Saturday."

"That sounds nice," she said, pushing thoughts of Hiro aside.

"How about if I pick you up about eleven. Actually, we'll have to walk. But it's not far, as you said. Maybe if we leave early we can beat the crowd."

"Okay. Well then, I'll see you on Saturday."

Walter greeted her father when he arrived, and told him about seeing the President.

"Now I can tell everyone that my daughter and her friend have met the President and his wife."

"Not me, sir. Just Grace."

Ken patted Grace on the back. "Enjoy your lunch."

She was relieved that Walter made no attempt to take her hand, or put his arm around her as they walked down the street.

She didn't want to have to explain anything to anyone who might see them.

A crowd had already gathered at the restaurant before they arrived, and they waited nearly an hour before being seated.

"I can see why the *Alii* liked it here," Grace said. "It's beautiful. Can you imagine living here?"

"Before I came here I thought the entire island looked like this. I expected to see grass shacks everywhere."

"Really?"

"Yes. It was weeks before I saw my first coconut or tasted fresh pineapple. Of course, that was right after Joey was killed, and I wasn't doing much of anything. It's hard to believe it's been a year already."

"And Richie's been gone three."

"Damn war," Walter said, and then added, "Sorry."

"I couldn't agree more."

They were seated on a patio in a grove of trees, surrounded by lush, fragrant tropical plants in shades of celery, moss, fern, jade, lime, and forest green. Flowers in riotous reds and pinks lined the edges of the terrace.

Grace drew in a deep breath. "It smells heavenly."

The waitress handed them a menu, and later returned to take their order.

"I'm glad I can't see all the people still waiting in line," Grace said. "It always makes me feel like I need to eat faster and pretty much ruins the meal."

"You wouldn't want to eat on base then," he told her. "We gobble our food like pigs."

Their lunch was delicious. Hawaiian music played in the background and fleetingly transported Grace back to the carefree life she'd known before the war.

"This is really nice. It's like home was before the war."

"I dream of home all the time. I'll bet all the guys do, although they might not admit it. Just like your brothers do, even if they don't say so."

"My brother Tom really misses home. Our letters aren't getting to him very regularly, and I'm afraid he thinks we're not writing."

"Letters are our lifeline. I don't think I'd survive without them."

Grace thought he sounded almost desperate. It made her think of Tom's last letter. It too, had sounded desperate, as though he were out of their lives *and* their thoughts. She was sad for both of them, and for all the other men who were so far from home and family.

Just then, she recognized the island song, "*Sanoe*" playing over the sound system.

"Oh, listen," she said. "This was written by Queen Liliuokalani. It's one of my favorites." She leaned back, closed her eyes and hummed along with the romantic melody.

"What do the words mean?" Walter asked her.

"I'm not sure. I know it's about a love affair, but that's about all. It was written by the former queen. She actually wrote a lot of songs, more than one hundred and fifty. '*Aloha Oe*' is probably the most famous."

"I've certainly heard that one a time or two."

The waitress came by with the check and took their empty dishes.

After he paid, Walter escorted her out of the restaurant. "Do you have time for a little trip?"

"Trip?"

"Yes. I thought we could catch the bus over to Pearl City Tavern. They have dancing there in the afternoon."

"You don't get enough dancing at the USO?"

"I have to share you with a hundred other guys at the USO."

"Hardly."

When she saw the disappointment on his face, she said, "Okay. I guess we could do that if you'd like."

"I certainly would like."

There were more men than women at the Tavern, but none of the other boys asked her to dance. Walter made it clear that she was with him. She was surprised at how quickly the afternoon passed.

"Are you going to the USO tonight?" he asked her on the bus back into town.

"I think I've done enough dancing for one day."

"What about a movie?"

"Actually, my friend Dorothy invited me to dinner."

"Are you tired of me?"

"No. I had other plans already."

"So, you'll go out with me again?"

She hesitated, not wanting to think of it as "going out."

"Grace?"

"I'll have to see."

Again that night after she'd gone to bed, she felt guilty. as though she were cheating on Hiro, even though they'd never made any agreement or promises to each other. She wished she could talk to someone, to help her sort it out.

When she got to work on Monday morning, she realized who that someone was.

"Anne, do you have a few minutes?"

"Sure. What's up?"

"I need some advice. Or at least an opinion." She closed the office door before sitting down. She told Anne about Hiro and Walter, and her confusion about it all.

Anne was quiet for a while. "Some say 'All's fair in love and war.' Is it true? When the two intersect, maybe it is. If you and Hiro never made a commitment, there's no reason you should feel guilty about seeing Walter. If you *do* feel guilty, maybe you think Hiro believes otherwise."

The minute Anne said it, Grace understood.

Hiro believed there was a promise.

CHAPTER 19

All week she worried about it: how to tell him; what to tell him; when to tell him. She had to do it, and she dreaded it. Just because it was the right thing to do, didn't mean it was an easy thing to do. In fact, it was probably exactly the opposite. Saturday came and she still hadn't figured it out.

"You're coming with us to the dance tonight, right?" Naomi asked.

They each had a grocery list, and were walking to the market together.

"Yes."

"Are you okay? You've been quiet all week."

"I'm fine. We're swamped at work, and I'm tired."

Naomi chattered on about one of the girls she worked with, how her family owned land on the big island, and she was here going to school at the university. Grace made appropriate comments at the appropriate moments, but in truth, she didn't hear a thing Naomi said. How to tell him, and what to tell him, were the only things on her mind.

Walter was already there when they arrived at the club.

"I've got a table," he told them.

He took Grace's hand and led them toward the back of the room, away from the dance floor. Naomi and Frank went off to dance immediately, while Chiyo sat down at the table.

"Ready for a dance?" Walter asked Grace.

She nodded subtly toward Chiyo. "Let's wait a bit."

"I'll get us some sodas," he said and went off to the bar.

Grace sat down next to her cousin. "Are you okay?"

"I suppose I'll always think of him here, always look for him. I see him all the time, you know, walking down the street, or at a store; a stranger in a navy uniform, who looks like him, but isn't."

"It'll get better. You'll meet someone else."

"I suppose," Chiyo said listlessly.

"Here you go," Walter said. He put a soda down in front of each of them.

Bobby joined them. "How are you doing?" he asked Chiyo.

"Fine."

"Would you like to dance? It's okay if you don't want to, I'm only asking."

Chiyo smiled for the first time that evening. "Sure."

Grace felt a rising anxiety as Chiyo and Bobby left the table, and she was there alone with Walter. She knew this was the time.

He reached over and took her hand. "Are you ready for a dance, too?"

She shook her head, "Listen, Walter. I…"

"Don't say it."

"I can't go out with you anymore."

He shook his head. "Please don't say that," he whispered.

"I have a friend. I told you about him before. He's with the 442nd. We were dating before he left. He thinks I'm waiting for him. I have been. We've been writing." She saw the misery wash across his face, and her heart broke. "I'm so sorry, Walter. I am. Spending time with you has been wonderful. Really. If it weren't for Hiro…"

"Is it something I did?"

"No, not at all. I just don't think it's fair to Hiro." She looked closely at him. "If you had a girl back home, would you want her going out with someone else?"

"No."

"I can't do this anymore."

"He's a lucky guy. Lots of girls in your situation would write a Dear John letter, and dump the guy, or not bother to tell him anything at all. Maybe that's why you're so special."

They sat together in silence for a while.

"What about the dances. Are you still going to come?"

"I don't know. I can't dance every number with you anymore. Are you going to be okay with that? Maybe it would be better if I weren't here."

"It wouldn't be better for me," he insisted. "You don't have to worry. I won't get drunk, and I won't make a scene."

"I'll have to think about it."

"Can I have a dance once in a while?"

"Of course."

"Could we have one now?"

"Yes."

He led her out to the floor, and they danced to "Moonlight Serenade." She felt so comfortable in his arms, so right. She knew she'd miss seeing him, but she was afraid that in the end, these dances would prove to be too painful.

She wrote Hiro when she got home that night.

I've been thinking about you so much these days. Tom says he hasn't been getting our letters. Have you? I hope so. Yours arrive regularly. I love your poems, especially the descriptive phrases. Vivian's dad says your mom is a teacher. Is that why you have such a wonderful vocabulary? I suppose all the books you read help, too. Oh, I have a bunch of paperbacks to send you. I got them from Irene at work.

Speaking of work, we've been really busy. There are so many more POWs now than there were a year ago. All their paperwork goes through our office. The various ARC divisions are packaging even more supplies for Uncle Sam, which need to be sent where they're needed most. So everybody's hopping, including yours truly. Fall is coming, which doesn't mean much except that the girls will be going back to school. We'll do that together one day soon. Meanwhile, here's my latest effort:

Brilliant red lava
devouring all it meets
Madame Pele's wrath

Please be careful and come home soon. Grace

She didn't go to the USO dances for the next three weeks. She told Naomi that she was so busy at work that she was too tired. A month after she'd broken up with Walter, she agreed to go with Naomi and Chiyo.

"It's like old times again," Naomi said, as they piled into the car Frank had managed to borrow.

Walter wasn't there when they arrived, and Grace felt both relief and disappointment. She danced with two sailors and three soldiers, none of whom looked familiar to her. She was sitting at the table drinking a soda when she heard an unmistakable voice.

"Would you like to dance?"

She looked up into his shy smiling face and said, "Sure."

It was so familiar, so natural, so comfortable. A part of her had forgotten how easily they moved together, but a deeper place in her heart, remembered.

"It's been a long time," he said.

"Yes."

"I've missed you."

There was nothing to say. She couldn't admit she'd missed him, too. It would only open it all up again.

He took her back to the table in silence.

"Thank you," she said.

"I'll see you."

She watched him walk away and realized that he headed straight for the front door.

She was sound asleep when the air raid siren went off. It screamed her awake like a wild animal. She jumped up and grabbed her robe, groped for her slippers, and raced out to the kitchen.

"I'm sure it's only a drill," Ken said, as he pushed Lilly and Grace outside toward the shelter, "but there's no way we could sleep through it anyway."

It lasted an hour and a half and then finally, the all clear sounded.

"There are a lot of things I won't miss when the war is over," Lilly said, "and this is at the top of the list."

On Monday, Grace noticed that Anne closed her office door at about nine o'clock and kept it closed until noon. Since she rarely closed her door at all, this was particularly strange. At four o'clock, Anne walked outside. When she returned ten minutes later, Frank Berry was with her.

"Hi, Grace," he said when he came in. "Could we have a few minutes with you?"

Grace was perplexed. Irene had already left, and she didn't understand why he couldn't talk to her at her desk. He stood there, indicating that she go into Anne's office. Why would he possibly want to talk to her? He had periodic meetings with Anne, but Grace had never before been involved. Besides, she'd seen him two days before at the USO dance, and he hadn't said anything was amiss then.

Confused, she went into Anne's office and sat in a chair across from the desk. Frank closed the door and sat next to her. Anne sat behind her desk.

"First I have to say that everything we talk about here today is to be kept strictly confidential. You are not to speak to anyone about it. Do you understand?" Frank asked.

Grace nodded, a sense of panic beginning to rise in her. Was this something about her father? Was he in trouble again?

"And you agree?"

"Yes."

"I'm sure Naomi has told you something about my job," Frank said. "Among other things, I interrogate the POWs who come through here on the way to the states. You already know that they all fill out the POW postcards. Anne tells me that you've processed them in the past."

"Yes." Had she done something wrong?

"This morning I came across something completely unexpected, and I confess I was shocked." He handed her a single POW card, exactly the same as the dozens and dozens she'd seen in the past. Exactly the same, except for the name on it: Richard Kawakami!

Richie!

"Richie?" she cried. She jumped up. "Richie is *here*? Where is he?"

"Grace," Frank said, taking her arm, "sit down. We have to take this one step at a time."

"If he's here I want to see him!"

Anne leaned across her desk and spoke in a low, almost harsh voice. "Sit down and listen, Grace. It's not as simple as that. The fact is, it's not simple at all."

Grace sat. Her heart was pounding and her mind was racing. Why wasn't it simple? If he was in Hawaii, why couldn't she see him?

Frank turned his chair so he was facing her. "Grace, this situation is extremely complicated, and Anne and I aren't sure of the best way to proceed. We need you to listen so you can help us. Okay?"

"Yes. Okay."

"Richie is here. He was captured. He's in the hospital because he has malaria. He is extremely sick."

"Is he…?"

"The doctors are doing all they can, but it looks like he's been sick for months. He's not responding as well as they would like him to."

Her mom would know what to do; she could help him. Elena almost blurted it out, but didn't. It was clear that they didn't want her to talk.

"The normal procedure would be to keep him in the hospital until he was well enough to travel, interrogate him, and then send him to the states for the duration."

"The duration?"

"Yes. That's the normal procedure."

"But he's a citizen. A United States citizen. He was forced to go into the Japanese army. My dad said he was conscripted!"

"That's part of the problem. Because he fought in an enemy army against the United States, he *lost* his U.S. citizenship. He is no longer one of our citizens. In fact, he's considered a traitor."

"No," she cried. "He didn't want to. I know it!"

"I'm sure he didn't. That isn't the issue. The unfortunate fact is, he *did*. And, that's what our government will be looking at."

"What are you going to do?"

"We're not sure yet. At the moment, he's too sick to be moved, so we don't have to do anything. We need to come up with a plan. That's where we need your help."

"My help?"

"Yes. We need to have a meeting with your parents, and we'd like you to tell us who else might be included. Who do you know who might be able to help?"

"My Uncle Yoshi is a lawyer," she said. Her mind was beginning to grasp the complexity of the dilemma. She thought for a moment. "The judge! Dorothy's father is Judge Reback. He helped when my dad was at Sand Island."

"Good," Frank said. "This is exactly what I was hoping for." He looked at Anne. "Where do you think we can meet?"

"Someplace neutral, not here, not at their house, and not at the base. What about a conference room at the Royal Hawaiian? Surely the Navy has a space big enough for about ten people to meet in private."

"Yes. Perfect. Now, how do we get them there?"

"Well, we certainly don't want military vehicles picking them up," Anne said.

"I'll talk to the judge," Frank said. "I can't very well lie to him. His position warrants a degree of trust, and his devotion to this family makes him the perfect ally. I'll try to arrange it for tomorrow evening."

Anne picked up the phone. "I'll check the hotel," she said, dialing a familiar number. "We've had meetings there in the past. I'm sure they'll accommodate us."

It took her only five minutes to arrange for a conference room.

Frank looked at his watch. "With any luck, the judge is still in his office. I'll give him a quick call to make sure he's available tomorrow." He went out to the other office and closed the door.

Grace looked at Anne with a wan smile. "Is he awake? Can he talk?"

"I don't think so. He's been sick for so long, and he's so weak, I don't think he even knows where he is. Two other POWs from his unit told Frank that he'd been sick for months; he hadn't done much fighting lately, if at all."

"Did you see him?"

Anne shook her head. "No. Frank hasn't even seen him. He just saw the card."

Grace glanced down at the card, which was still in her hand. Richie had somehow given them his name and address, right here in Honolulu. No wonder Frank noticed.

Richie was there. They had to figure out how to keep him there.

The judge told Frank he was available for the meeting and would do everything in his power to help Richie. Frank sat down again next to Grace. "I'll call your parents and your uncle tomorrow. I'll tell them we need to talk to them about your dual citizenship. I'm quite sure that will get them there."

It did.

They sat together at a long conference table at the Royal Hawaiian, in a room which opened out onto the beach. Frank greeted her parents and Yoshi when they arrived, and then Anne, Grace and the judge joined them from an adjacent room.

Lilly and Ken looked at each other with alarm when they saw Grace. "What's this all about?" Ken asked, clearly agitated.

"It's nothing about me, Daddy," Grace reassured him. She sat down in the vacant chair next to her mother. "Everything is good," she whispered to Lilly.

"We're here because of Richie," Frank said. "We're going to try to figure out how we can get him back home."

And with that, he began the long explanation of Richie's capture, and the legal and military problems which they now faced. For three hours, the group talked about his health, his legal status, and the numerous complications which needed to be addressed.

"I'll have to check precedent," the judge said, "but I'll tell you right here and now, I'm willing to move mountains to get this young man home where he belongs."

"I'll do whatever I can to help James," Yoshi told them.

"I'd like to talk to the doctor in charge of his case and see what protocol they're using," Lilly said.

"I'm not sure that will be possible," Frank told her. "He's a prisoner. A military doctor might not be willing to discuss his case. On the other hand, some of the civilian doctors at Queens also work at the military hospitals. Maybe we could find one who would be willing to bend the rules a little. Why don't you pursue that avenue," he told Lilly.

"What we need is a politician who can cut through the red tape," Anne said. "I'll call the governor's office. He owes me a favor or two."

"I could write Mrs. Roosevelt," Grace offered.

Lilly laughed.

Anne and Frank looked at each other.

"That's not a bad idea," Frank said.

"It certainly couldn't hurt," Anne agreed.

Frank thought for a moment and then said, "You write her, Anne. In fact, we'll all write her. Yoshi, you put together a brief. Judge, we'll need your perspective of the family. Ken, a father's viewpoint. Lilly, you too. And Grace, remind her that she spoke to you when she was here last spring. Get them all to me, and I'll put them in a diplomatic pouch. That should get someone's attention."

"I know we can't see Richie," Ken said, "but could I write him a letter?"

Frank considered it. "Yes. It would have to be brief. Anne should see it first, as a representative of the Red Cross. And then I'd have to read it. I'm not sure he'd be aware enough to understand it right now, but we'll be monitoring him closely, and we'll know when he is."

He looked around the table. "This is a sensitive matter. Information of this sort in the wrong hands can do serious damage to our cause. So, nothing goes beyond this room except among yourselves. *No one* else is to know. Understood?"

Everyone agreed, and the meeting was over.

The next few days, Grace and her parents could only think or talk about Richie. They were all careful not to mention anything in front of Makiko or the girls, but when they were alone, it was all they spoke of. Grace found it nearly impossible not to tell Tom when she wrote to him, but Frank's words were clear and like all the others, she understood the necessity to abide by them.

Anne composed a letter to Mrs. Roosevelt and read it to Grace.

"Dear Mrs. Roosevelt,

Your visit to Hawaii last spring was one of the highlights of our year. I will never forget your kindness or your invitation to visit you at the White House. You've helped out so many of our fine boys in uniform, and I am hoping that you might help out one more. His is a very special case, but it is not the uniform you are accustomed to helping."

The rest of the letter told about Richie's circumstances, his background in Hawaii, and his service in the ROTC at the university. Anne assured the president's wife that he would only have gone into the Japanese military under duress, knowing that his grandmother's life was in jeopardy.

Yoshi and the judge wrote letters of a legal nature, citing cases in the past which might add weight to their argument. Ken wrote about Richie's hard work at school and at the store, and his willingness to go with his grandmother into war-torn Japan. Lilly wrote from one mother to another, hoping a maternal plea might help persuade her.

Grace wrote a simple note reminding the First Lady of their meeting, and asking her for her help in rectifying Richie's untenable predicament.

All the letters went to Frank, who read them carefully and, with his approval, had them sent to the White House.

And then the wait began.

Although Grace thought about Richie constantly, she was on guard against mentioning his name. Even at work, she and Anne rarely spoke about her brother, and then only after hours and in a closed office. She was distressed that she couldn't tell Tom that Richie was in Hawaii, since she knew how much it would mean to him. However, she also knew the consequences of such a rash move and was careful not to disclose the news.

At the end of October she received a jubilant letter from Tom.

Dear Grace,

Yesterday I got twelve letters from home. Twelve!! It was the most wonderful day. You haven't forgotten about me. Everyone wrote—you, the folks, Chiyo, Naomi, and Vivian. The guys here are so jealous! Hiro got mail as well, so he is happy, too. Things around here are about the same. Lots of moving and lots of fighting. I'd been feeling pretty down, but life looks a little brighter today. Hope you are okay and working hard at the RC. Those folks do their best to make things better for us wherever we go. Say hi to everybody and keep those letters coming. Tom

Grace was relieved. He sounded happier than he had in months.

"Did you hear from Tom, too?" she asked Vivian. They were at the park watching some of the neighborhood girls practice the *hula.*

"Yes. Big difference in his attitude since he got our letters. I wish they didn't take so long. By the time I get an answer, I've forgotten what I asked him in the first place."

"I know. I told him they'd lifted Marshall Law, and when he said he'd read it in a newspaper he'd found at the post, I didn't even remember that I'd mentioned it."

"Do you still hear from Hiro?"

"Of course."

"And he still writes *haiku* for you?"

"We both write one with every letter. His last one was so sad. They're changing as the war goes on. I'll tell you, let me think." She paused a few moments and then recited:

"Hills roll with thunder
Blasts of gunfire and bombs
Wreak total havoc."

"I suppose they can't get away from it. I read about the battles, and I know guys are getting killed, but I can't imagine what it must be like to have something explode right next to you."

"I'm not sure I could stand it if I did know."

Frank kept them updated as often as possible about Richie's condition. Lilly had found a doctor who visited the military hospitals regularly, and was able to give her the reassurance she wanted. Ken wrote Richie a letter, which Frank approved. Now it was up to Richie to get well enough to understand it.

It was nearly Thanksgiving when the first response came from Mrs. Roosevelt. In a letter addressed to Anne, an aide reported that the First Lady had received their letters and the matter was under consideration. The closing words were, "Mrs. Roosevelt wants you to know she is doing her best to resolve this situation."

Christmas came and went without further word. Then, during the second week in January of 1945, there was a brief note from the White House, saying that Richie had been granted a Presidential pardon.

He would be released!

CHAPTER 20

"When can we see him?" Lilly asked Frank. He had brought them the official word of the pardon.

"We have to get him transferred to Queen's. The doctor says he's far from being out of the woods. At this point, he still sleeps most of the day."

"Couldn't we just bring him home?"

"I asked. I told the doc you're a nurse. He advised at least a couple of weeks more in hospital. But you'll have plenty of medical opinions available at Queen's."

Frank stood. "One more thing. The less said about the pardon the better. We don't want it to look like you got special treatment."

The transfer took three days.

Lilly, Ken and Grace were at the hospital within minutes after being informed of his arrival. They took the elevator to the third floor.

"What room is he in, Mom?"

"Three twenty-seven."

She led them down the hall to a southern facing room at the end of the corridor. Sunlight flooded in the window, and drowned the bed in bright yellow light. A frail boy lay under the white blanket, and Grace thought with annoyance that the attendant had given them the wrong room number. However, Lilly pulled a chair over next to the bed, took the boy's hand and said softly, "Richie?"

Slowly he opened his eyes, looked around the room and finally focused on his mother. Then, he sighed deeply and closed his eyes again.

He'd lost so much weight that his body barely showed under the covers. His cheeks were sunken, his eye sockets dark, and his skin, dull and sallow. His arms, which lay inertly on the blanket, looked like those of a twelve-year-old child.

"Richie," Lilly said again, "it's Mom."

"I know," he said. His voice was hollow and unearthly, as if it hadn't come from him at all.

"You're home, Richie. You're back in Hawaii."

He opened his eyes again and looked at Lilly. "Mom?" He glanced around the room. "Grace?" he said, his voice uncertain.

She walked to the bed, and took his other hand. "Yes, it's me. You're home."

He tried to sit up. "Dad?"

"Yes, son. We're all here."

"Where's Tom?" he asked in a whisper.

"He's over in Europe. He's in the army."

He shrank back like the word itself wounded him.

"Tom is okay," Lilly said. "We got a letter from him last week. He's fine."

"Where are we?"

Lilly looked uncertain. "We're home, in Hawaii."

"No. Where *are* we? What is this place?"

"Queen's Hospital. You're at Queen's."

"Your hospital," he said. A smile slowly washed across his face.

"Yes, my hospital."

"That's good."

Grace heard both relief and exhaustion in his voice.

His smile faded and he fell asleep again. They stayed with him for two more hours, but he never once stirred.

Grace rode home in shock. This shell of a man was not her brother, was not the vivid person she watched leave on the ship to Japan. Her mother had told her the symptoms of malaria: nausea, vomiting, chills, fever, sweats, and fatigue, but she hadn't said it could turn someone into a skeleton. No wonder they thought he needed to stay in the hospital.

"How long before he gets better?" she asked her mother.

"It depends on how well the medicine works. The symptoms can last for months and can return periodically. So, even when he seems better, he can relapse or have a serious setback. We have to do our best to help him get stronger and gain weight."

"Can we write and tell Tom now?" Grace asked.

"Yes," Ken said. "Frank told me to keep it simple, but that we could let him know that Richie is home."

They visited him every day. As the week progressed, he was awake more and eventually began talking about Japan. On Sunday, Lilly prepared his favorite chicken dish, and they took him his dinner. He ate slowly, and smiled often at his mother. When he'd finished he lay back against the pillows. He was so still that Grace thought he'd fallen asleep.

"Grandma is dead," he said without preamble.

Grace reached for her father's hand.

"We thought she might he," Ken said, although Grace doubted that he'd thought any such thing.

He looked at his father. "They said they'd kill her if I didn't go with them."

"You mean the army?" Ken asked.

"I could see how hard it was for her. We knew for days they'd come for me and she struggled. She wanted me to do my duty." He closed his eyes for a long time and then opened them again. "I don't think she could figure out who I should be dutiful *to*. Finally, she told me, 'Go hide…and live.'"

Grace watched the torment play across his face. She knew that the *samurai* code ruled her grandmother's life, and she realized that her divided loyalty to Japan and her grandson must have caused her tremendous anguish.

"I couldn't leave her. She was still so weak." His voice trailed off. "So, they came, and I went with them. The uncles wrote to me. It was only a month later." He looked at his father in despair. "It was my fault. I should have done what she said."

Ken shook his head. "No, son. If you had, they would have tortured them all, to find out where you were. Your grandmother wanted to protect you, and you were trying to protect her. No one could ask for more."

Tears welled in his eyes, and spilled onto sunken cheeks. "Can I come home?"

"Of course," Lilly said quickly.

"I thought you might not want me."

"Oh, Richie," she cried, sitting on the bed and hugging him. "Of course we want you home. You just have to get a little stronger."

He let her hold him, and then he sank deeper into the pillows. "I'll try harder," he said. But Grace could see that even their short visit had exhausted him. He still had a struggle ahead of him before returning home.

On the last Sunday in February, Grace and her parents were reading the morning paper, when a dark car pulled up in front, and two men in army uniforms got out.

Grace stood up. "That's strange," she said as they came up the walkway. "Maybe it's something about Richie," she said, and she started toward the door.

Lilly stopped her with her arm. "It's not about Richie."

The unearthly sound of Lilly's voice made Grace's skin turn cold.

A look passed between her parents that made her shiver with fear.

Ken walked to the door and opened it slowly.

"Kenneth Kawakami?"

"Yes," her father said, his voice barely squeezing from his throat.

The man introduced himself and then said, "May we come in?"

Ken stepped aside, as the men came into the living room.

Lilly eased herself down on the sofa.

"Mrs. Kawakami?"

"Yes."

"I'm sorry to have to inform you that your son, Private First Class Tomoaki Kawakami, was killed in the line of duty on February 2nd. JuneYou have our deepest sympathies, and the appreciation of a grateful nation."

Lilly covered her face with her hands.

Ken sat down and put his arm around her shoulders.

They were both utterly silent.

"Where is he?" Grace managed to croak.

"He was buried in a small graveyard in Italy, with twenty-three others from the 442nd."

Lilly looked up. "You mean he won't, he can't, you aren't going to bring him back home?"

"No ma'am. I'm afraid that isn't possible."

Tom was dead.

Tom was buried.

Tom wasn't coming home.

"Do you know how he died?" Ken asked.

"No, sir. I'm sorry I don't. We only get the names. All I know is that the 442nd is one heck of a fighting unit." He paused and then added, "They've had a lot of fatalities."

They stood and waited respectfully, while Ken and Lilly grappled with the tragic news.

Ken finally looked up again. "Is there anything we need to do?"

"No, sir. Nothing. You'll get all the papers you need by mail. If you have any questions, you can call this number." He handed Ken a card. "Is there anything else we can do for you?"

Ken looked at Lilly who merely shook her head.

"No," he said.

"Again, we're sorry for your loss."

"Thank you," Ken said absently, and went to open the door.

"Take care," the officer said as they left.

Lilly looked at Ken in utter despair. "We can't even bury him. He'll be in a foreign country forever. We can't even visit him. No one will put flowers on his grave."

"We can go to Italy, Lilly," Ken said. "I'll take you there."

"I want him home," she said in a hoarse whisper, and began weeping.

Grace sat down next to her, tears streaming down her face. "How are we going to tell Richie?"

And then Ken, son of a *samurai*, broke into anguished sobs.

It wasn't until late in the afternoon, that they were composed enough to take the sad news to Richie. They talked briefly about not telling him, but Lilly was sure that Richie would know something was wrong the moment he saw them.

When Ken told him, Richie didn't seem to understand. "Tom?" he asked, as if he didn't quite catch the name.

"Yes," Ken said. "He was killed in Italy."

Richie looked at Lilly. "You said he was fine."

"I know. We thought he was."

"I thought he was fine. That's what Mom said." He started rubbing his hands on the blanket, as though they itched uncontrollably. "She said he was fine." He began rocking back and forth. "I don't know what happened. He was supposed to be fine."

Grace rushed to sit by him.

Lilly left the room, and came back shortly with Richie's nurse.

"Time for your medication," she said, and handed him two tablets, and a glass of water.

Richie looked at her with a confused frown. "My brother, Tom, is dead. Remember I told you about him? Mom thought he was okay, but he wasn't."

"I'm sorry, Richie. I remember you telling me how special he was." She nodded toward the glass of water. "Why don't you take those? It'll help you relax."

Richie took the medicine and within a few minutes, he was asleep.

They sat quietly with him for a while. The nurse came back into the room and put her hand on Lilly's shoulder. "You should go on home. I'll keep an eye on him. I'll call if he needs you to come back."

"Are you sure?" Lilly asked her.

"I'm sure."

"Thank you, Suzanna. I appreciate that. We have some calls to make."

On the way home in the car, Lilly said, "We need to tell Vivian." She turned to look at Grace. "Can you do it, or shall I?"

"I'll do it. Will you drop me off?"

They stopped in front of Vivian's.

"You're sure?" Lilly asked.

"Yes."

Vivian answered the front door.

"Hi. Come on in. What's up?" When Grace didn't answer right away, Vivian looked at her more closely. "What's wrong? Grace?"

Grace couldn't find the words.

"Grace, is it Richie?"

She shook her head.

Vivian pulled her over to the couch and sat. "Is it Tom?" Did something happen to Tom?"

Grace began to cry. And still the words would not come. Finally she managed to say, "They came and told us this morning."

"Told you what? Is he hurt?"

"He's dead," Grace said, the words sounding like a knife scraping on glass. "He was killed in Italy. They buried him there. He's never coming home."

Vivian's face contorted with pain. "No. No, no! It's a mistake! It has to be." Her voice slid into tears.

Grace stayed until she couldn't stand the weight of Vivian's pain on top of her own. But the despair she found at home only compounded her own misery. Her parents sat in morbid silence at the table, drinking invisible tea. She went into her room, lay down on her bed, and fell into merciful sleep.

During the next week, she discovered that she could escape from the sadness when she was at work. The office became her refuge, the one place in her life where all those around her weren't miserable. Anne and Irene were sad for her, but they weren't sad. At least not until the following week.

On March 12th, President Franklin Roosevelt died of a massive stroke. From that moment on, the rest of the nation joined her in grief.

To make matters worse, she hadn't heard from Hiro in weeks. At first she wasn't concerned, since the mail had been so erratic. When two months had passed, she began to worry.

"Why don't you call his mother," Naomi suggested. "I'm sure she'll tell you if there is anything wrong."

So, on the weekend she did just that. She thought carefully about how to word her call in case something had happened to him.

"Mrs. Sato? My name is Grace Kawakami. I'm a friend of Hiro's. I've been writing to him, but it's been a long time since I've gotten a letter back. I wanted to know if everything is okay."

"Ah, so you must be the Grace I've heard about. He never said your last name, or I would have tried to call you."

She didn't like the sound of Hiro's mother's voice. "Has something happened to him?" she asked, hardly daring to imagine the answer.

"Yes. I'm afraid that he was hurt at the beginning of last month. He's in a hospital in Italy." She stopped, and yet, Grace knew there was more. "He was hurt badly, but he's doing better now. One of the nurses wrote to tell me."

Still Grace waited.

"He was hit in the leg. Like I said, it was bad. They had to operate three times." She paused, and then said in a choked voice, "They couldn't save it."

"Oh!" Grace heard herself say. "Oh, I'm so sorry."

"He'll be okay. He'll be coming home pretty soon, I think."

"Coming home. That's good. Uh, do you think he'd like a letter from me?"

"Yes, I think he'd like it very much."

She wrote him that night, and told him she'd spoken to his mother. She told him about Tom. She told him Richie was still in the hospital. She told him she was looking forward to seeing him as soon as he got home. She ended with a *haiku*:

Though torrents of rain
Wash away life's precious dreams
Spring brings forth new life

She sent it with high hopes. She thought perhaps he hadn't written because he couldn't face telling her what had happened to him. Now that she knew, it would be easier for him.

But apparently, that wasn't the case: there were still no letters.

After hearing about Tom's death, Richie was even more determined to come home.

"I'm tired of being here," he told the family when they came to visit the following week. "I want to be home for Easter."

"You might not have to wait that long," Lilly said. "The drugs have taken hold, and your blood work looks good. We may be able to get you out of here by the end of this week."

He hadn't gained much weight, but he did appear stronger, and he hardly ever slept during the day any more. Grace wondered if, by coming home, Richie was trying to help their mother cope with the sadness she carried around with her like a dark, heavy satchel.

The doctor agreed that he could be released, provided he continued with the same regimen at home.

The house felt fuller and more complete once Richie was back. He brought with him his good nature and quick laughter. He and Naomi once again became the daring duo, always ready for a challenge or an adventure. "Let's redecorate the bomb shelter," or "You go shopping, I'll fix dinner." There was still a hole without Tom, but Grace felt the burden of being the only child fall from her at last.

On May 8th, the war in Europe ended.

On June 1st, Hiro came home.

Neither event changed Grace's life at all. The war still raged both in the Pacific, and in Hiro. He didn't call her, but his mother did.

"He's depressed," she told Grace. "He doesn't want to see anyone, but he won't say why. He won't talk about Tom at all. I think it must have something to do with your brother dying. It was obviously very difficult for him."

"Maybe after he's been home a while, it will get better."

A month brought no change.

Naomi asked Grace and Richie to go to the USO dance with her and Frank.

"Come on. It'll be fun."

Richie finally gave in. He was no match for Naomi's persistence. Even Chiyo consented to join them. Grace was relieved that Frank was able to borrow a car. Even though Richie was vastly improved, she thought that the walk on top of the dance would be too much for him.

She wasn't surprised to see Walter when they arrived.

"Come join us," Naomi told him. "This is my cousin, Richie...Grace's brother."

"It's nice to meet you," Walter told him.

They found a table, and as soon as they were settled Walter asked Grace to dance.

"I've missed you," he told her as they walked out to the dance floor. He put his arms around her, and she felt as if she'd come back home.

"I heard about Tom. I'm so sorry. The 442nd has suffered a lot, way more than their share."

"Thank you," she said. "It's true. So many of his friends are gone." She had heard about dozens of others besides Tom who had been killed or injured. Their friends were suffering, too.

"What about your boyfriend?" he asked cautiously.

Boyfriend? The one who wouldn't see her? "He got hurt pretty bad. He lost a leg. He's home but..."

"But what?"

She didn't *know* what. "He doesn't want to see me. I guess he doesn't want to see anyone. His mom says it's because of Tom. I don't know."

Walter didn't reply, and the music ended.

"Can I have another dance?" he said finally.

She felt torn. Although she loved dancing, with him, she was afraid that she might be creating a problem. However, the music started as they stood there, and he simply put his arms around her again and began dancing.

The entire evening progressed in the same way. They never returned to the table. When the last dance was announced, Walter said, "I think this one is mine."

She couldn't argue.

After only a few bars of the music Walter said, "If things don't work out between you two…"

"I know," she told him.

"If it weren't for him, I'd have a chance, wouldn't I?"

She knew he would, but it seemed pointless to tell him so. She was fond of him. If it weren't for Hiro, she knew she would be dating him. He'd actually been the one constant through it all, through the awful months of waiting and hurting.

She looked at him then, and wondered if she'd ever really seen him without Hiro standing between them.

"Yes," she said gently.

He tightened his hold on her almost imperceptibly.

She felt an unexpected excitement and an unsettling confusion. What was happening here? She thought she had settled this months ago.

He leaned back slightly and looked down at her, and she realized he'd sensed her uncertainty.

"I'm still here," he said. "I could always stay, if this is where you want to be."

Was he proposing?

She buried her head in his chest. There was no way she wanted to have this discussion, at least not now.

He walked out to the car with them.

"I'll call you," he said.

It wasn't a question, and she didn't argue.

Hiro had been home for six weeks. Grace decided it was time to go and see him, whether he wanted her to or not. She chose not to call and check with his mother, thinking that he would likely refuse her request. She knew where they lived. She made up her mind to walk to their house in the afternoon, on her way home from work.

It was a beautiful summer day, with blue skies that extended forever and the sweet fragrance of island flowers everywhere.

His mother answered her knock on the door. "Yes?"

"Hello, Mrs. Sato. I'm Grace Kawakami. I wanted to say hello to Hiro. I'll only stay a couple of minutes."

The older woman looked uncertain. "I'm not sure…"

"I know he hasn't wanted to see me, but maybe it would help."

"Maybe." She opened the door to let Grace in and led her through the kitchen to a door which opened up onto a small patio. Hiro sat in a wheelchair reading a book.

"Hiro, your friend Grace is here."

"Send her away," was the swift reply.

"Hiro," Grace said.

"Go away!" He threw the book at her. She recognized it immediately. It was the book of *haiku* that she'd sent him. He still had it.

"Please, Hiro," she said.

"Go!" he screamed. "I don't want you here."

"I'm so sorry," she said to his mother, and she left.

When Walter called the next evening, she agreed to go out with him.

"What happened to change your mind?" he asked her, when they met to go to the movies.

She knew exactly what he meant, but she wasn't sure how to answer.

"Have you seen him?"

"No. I tried. I went to see him. He told me to leave."

"So, it isn't really settled."

"According to him it is."

"I don't think so. He's waiting."

"Waiting for what?"

"To see how determined you are. To see if you come back." He led her to a seat in the very last row of the theater, where their whispers would not disturb anyone. "Are you going to go back?"

"I don't know."

And, she honestly didn't know. His anger had given her second thoughts, and she wasn't sure she was prepared to fight her way through it. At the same time, their letters and poems connected them in a very special way, which had not been severed, even by his rage.

When the lights went down, Walter put his arm around her shoulder. She expected him to say something else. He didn't. That was when she realized, he was waiting, too.

They saw each other every weekend; on Saturday at the USO dances, and on Sunday for a movie or a picnic. He didn't ask her about Hiro, but it was clear that he didn't consider the issue resolved. There were several times he started to say something and then stopped himself. Although each time it happened she felt relieved, the longer the uncertainty persisted, the more confused she was.

"Are you getting serious about Walter?" her mother asked, after she'd been seeing him again for about a month.

She wasn't sure what to say. "I like him," she admitted.

"What about Hiro?"

"I don't know. He wouldn't even talk to me."

"Maybe you should try writing him. He might feel less pressure if he didn't have to respond on the spot."

"Maybe."

The more she considered it, the more she thought her mother was right. She decided on Friday that she would spend the next day composing a letter. When she went to bed that night, she couldn't sleep. What did she want to tell him? What was it that he was so upset about? Could she make things better, or would it only make them worse?

She was just as uncertain the next morning. She started a dozen times, but ripped up each attempt. There were so many things she wanted him to know, so many things she hoped might make a difference. But none of them sounded convincing when she read them over. Finally she wrote:

Life's anguished changes
bring our tempered souls closer
to true contentment

She wrote it on a beautiful piece of origami paper and folded it, as nearly as she could, the same way he had folded the first one he'd given to her. She went by his house and put it into the mailbox.

Then she waited.

The following week his mother called. "Hiro would like to see you. Would it be possible for you to come by on Saturday?"

"Yes, of course. What time?"

"In the afternoon, say about two o'clock?"

"Yes. I'll be there."

"Good. We'll see you then."

Uncertainty accompanied her everywhere for the rest of the week. She had no idea what either one of them would say.

Mrs. Sato answered the door when she knocked on Saturday afternoon. "Please, come in."

"Thank you."

"He's out on the patio. If you don't mind, I'm going to run to the market while you're here."

"That's fine."

She walked through the kitchen and out to the patio. He was sitting in the wheelchair exactly as he'd been the last time.

"Hiro," she said gently, hoping not to set him off.

"Hi." He turned just slightly. "Come over here and sit." He pointed to a chair that faced him.

She did as he asked and then, for the first time in over two years, looked into his eyes.

They were full of misery.

She noticed, then, that he held her *haiku* in his hand.

He looked at her, a weak smile curling at the edges of his mouth. "Tempered?"

She paused and then said, "Yes."

He looked down at his single leg. "You think this can bring me contentment?"

"I think the fact that you survived gives you the chance," she said as gently as she could.

"As compared to Tom."

"Yes. Not to mention hundreds of others."

"It's hard to be contented when you've been where I've been."

"You mean in the hospital?"

"The hospital was easy compared to the rest of it."

"Can you tell me about it?"

"You don't want to hear about it, Grace. It would be best for everyone if we said goodbye to the past, and went on with our lives."

"You mean go on separately?"

"Yes."

"What is it you're afraid of, Hiro?"

"I don't want you to hurt any more than you already do."

"I don't understand. What is it that happened?"

He looked suddenly tired and defeated. "Tom died saving me." The words came out in staccato sharpness. "We were under heavy fire. My gun jammed. He put himself between me and them, while I tried to fix it. It only took ten seconds. Ten seconds!"

Pain bloomed in her chest and rose to her face. She felt the air sucked out of her lungs. "He saved you?"

"Yes. How can that produce contentment?"

She looked down. "I don't know."

"I'm so sorry," he said. The anguish in his voice rivaled her own grief.

She stood. "You're right. I had no idea. I'm sorry." She looked around as if to get her bearings. "I should go."

"Yes," he agreed. "That would be best."

The following week the United States unleashed the unprecedented power of the atomic bomb on Hiroshima and Nagasaki. Japan surrendered and the war was over.

Honolulu celebrated for three days.

Grace walked around in a daze, carrying Hiro's awful confession everywhere with her; carried it like a blade that rubbed against her heart with every breath she took.

"Come to the dance with us," Naomi urged. "It's going to be the best one ever!"

She didn't want to go, didn't want to do anything, and certainly didn't want to explain why. Still, she went.

Of course, Walter was there. She couldn't hide her feelings from him.

"You saw him, didn't you."

"Yes."

"Tell me about it."

She hadn't told anyone what Hiro had said. But it spilled over, one agonized word tumbling over another, in anguished relief. And she was glad, now, that it was out.

"So, he blames himself."

She nodded.

"Just like I did."

"Yes."

"And you blame him."

"Yes," she whispered.

"Ah..." He paused, then asked, "What would Tom say?"

She looked up at him, surprised. "I don't know."

"Oh, but I think you do."

Tears filled her eyes. "He'd say, don't blame Hiro."

"I'm sure that's exactly what he'd say." He held her. "I'll tell you something else. Tom died a hero. Blaming Hiro diminishes Tom's sacrifice. He knew what he was doing. Don't take that away from him."

Tom died a hero.
He made the decision.
He made the choice.

Walter's simple words brought her a peace that she hadn't known for days. She felt her entire being relax; she could bear the loss of her heroic brother.

"Do you think Hiro can ever forgive himself?" she asked, her voice barely audible.

Walter held her one last time. "Yes. I think that with your love, he has a chance."

Two years later, the entire family stood on the bank of the Ali Wai canal, to celebrate the *Bon* festival. Between them, they carried three lanterns. Dorothy held Becca in her arms as Paul quietly distracted the toddler. The Judge held the first lantern while Lilly lit the candle. Then, Ken lit one for Grandfather, and Makiko, the one for Grandmother. Carefully, they placed the lanterns in the water, and watched them drift gently among the many others. Although there had been no *Bon* dance, Japanese families were honoring the souls of the thousands of dead, who had perished during the war years.

Grace knew that Chiyo had wanted desperately to wear a *yukata* that day, but Yoshi had said no. Instead, they were all dressed in their finest clothes to mark the occasion.

Hiro held Grace's hand.

She smiled at him.

"I wish Tom could see the two of you together," Richie said gently.

Grace put her hand on her slightly rounded belly. "Maybe there will be another little Tom around soon."

The End

Glossary of Japanese words

Andagi: sweet, deep fried buns
Arigato: thank you
Geta: thong sandals with an elevated wooden base
Gyoza: crescent shaped vegetable or meat dumpling
Haiku: three line poem with seventeen syllables
Issei: first generation Japanese who emigrated to the US
Kakimochi: rice crackers
Kamaboko: fish cakes
Karaage: deep fried chicken or fish
Kimono: full length, straight-lined robe, often of silk
Kuri-manju: bean paste dessert
Kushi katsu: breaded, deep fried pork
Maru: designates a passenger, not a military ship
Musubi: rice held together with meat and seaweed
Nisei: first generation Japanese born in the US
Obi: long sash used to secure a kimono or yukata
Obon: festival to honor the souls of the deceased
Osechi: New Year's foods
Ozoni: rice cake soup
Samurai: powerful military aristocracy
Shikata ga nai: it can't be helped
Toro nagashi: floating of lanterns during Obon
Yagara: stage or platform at the center of bon dance
Yukata: lightweight, cotton robe

Glossary of Hawaiian words

Alii: Hawaiian royalty
Aloha: hello, goodbye, love
Aloha 'oe: alas for you
Haole: Caucasian
Hapa: half
Hula: traditional Hawaiian dance
Iolani Palace: home of the Hawaiian royalty
Kalihi'Kai: neighborhood near downtown Honolulu
Kama'aina: long time Hawaiian resident
Kapa'akea: father to Lili'uokalani
Lei: long necklace made of flowers
Madame Pele: Goddess of fire and volcanoes
Mauka: the inland direction
Nuuanu: cemetery and memorial park in Honolulu
Pali: mountain precipice
Poi: paste made of sweet potatoes, formerly a staple of Hawaii
Sanoe: mountain mist

Japanese Americans and WWII

The 442d Regimental Combat Team (the 100th Battalion was incorporated into the 442d Regiment), fought in the European Theater during WWII. The 442d became the most highly decorated regiment in US history: 18,143 medals, including 21Congressional Medals of Honor, were awarded to members of the unit.

During WWII, more than 120,000 residents of Japanese heritage, 2/3 of whom were US citizens, were sent to "relocation centers." These camps were enclosed by barbed wire and guarded by armed sentries. The internees included Japanese-American veterans of WWI.

Although rumors abounded throughout the war, no verifiable incident of espionage or sabotage by a Japanese American was **ever** discovered.

It is estimated that internees lost a total of approximately $380 million in property and goods during the period of internment.

In 1988, President Ronald Reagan signed the Civil Liberties Act of 1988 that provided redress of $20,000 for each *surviving* internee of the relocation camps. This was more than 40 years after the end of the war!

Linda McGinnis
is the author of:

The Cloud Dancer Series
Pueblo Summer
Second Summer
Summer Ghost
Summer Vows
Summer Light

The Sweet Refrain Series
Till I Kissed You
Devoted to You
Let it Be Me
Love of My Life

The Bridal Ball Series
The Bridal Ball
The Bridesmaid's Waltz
The Bridegroom's Toast

You can visit her on the web at
LindaMcGinnis.com
or follow her on Facebook.